A
CANDLELIGHT GEORGIAN SPECIAL

CANDLELIGHT REGENCIES

A Marriageable Asset

Ruth Gerber

A CANDLELIGHT GEORGIAN SPECIAL

Published by
Dell Publishing Co., Inc.
1 Dag Hammarskjold Plaza
New York, New York 10017

Dell ® TM 681510, Dell Publishing Co., Inc.

ISBN: 0-440-14974-6

Printed in the United States of America

First printing—January 1981

To the memory of my loving mother,
Clare Werther Gerber

CHAPTER ONE

On the infrequent occasions when the hounding of his creditors induced him to leave London, Sir Lucius Charldon instituted stringent economies upon his household, which invariably included that of denying himself the luxury of a fire in any room he did not frequent.

This bleak January day being one of those times, the customarily frigid library was quite the most comfortable apartment in the manor, for here the master lay upon a threadbare sofa, wrapped in shawls and flanked by as many nostrums as would fit upon an adjacent console. As he had not as yet decided to which of a variety of ailments he was most likely to succumb, Sir Lucius fortified himself by frequent application to a decanter of fine brandy, which had reached this side of the Channel despite the opposition of the excise.

Serene in the knowledge that even the most importune of creditors would hardly pursue him to this remote area of Dorset, Sir Lucius nevertheless felt a momentary disquiet as his butler presented a letter.

Communications these days—whether by post, or, as this had come, by messenger—more than likely contained a scarcely veiled demand for settlement of some long outstanding account or presented him with a sheaf of new debts incurred by the restless young woman he had married.

Feeling his business was with the master, the roughly dressed man followed on the heels of Bassett, the butler, although he had been directed to wait in the hall. Thus he had the doubtful privilege of hearing Sir Lucius's diatribe on the thoughtlessness of daughters in general and the abysmal worthlessness of his own in particular.

With a roar amazingly at variance with his invalidism, Sir Lucius accosted the hovering fisherman-turned-messenger.

"Not skulking, yer honor, if yer please," he said, eager to explain his presence in the room. "I was ter ask yer honor if there be an answer."

"This was written more than a fortnight ago."

"'Tis gettin' a mite too crowded for delivery hereabouts," the man offered by way of excuse, but it was the wrong thing to say, for Sir Lucius was moved to deliver a thunderous dissertation on the unreliability of every "gentleman" engaged in the Trade and the sticky end to which all would undoubtedly come.

The placid fisherman waited patiently for the choleric lord of the manor to finish tearing his character to shreds, as he did every time a shipment of brandy was delayed. In the mildest of tones he attempted to pacify Sir Lucius, who had paused for breath, with a pledge to do his best. Fearing that his patron was fast regaining his wind, Abel Trowbridge hastily, if awkwardly, bobbed himself out, several much begrudged shillings in the pocket of his dark jacket.

Turning up his collar against the slanting rain, Abel heaved his box to a brawny shoulder and, giving the money in his pocket a final pat, stepped out with a distance-consuming stride in the direction of the Rose and Garter, where he was assured of a welcome, the innkeeper's wife being his sister. With any luck at all, he thought as his fingers rubbed reassuringly against his coins, he'd have Sir Lucius's daughter home inside the week. He sighed and shifted his burden to the other shoulder without losing a step.

Poor lass. The way he'd heard it, and Bassett wouldn't lie—butlers being too stiff-rumped for that—Miss Vanessa could have stayed in France for all Sir Lucius cared. But now he'd found a fine profit in arranging a marriage for her. Aye, Bassett must have heard wrong about something, for what would the Earl of Melcourt be doing offering for a modest, innocent young girl like Vanessa Charldon, whom he'd never met, at that. Even the servants hereabout knew the Earl's tastes ran to wanton hussies like Miranda Charldon, Sir Lucius's lady. Always throwing out their lures to him they were. Abel knew what to call it when a woman sought out a man, be he lord or be he lackey. If Lady Charldon had any say in it, there'd be no wedding between the Earl of Melcourt and her stepdaughter—that is if there was any truth to the story in the first place.

He'd see the little miss safely home as he'd promised, but somehow he couldn't help think as how she'd be better off with the Frenchies. At least she'd know who her enemies were.

* * *

A raw wind off the coast of Brittany blew into the kitchen at Raoul's heels, and Vanessa waited in silence as he shrugged off his sodden coat and almost angrily threw it toward a rough bench near the hearth.

"It is arranged," he said. "The fishing boat will go out in two days. They will transfer you mid-Channel"—he eyed his young companion warily—"with the rest of the goods that are to be smuggled into England."

The boyish figure refused to rise to the bait. "If the rain stops," Vanessa countered.

"The rain will not change anything."

"I might get seasick," she told him complacently, leaning back in her chair and stretching out her long, booted legs.

"And you the perfect sailor? What nonsense!" Taking a more careful look at her, he frowned. "You gave your word, Vanessa."

She jumped up, her hands clenching and unclenching in a nervous gesture.

"The word of a Charldon is never retracted," she flung at him in a voice grown suddenly husky with unshed tears.

"Forgive me, little one, I am a fool. You are all that is honorable," he murmured contritely while his hands gripped her slight shoulders.

With the burrowing movement of a small animal she relaxed and nestled against him.

"Oh, Raoul, must I go?" she pleaded. "I have passed safely through the Terror and you did say that things have been better since the Girondists were called to the convention."

"Ah, but have I not also told you these many days that it will not last, my dear? Already there is talk of restoring the churches, and soon we again will hear the grumbling of the people." He sighed sharply. "France is not yet ready for a return to the old regime."

Raoul took one step back, releasing her.

"Then I must go?"

He felt pained at seeing her so forlorn—almost as she had been when she had first come to France— poor, unhappy child. Her courage had supported them these last years; without her, Grandmère and his wife, Jeanne, never would have survived. Such a gallant child— No! She was a child no longer; she was a woman, very lovely and very suspicious.

"Something is wrong!" Vanessa almost snapped. "You have been as unhappy as a cat on a raft since we left Vitry."

She ran her hands through her shaggy, cropped hair as she watched Raoul pace the floor. Suddenly he stopped in front of her.

"It had to be Fouché! I know it was!" he exclaimed.

"What do you mean?"

"I'm sure I saw him in Vitry—at the Chat d'Or. What bothers me is that he was with someone I know, someone I can't place."

"The man in the corner?" Puzzled, she continued, "If it was Fouché, would it be so important? After all, we got away, so obviously he didn't recognize you."

"Perhaps. It will come to me, but I can't be easy in my mind about it. I keep expecting to meet him at every turning. I wonder will you get away, or will he stop us? Is he waiting for me to lead him to the others, or did we accidentally stumble into a meeting with one of his spies? It is a dangerous situation—for me, for Jeanne, for us all. You are English."

"He doesn't know me."

"Don't talk like a child. He knows everyone and everything. What is to stop him from accusing me of harboring an enemy agent—you!"

"Oh!" she gasped.

"For all our sakes then, Vanessa, don't fight this."

"And why didn't you tell me of this before now?"

"You might have argued anyway."

He was right, she conceded silently, and threw up a hand in the manner of a fencer signaling a hit.

Raoul was amused at her gesture and, at the same time, relieved at her capitulation.

"It is well we understand each other. Now listen carefully. If by any chance you cannot reach the Strand at the appointed time, you must go to the innkeeper. He will make new arrangements to have the fishing boats take you out."

"And he might steer her straight to the arms of the guillotine." From the depths of the chimney corner came the dry voice of Raoul's former nursery maid, Blondine. "You were too trusting even as a child, M'sieu le Comte, but it is a luxury you can no longer afford; the price is too high. Once she sets foot outside this door, Mademoiselle Vanessa will be at the mercy of anyone who sees her. You cannot depend on their loyalty to the family of the Comte de St. Varres."

"Are you sure of this?" Raoul's voice cracked like a whip.

Blondine snorted, annoyed that a former charge of

hers should question her warning. "I am so sure, M'sieu le Comte, that I would rather you take Mademoiselle back to Paris than inform anyone she is at hand."

The Comte was thoughtful, assessing the news with his usual calm, but Vanessa's blue-violet eyes grew large as she considered the existence of some unknown enemy.

"But who . . . why . . . ?"

The elderly woman shrugged at the girl's persistence. "Is it possible to read a man's mind or look into his heart? Someone hates the family of de St. Varres." Vanessa's quick-drawn breath was stilled by the touch of Raoul de St. Varres's hand on her shoulder. *"Non,* do not tell me you are related only by marriage," continued Blondine. "It is enough if one has so great a hate. There are others who wish to destroy all English and would see you dead, if only for that. And there is always the one who seeks to do a mischief for its own sake, heedless of the evil he unleashes." Old Blondine heaved a sigh that sent shivers through her massive frame.

"And now, M'sieu le Comte, you see why you must go back to Paris and leave Mademoiselle to me, for have I not found an old friend of Mademoiselle's who used to take her fishing when she was thought to be locked in her room?"

"Abel Trowbridge!" the girl exclaimed, hugging the buxom woman in delight.

"It is indeed he, but you are not to know him, for he is with men who very much desire to be nameless." She let her eyes sweep over the girl. "Not that he would know you," she said with a sly smile. "You are very much the young gentleman. It is enough that I have told him you are traveling as André Vallier. This Abel, he was not surprised, and me, I know you have done things of a wildness before. But not disguised like this, I do not think.

"And now for you, M'sieu le Comte," Blondine told him with mock severity, her eyes still bright above apple cheeks, despite her more than seventy years. "You will obey me now as you did when you were my charge. Make your good-byes and then be off with you. I cannot answer if you delay us." She cocked her head and listened. "Even now as we have been talking, the rain has stopped."

"Old clackety-tongue," he told her with affection, "I realized that myself a quarter hour ago."

CHAPTER TWO

The *Ella K.* skulked off the Dorset coast, awaiting a chance to elude His Majesty's red-shirted, blue-trousered Preventives. Her helmsman whistled silently between his teeth in dismay as the fog cleared just enough to disclose the outline of a ship where no ship should be.

" 'Tis that cruiser again, Cap'n," he warned

hoarsely, intent on keeping his voice unheard more than a few feet away.

They had been playing hide-and-seek with the Preventives since reaching the English side of the Channel and might have been nabbed long since had their captain been a less cautious man. Thirty years of fishing these waters, and occasional trips to Holland and France, had enabled the captain to take advantage of an increasingly profitable trade, Mr. Pitt's lower tariffs notwithstanding. Welcomed by the French, who knew of no better way to lure English gold into a deplorably impoverished economy, and well paid by the many clients for whom he supplied contraband luxuries, the captain had no intention of making known to the authorities the existence of this small, secluded cove, which he found so useful for his activities. To protect his anchorage against possible informers, all passengers were blindfolded before reaching shore and remained so until they were well away from any recognizable landmark.

Carrying out his captain's orders, one of the crew picked his way across the deck to where their lone passenger sat huddled against a bale, seeking protection from the spray cast up as each wave smashed into the hull. "We be headin' for land, me lad, and no need to worry about the damn' Preventives," he chuckled as he tied the blindfold. "They might as well be wearin' blinkers too, for all they'll see this night."

The job completed to his satisfaction, he grunted and moved off, never to know that all his precautions would not serve to keep Vanessa Charldon in ignorance of their rendezvous. She was aware of the sharpness of wind upon her face, the heady tang of

15

the air—half taste, half smell—the rhythmic throb of the waves as they beat against the rocky outcropping. No matter how obscured her vision, how muffled her hearing, her other senses and, perhaps most of all, a faculty as yet undefined told Vanessa she was close to Shelburne Cove.

Since discovering she had no choice but to leave France, Vanessa's only consolation had been her pride in the ownership of historic Shelburne Hall, which had been left to her by her grandfather; it was a refuge, someplace to go in time of stress, always awaiting her return.

Nothing seemed to have changed. The handkerchief placed over her eyes by the seaman's rough hands was an unnecessary precaution; she would never betray her own people. But if they had secrets, so too did she, and she had no intention of divulging her identity. It might prove embarrassing, as it was one thing to make free of Shelburne's beach without her knowledge and quite another to involve her in their dealings. Not that she would require payment, but these men would not be beholden to anyone.

Vanessa realized suddenly that danger existed here. She had been wrong to imagine that there had been no change. The years had wrought great changes in her and in the character of these once simple fisherfolk. Their country was at war and they were engaged in profitable commerce with the enemy, even to the point of transporting possible spies between the two warring nations. It was as much for her own sake as for theirs that she dared not reveal her identity. Once they would have accepted her, but no longer.

Despite the blindfold she knew exactly where they

would beach. In that sea there was but one protected inlet, one lonely stretch where, sheltered from both storm and prying eyes, the illegal cargo could be unloaded.

No wonder Abel had cautioned her to silence! What a fool she had been to fret about his coming for her as if she had been a child, she thought as she stumbled off the boat. She owed him an apology and, remembering what Blondine had said, perhaps her life.

Impersonal hands perched her atop a tower of boxes and bundles and the cart upon which this structure rested began its lumbering journey north. The air, like thickened mist upon her face, presaged yet more rain. It was an appropriate welcome, she thought as they pressed on.

"Let old Abel unbind yer eyes, missy. There be no one but us about." Harsh, familiar, his voice broke the silence, and relief went through her like a purge, leaving her exhausted and defeated. Even her apology was tendered in dull, unemotional tones quite unlike her own. Abel's reply was equally colorless, the words meaningless to her and coming as if from a great distance.

In this detached, almost somnambulistic state, Vanessa Charldon entered the busy kitchen of the Rose and Garter while Abel fetched his sister.

One look at the drooping figure, and Betsy Plunkett took charge in that bustling way that could be so comforting. Vanessa soon found herself undressed, washed, and snugly tucked up in a warm bed, blissfully unaware of the hurried exchange between a maidservant and the innkeeper's wife, ending with a sharp admonition delivered by Mrs. Plunkett to the ef-

17

fect that Miss knew how to keep her mouth and her ears shut, which was more than could be said for others.

Not being the fool Mrs. Plunkett imagined, the servant knew better than to oppose her mistress. If Mrs. Plunkett chose to disregard Mr. Plunkett's orders to keep everyone out of this room, it was certainly not her business. She had done her duty. There was no reason for some people to act so superior when they had been servants themselves not too long ago. She left the room with a most audible sniff, which would have conveyed a world of meaning to Mrs. Plunkett had she been in the least concerned. At that moment, however, she was indecisive about further disturbing the drowsy girl and wondering what Plunkett would say.

Due to some accident—if a plan, it was so long ago that no one knew—the chimney that served this room and one other carried sounds as well as smoke. Betsy Plunkett knew it was for this reason that her husband had ordered this bedroom to be left empty. But what was she to do with not a spare room in the house, aside from this one, and Miss needing a place to stay? As if a wee slip of a girl could be interested in the quiet little man from London.

She looked down at the shivering girl, and her face softened. Of course she wouldn't disturb Miss Vanessa. Men and their foolishness! She sighed, blew out the candles, closed the door as quietly as she could, and went about the business of keeping the Rose and Garter a well-run inn.

Left to herself, Vanessa gradually relaxed as the warmth of the fire spread throughout the room. Presently her teeth stopped chattering, and she lay as if rendered senseless.

Sometime during the night, she stirred, uncomfortable now in the chill that had invaded the room. Still somewhat befuddled, she arose and managed to stagger toward the fireplace, thinking to prod a little life into the embers before adding more fuel. In the quiet of the room an insistent murmur of indistinct voices was impossible to ignore. They seemed to come from the chimney itself. Believing her imagination to be playing tricks on her hearing, Vanessa was about to stir up the fire when she realized that the conversation had something to do with her. Not every word was distinguishable, but there were two voices: one deep, the other curiously nondescript.

"At Shelburne? The Excisement has been ordered to investigate?" This was the deeper voice.

"As for the Riding Officer . . ."

"There's been trouble with the navy. Do we have to contend with land officers as well?" The speaker with the deep voice must have turned away, for she missed his next words.

The other man laughed. "Which would halt the traffic," he said in a precise voice.

There was momentary silence. Then: "Yes, I see what you mean," the deep voice drawled. "A few obstacles will create an element of authenticity."

"Exactly, my lord. If it is too easy, they will become suspicious."

Both voices were clear now. The sound came through the fireplace as if it did not exist.

"And the Riding Officer?"

"There have been reports of lights on the beach and

in the Park as well as within Shelburne Hall. It is common knowledge that only the caretaker and his wife are in residence and would have no occasion to be out after dark—as well as not having the stomach for it. Therefore," the voice went on pedantically, as though the speaker was ticking off the items on his fingers, "therefore, you had better proceed with caution. It would never do for the Earl of Melcourt to be found engaged in a matter of questionable legality. And, needless to say, our friend would not be pleased if our plans were to be upset."

Caught up in the discovery of the identity of the deeper-voiced speaker, Vanessa lost part of his response.

". . . by my mother, Lady Presteign. I have discovered that the Charldon girl is due back in England, and if I must marry her to obtain the property, marry her I will."

The Charldon girl! That was she! No one was going to marry her for the sake of Shelburne Park if she had anything to say about it.

"Very good, my lord."

The scraping of chairs seemed to signal the completion of their conference. Vanessa knew, as surely as if she had been in the room with them, that one of the men would be leaving in a matter of minutes. Her bare feet made no whisper of sound as she crossed the icy floor. She was attempting to push open the casement when she spied a tall figure emerge from the shadows beneath the overhang and take the reins from the hands of a stableboy who had just appeared with his mount from around the corner of the building. Afraid that a sudden movement might catch the eye of the horseman as he turned to leave, Vanessa drew farther into the shadows.

Only once did the rider look back, but Vanessa remained motionless and made no effort to withdraw until he had disappeared from sight. Then, stirring up the fire and putting aside all thought of rest, she gratefully slipped her weary self between the cold sheets and prepared to mull over all that she had heard. Due to the perverse nature of sleep, she knew no more until morning.

While an exhausted Vanessa slept on, untroubled, the Earl of Melcourt sat before his fire damning his obligation to William Pitt.

He might very well be put into a precarious matrimonial position if he was obliged to offer for the girl for the sake of an empty house and a deserted stretch of beach. But Shelburne's sheltered cove and secret tunnels afforded safety to the men who risked their lives for the information wanted by His Majesty's government.

That he, the Earl of Melcourt, had allowed himself to be talked into volunteering for some of these missions did not trouble him in the least. Nevertheless, he might wish that Pitt had selected another base for his operations, not for any distaste Melcourt felt for the illegal trade, but because of the personal problems that were arising. After all, every youngster brought up in that part of the world accepted smuggling as commonplace and consumed with equal enjoyment daily rations of bread, butter, jam, and tales of the great gangs of the past.

The Earl had been sure that Pitt would prefer the

Cinque Ports to this part of Dorset, but in the position of First Lord of the Treasury, he had done his best to destroy the trade, starting at the Deal beaches. Now, to gain secret information for Pitt he, Sylvester Vinton, ninth Earl of Melcourt, was supplying patronage to one of the few illicit crews still functioning, and for a man who was not even a Whig! He had promised Pitt what had seemed little enough at the time—to gain possession of the Shelburne property—but he had no idea that he would have to do more than purchase it.

Perhaps, as he had told Pitt's man, Leeds, at the Rose and Garter, his mother would know of some way to approach Sir Lucius Charldon to gain his consent to at least rent the property. The older man was constantly in the hands of the moneylenders and could certainly use the money—unless he was holding out for a marriage settlement. And, of course, Pitt could not be burdened with these most unusual legal entanglements. As Melcourt now sat before his fire, he wondered if his mother was aware of the deucedly strange disposition of the Shelburne estate.

He must not forget another thing: to stop at the inn and ask innkeeper Plunkett about the room above the one Leeds had occupied. There had been no sign of an arrival, and undoubtedly Plunkett would have warned him if anyone had taken that room, yet he was almost certain he had seen someone at the window. If he was not mistaken, there could be the very devil to pay.

All thoughts of solving Mr. Pitt's dilemma were put aside as his lordship perused the contents of a letter handed to him by his butler.

"Damn!" he muttered beneath his breath. "Has she no sense?" He crushed the engraved paper in a convulsive grip and flung it from him.

"Did your lordship mean to burn this letter?" Parker asked as he picked up the paper.

"I suppose it's necessary," the Earl remarked with rueful humor. "Is it common knowledge that I have an interest in Shelburne Hall, Parker?"

"Merely suspicioned, my lord, and not for the real reason. I had it from Mrs. Clemson, who had it from her niece, who had it from Lady Charldon's personal maid that you and Lady Miranda Charldon . . ."

"Spare my blushes, Parker. When Lady Charldon first began to send me these letters, we thought it would be a good idea if Pitt used the same letter paper."

"It was an excellent idea, my lord," said Parker. "The Charldon cipher is as well known in the neighborhood as your lordship's. There is also good reason to burn your correspondence. Not that you have to concern yourself with *our* people, my lord, but from time to time we have to use village girls," he added almost apologetically.

"Poor Mrs. Clemson," said the Earl with a smile. "If I do marry Miss Charldon, Parker, I will have to see that our permanent staff is augmented here at Melcourt. With a new Countess in residence all year around, the housekeeper will have her dearest wish." The Earl stretched out his long legs toward the fire. "I would burn all Lady Miranda Charldon's letters without opening them, but how then could I tell them from Pitt's?"

He frowned thoughtfully, regarding the blaze upon

the hearth. "And since in all likelihood I will marry Lady Charldon's stepdaughter, Vanessa, my correspondence could create complications."

Completely but silently in agreement, and having satisfied himself that his lordship needed nothing more that evening, Parker wished him a good night and withdrew from the room, leaving the Earl to his thoughts.

The fact that people talked about Lady Charldon meeting him at Shelburne had worked to his advantage, but now he had no intention of encouraging her. Miranda was becoming tiresome in her demands and entirely too possessive. She was also much too free with her tongue in front of friends and servants alike. The relationship was becoming tedious.

Perhaps the return of Lady Charldon's stepdaughter would serve a dual purpose—one having nothing to do with Pitt. As for complications arising from Lady Charldon's letters to him, he would have to take his chances.

He shrugged athletic shoulders out of his close-fitting superfine coat without the help of his valet, then loosened his elegant cravat—neither of which he had ever found necessary to do for comfort, being a man who wore his clothes rather than the other way around—but something was feeling too tight.

CHAPTER THREE

"Truly, I am happy to see you, Addy dear, but how impossible of Abel to drag you out on such a morning!"

"'Twas I did the dragging all the way here to the Rose and Garter, Miss Vanessa."

The damsel so addressed looked at her old nurse appraisingly. "Still running things, are you?"

The old woman seemed to increase in stature and a militant sparkle in her eyes made her appear much younger. "Aye, that I am." A smile touched her lips. "Even the housekeeper at the manor is wise enough to come to me with her problems. She says she don't know how they got on without me when I was in France with you. And that, miss, is why I'm here asking you not to go home until tomorrow. They're all a-twitter this morning, not knowing what to do next what with your whole family coming, two of the housemaids flat on their backs, and cook barely on her feet again," she said by way of explanation. She looked at her former charge critically. "I do believe you could do with a little working on before you're inspected by them. Even such a one as Abel noticed you're not in very good looks."

Vanessa shivered. "I'm not sure I want to be presented for their inspection, Addy." Once saying that, Vanessa began to tell her story, although she was beginning to feel that Addy might be alarmed out of all proportion by it.

The woman was pensive. "It might be that Sir Lucius has something in his mind, for 'tis true he's been asking me for some time whether convent life made you more biddable," she said, a frown ridging her brow. "I never told him that you were never in a convent in your life. He deserves no sympathy after getting rid of you the way he did." Addy looked darkly at the young girl. "And as for you, Miss Vanessa, you shouldn't have let the Comte send me away before you left."

"You did the only thing possible by leaving when you did," said Vanessa. "If you had remained in France, neither of us would have been able to get away." She shrugged. "As it was, Raoul and I had to travel halfway across France as though pursued by devils, as likely we were."

"And what of the young Comtesse? Why didn't she come with you as Comte Raoul wanted?"

"She's expecting a baby, Addy. She hasn't been well, so she'll have to stay in the mountains with the other Girondists. Even with Robespierre dead, Raoul is afraid for her," Vanessa concluded with a shudder.

"What a sad thing that the old Comtesse did not live to see an heir born to her grandson."

"She knew, Addy. She tried to hold on, but she couldn't." Tears were in the girl's eyes. "It was that terrible winter . . . not enough food . . . no medicine . . ." She choked, unable to continue.

Addy continued to reminisce matter-of-factly, giving her young mistress a chance to regain her composure. "If it wasn't for those strange people who brought the firewood and food, none of us would have made it through the winter. It's surprising that they couldn't get medicine for the old lady."

"But they did, Addy. They tried, but she wouldn't take it. She said I should thank them and tell them it should be saved for the children as she was so old it didn't matter. But it did matter, it did. That was what she said, but, Addy, I know that wasn't the real reason she refused what they brought. I could see it in her eyes! She was contemptuous of them. To her they were the *canaille* who had destroyed her Paris.

"With every piece of wood we placed on the fire, I think she shriveled, for some of it was fine furniture looted from homes she knew. I think at the end she was sorry she had refused their help, for she wanted so much to see her great-grandchild." Her voice broke on the last words.

"No, Miss Vanessa," came the calm, reassuring voice. "As much as she may have wanted that very thing, she would never go against her beliefs." Addy patted the girl's hands, which had tightened into fists, making them relax.

Vanessa was silent for a moment. "How well you knew her. Better than I. I have a lot to learn, haven't I?" She sighed ruefully. "I wouldn't have turned them away."

"I'm so much closer in age to her, Miss Vanessa, so I can understand how she felt. But had she been your age, she'd have felt it cowardly to lie back and die. She'd have joined you and those wicked youngsters who went with you—and a more rascally set of villains I've never seen. They looked like they belonged in prison."

"Some of them had been in prison, Addy, and most—no, all of them stole. Honesty does not put food in one's mouth, after all. Raoul and I were lucky that a little money bought their services and a little more kept them loyal. He and I were able to leave Paris as Citizen Deputy Gaudet and his secretary, Citizen André Vallier, while the real officials were kept hidden in some cellar."

The old nurse, relieved that Miss Charldon was absorbed with the telling of the story and no longer in danger of abandoning herself to tears, proceeded to busy herself with the pitifully few things her young mistress had brought with her. Hoping to find something more suitable than the girl's present masculine attire, she shook out the folds of a habit that had obviously seen better days, and as she did so, something dropped to the floor. Retrieving and examining it, she was about to scold Miss Charldon for her carelessness when that young lady saw what she held.

"Oh, no! How could he! Only see, Addy, this opens when you press it here. . . . Look inside!"

Thus directed, the old woman trained her eyes upon the twin miniatures revealed in the open locket.

"Comte Raoul and his lady!"

"He must have slipped it among my things while I was sleeping, and I never heard him," she mused. "He could have done it at any of the inns where we shared a room."

Addy looked at her sharply, and she had the grace to blush. "It sounds worse than it was," she answered defiantly.

With the familiarity of an old family retainer Addy extracted a full, if blameless, confession from a reluctant Miss Charldon. When she had finished, her former nurse stated bluntly that no one with any sense would think any the worse of her, but as everyone knew, society was made up of a bunch of ninnies so they had better hope the story of her mad escape from France in the company of a dashing young nobleman would never be heard.

"Oh, fiddle!" Vanessa exclaimed. "I can't worry all my life, waiting and wondering if someone will discover that I dressed like a man and behaved in a manner that would choke a few old biddies."

Not even to Addy would she divulge that she and Raoul had been inseparable, even to sharing the same bed for one night. Innocent as it had been to him, she still felt rattled by it, in spite of Raoul's laughing protestations and his likening her to a new puppy. She hoped he would have the good sense to tell Jeanne the truth—that they had shared the one remaining bed in the inn because she had been shivering, both of them so tired that they ached, and with still another hard day's ride before them.

She looked down at the miniature of Jeanne. Would she trust her husband? Her eyes traveled to the other likeness. Of course, she chided herself. Even the artist had captured something of their trust and affection for each other; perhaps it was the way they seemed to look at one another.

"People tell me I look like my Cousin Jeanne. I

wonder if one day I will have a husband I will love as she loves Raoul. And," she said on further reflection, "will ever a man feel for me what he feels for her?"

Surprisingly, Addy answered her. "A beautiful woman will draw many men, like moths to a flame. You will have to pick the best."

Vanessa was startled. She had not realized she had spoken aloud. She quickly recovered her composure and commented wryly, "There is a touch of the philosopher in you, Addy. In any case it is not my wish to have a man desire me for my looks alone."

"And I dare say none will, if you continue to look a fright." Addy made a face as she ran her hands through the girl's hair. "Did this have to be cut so short?"

"That was Raoul's idea. I had to look the part."

"And the color! Faugh! If it won't come out, you'll have to wear a wig."

"Jeanne said my hair would be like a torch leading the Bureau of Police our way."

Grudgingly, Addy commented, "If she said that, I warrant she was right. But your skin, surely . . ."

"That was my idea," Vanessa said with a gamine grin. "The clothes and the hair, and of course the calling, did not go with such white skin. André Vallier would be a sallow youth. Add a pair of eyeglasses that Dr. Franklin had left so many years ago when he had visited the old Comtesse—*et voilà!*"

All day Addy worked on a protesting Vanessa. She had to concede that staining her complexion had been the only thing to do, else those blue-violet eyes of hers would have betrayed her, the eyeglasses notwithstanding. Willow-slender, delightfully curved, scarcely reaching middle height, Vanessa conveyed the impression of being a much taller girl—due, no doubt, to the fluid grace of her carriage. Even with her hair this muddy color—now several shades lighter, to be sure, but with barely a trace of the glorious red that had earned her the childhood nickname "Firetop"—she was a beauty.

By the next morning Addy was more exhausted than she wished Vanessa to know and could not wait to send her out for some air. Nothing loath, Vanessa took advantage of the opportunity and cajoled Addy into returning to the manor during her own absence, as there was surely no need for them to travel together.

"I am not going to get lost, Addy, and you should be happy not to have me underfoot." Vanessa, seeing that she was gaining headway, promised to arrive in good time. "Though I wonder why it is necessary when my stepmama is not expected until late and my father, from what I remember, spends his time away from the gaming tables filling himself with brandy."

"I wouldn't know, miss," sniffed Addy, now very much the upper servant, in the tone of one administering a rebuke. She turned to fasten the unusual pendant around Miss Charldon's neck. Although she remarked once again that Vanessa might have been the model for the miniature but for the eyes and hair, the young Comtesse's being brown, the disapproving expression on the old face did not soften. Vanessa arranged her locket to better display its fine workmanship and paid no heed to the sour face. She kissed the wrinkled cheek and, undaunted, went off to see what the stable of the Rose and Garter had to offer.

She found a nag suitable for her requirements, and declining the offer of a stableboy to accompany her, but helping herself surreptitiously to a lantern, Vanessa set out determined to investigate what the years had done to Shelburne Park.

CHAPTER FOUR

Scores of gnarled oaks hunched over the old drive. Frisky squirrels played tag on the bare branches and a few hardy birds flashed between ancient trunks. Vanessa gave the horse its head, allowing it to pick its way through the underbrush that narrowed the long neglected road. Even after all this time it still hurt to recall the last summer, when she had never once entered Shelburne Hall the conventional way and had delighted in confounding Travers, her grandfather's butler. He invariably had attributed her unannounced presence to laxity on the part of some young footman, although, when taxed, all denied that they had seen little Miss Vanessa. In truth, they had been just as puzzled as old Travers; Vanessa and her grandfather had dared not look at each other as a very perturbed Travers served them a light luncheon, surrounded by the ceiling-high bookcases and linenfold paneling of the library.

Although at the time it had seemed incredible that no one had stumbled on the secret entryway to Shelburne Hall, Vanessa and Lord Redmont soon realized that only their unearthing of the most explicit directions—along with a floor plan of the original building—had enabled them to make their discovery. So far as they knew, the panel served as an entrance only. They had never found a way to operate the mechanism from within the library.

Vanessa thought fondly of her grandfather as the horse threaded its way between upright yews guarding the tomb of one of Shelburne's former owners. It was strange that no one had questioned the desire of this particular Vinton to have a memorial built for himself outside the family burial grounds, while Cromwell was one step behind him. They were so unimaginative, those Roundheads, but then, as now, the dark-eyed Dorset country folk were not inclined to talk with strangers.

"The secret of the crypt," Vanessa chuckled, and the sound reverberated hollowly. A certain eerie ring to the phrase made her wonder if Mrs. Radcliffe might not relish it for a title. She shuddered as she brushed aside a particularly revolting spider nested beneath an innocent-appearing metal ring set below the Vinton family crest. For a moment there was silence as she turned the ring. Allowing barely enough time to wonder whether the passage of years had inflicted damage to the mechanism, there was a slight movement of the casket cover.

Quickly she raised the dusty lid, revealing a steep flight that might have been hewn out of rock. Almost without thinking, Vanessa lifted her lantern and de-

33

scended into the depths. She navigated the precarious stairway more by feel than by sight, for it was so precipitous that she was quite unable to look down at her feet. At the bottom of the steps she hesitated, going neither right nor left. Then, with the air of one making a sudden decision, she walked straight ahead and the feeble light from her lantern merged with the shadows.

Vanessa let the panel slide smoothly closed behind her.

"Sit down, girl."

She spun around, looked toward the massive, flat-topped walnut desk where her grandfather had sat while she had curled up in the deep chair beside him, and her breath caught with a little choking sound. For a moment her thoughts had been so real she had heard his well-loved voice. She could almost hear him turning the yellowed pages of an old journal—almost see him squinting through his new eyeglasses, complaining that they were not as comfortable as his old pair—almost hear him clear his throat as he always did when he was about to propose some secret venture the two of them would undertake—without her grandmother's knowledge.

"Ahem . . . On the first clear day we must up and see if it is still possible to get into the Castle from the crypt. I daresay you might be able to leave by the old escape route too, you're such a little monkey," he told her with affection, "but your grandmother would never allow it."

"We don't have to tell her, Grandfather."

"She's a good one for ferretin' out secrets, m'dear," he responded with a sigh.

34

"Has she found out about your new hunter?"

Lord Redmont's eyes brightened. "Can't say she has, but she's not home, remember. I promise myself a ride before the week is out."

"It's too bad we never found a secret way out of the library, for then you wouldn't have to ride before Grandmama comes home from Bath," Vanessa said roguishly.

He snorted. "Wise, ain't you? Have your brother beat four times over and then some. No spunk, that Andrew. That's why I'm leaving Shelburne to you and tied up so neatly that that father of yours can't get his hands on it. When he's twenty-five, Andrew will come into the money I put aside for your mother. A pretty penny, that, if he's not a fool. It's you, girl, that I have to protect."

"But, Grandfather . . ."

"No buts, child. You'll give me your arm and we'll visit that black rascal of a horse," he said, a smile lighting his craggy countenance as he put his notes inside the small journal. "Just place this book on a shelf for me. Those pesky housemaids will be tidying before your grandmother returns, and there's no telling where they'll hide it," he chuckled. "This way it will be there for another day."

That day had never come. Her grandfather had taken the ride he had promised himself. Both horse and rider had fallen, and Lord Redmont had been killed instantly.

The smell of books, leather, and polished wood was just as it had been. The bas-relief above the mantelshelf was as dust free as if the maids had to answer to her grandmother. Evidently the place was well cared for, which was surprising. Travers (if it was indeed her grandfather's former butler) had been an old man when she had been a child. Of course, it was possible that he had been replaced by someone younger, although she did not think it likely that her father would spend money on a caretaker, even if it was her money. She should have checked with the estate agent. It was no longer necessary for her to do things in secret; her father would not be able to prohibit her comings and goings, and it would save him the trouble of consulting with the agent if she took over the management. Naturally it would serve to occupy her time too. Yes, tomorrow she would see about taking the reins into her own very capable hands. She would see, too, that Travers was well rewarded for his pains, Vanessa decided as she found the journal just where she had put it eight years ago. She shivered. The room felt as if someone had merely stepped out for a few minutes.

The afternoon sun won out momentarily over the gray clouds that had menaced her ride all morning and, in so doing, sent a shaft of light through the mullioned windows and across the library table. The prismatic effect of light breaking up into its diverse colors suddenly caught Vanessa's eye. She stiffened, unable to credit to imagination what her eyes showed her. Surely, if the crystal decanter and partially filled glass on the library table were any indication, whoever had been interrupted would soon return. Not Travers, surely. His taste had never run to fine French brandy, and brandy it was, Vanessa knew as she passed the glass beneath her nose.

Undoubtedly it would be wiser to postpone her

visit than to satisfy her curiosity, she thought as she opened the library door the merest crack, but she was rarely wise, as Vanessa would have been the first to admit. She simply hoped that the library's previous occupant was too far away to cause her any concern.

"You can't mean to offer for her?"

A woman's low, sultry voice reached her ears, and Vanessa realized that the speaker was no more than a yard from the door.

"I don't know. . . . Well, I suppose I do. I'd put up with almost anything to get Shelburne Park into Vinton hands again."

"You must have a friend—someone who could marry her and then sell the property to you, Melcourt."

He laughed. "Is she so bad then, your little step-daughter?"

Her father's wife! What was she doing here with the Earl of Melcourt? And talking about her! Vanessa stood frozen to the spot.

"Don't tease me," the indelicate creature pleaded. "You know how I feel about . . . us. Lucius is a very sick man," the voice almost purred. "His doctor assured me . . ."

"Don't bury your husband before he is dead, my dear Miranda; it is in very bad taste. Besides," he said sardonically, "he may fool you, after all."

"But, Sylvester, I thought that you and I—"

"No, Miranda," he interrupted firmly.

"Don't tell me you plan to set up your nursery?" she jeered.

"That, madam, is something a man discusses with his wife, not his future mother-in-law."

The unseen object of the Earl's matrimonial plans

thought he was taking entirely too much for granted and opened the door a hairsbreadth more to see this paragon.

Miranda laughed hysterically. "I wish you luck," she said.

"Do you, my sweet, when it means our relationship will be somewhat changed?" He grinned wickedly. "Tell me, do you dislike her so much, the little stepdaughter?"

"You might say I don't know her at all. You might also say I don't want to know her. Eight years of backboards, embroidery, and 'Lower your eyes, mademoiselle' in a French convent is enough to turn any female into a wax doll."

"You must have something wrong there, Miranda."

"I have nothing wrong. I hope you're not disappointed in your choice of a bride."

"Vixen! That is exactly what you're hoping, aren't you? But now, my dear, you must be on your way. They expect you at Charldon Manor, and your servants, quite unlike mine, don't know how to keep their own counsel."

From her vantage point in the library, Vanessa Charldon watched the Earl escort her stepmother through the doors of the Great Hall. If only she had kept the panel open—a vain wish, now. There was no telling how long Miranda would keep him busy. With no way to go but up, and still clutching the borrowed lantern, she made a wild dash for the stairs. She had almost reached the top before she realized that the pounding in her ears came entirely from her heart and not from her noble pursuer. Risking a glance over her shoulder, she saw him enter the Hall. A final burst of speed and Vanessa flew into a room near the top of the stairs, praying that he had not seen her but fearing that she had not altogether escaped his notice.

Her breath was loud in her ears as she struggled to open a window and then concealed herself behind the holland-covered portieres. The Earl, just as she had hoped, ran to the open window upon entering the room. Without hesitation she struck out at him, the full weight of the heavy lantern behind the blow. He fell with a thud, stretching his full length on the floor.

She placed the lantern on the floor beside him as she leaned over him. Her hands were quite steady, she was pleased to note, as she checked his heart. He would be blessed with a thundering headache—which he richly deserved, thought Vanessa with satisfaction as she drew the door shut behind her and descended the stairs. Invite his women to her house, would he!

Dashing tears of anger from her eyes with the back of her hand, she swore all manner of revenge on the man who was planning to make her his bride. She struggled with the doors leading from the Great Hall as if attacking them; the desire to kick, scratch, and bite anything barring her way was overwhelming. How she wished she had that—that—coxcomb—in front of her. She'd soon sharpen her claws on him. Demure little convent miss was she! Did these people think that nothing had happened in France, then? And as for his noble lordship, he would condescend to marry her even though he might find her repulsive! How she would make him suffer! The doors slammed behind her, echoing the violence of her thoughts.

Checking the pocket of her riding habit to make sure she had not dropped the journal, she began the long walk to where she had tethered her horse. She did not notice that the slim gold chain that had supported her most prized possession was no longer about her neck.

CHAPTER FIVE

"Oh, how I hate them!"

"There, there, pet. 'Tis all upset you are, and soaked through most like. Let Addy help you undress and then you can sit by me and tell me all about it."

Minutes later, warm and dry, her slight body nestled close to her former nurse, Vanessa's agitation was the only remaining sign of the violent storm that had overtaken her on the way to Charldon Manor.

Several times during her narrative, a comment was forced from her unwavering advocate. "That wretched woman! It was bad enough your father sent you away from your own home because of her—and his fault too for lettin' you hobnob with the grooms."

Vanessa could not but protest that since the death of her grandfather her happiest hours had been the ones spent in the stables, causing her servant to turn her eyes upward and address a higher authority.

"Aye. And 'tis that not what I've been saying? All her time spent with servants and"—she threw a dark glance at her charge—"and with the Gypsies, I'll not be doubting, and her father wondering why she was a little savage."

Once started, the old woman was hard to stop, and Vanessa, sensing in her an indignation to match her own, had no intention of curbing her champion. "Not being asked to your own brother's wedding, and Gwenyth Vinton never even knowing that your scatterbrained brother Andrew had a sister until her mother—your godmother, dearie—demanded to see you. And then your fine Aunt Clemency telling you that your mama-to-be was scarcely older than you and beautiful and accomplished. You so hurt over losing your grandfather, I could have told your father what would happen."

"I remember Grandmama crying, Addy, the day you took me to see her. It was my father made her cry, I think, because he was storming down the steps when we got there." Vanessa shivered. "I tried to talk to him, but he looked right through me."

Addy nodded her head as if she too had cause to recall that day. "Your grandmother hadn't been well since your grandfather died, Miss Vanessa, and your father had told her he was about to remarry and wanted to send you off to a convent. They argued until she gave in, but she insisted on making the arrangements. That was all right with your father—if she paid.

"Your grandmother wrote to her old friend, whose grandson had married your Cousin Jeanne. They made up this scheme between them, the two old ladies, and all the while everyone thought you were in a convent."

41

"That's what Miranda said," Vanessa explained. "I wondered why she said that."

"It's what they all believe—and all the time you were with your cousin's family."

Vanessa sat up with a start. "But why do they think I was in a convent all this time? Aren't they aware of what was going on in France?"

"Sit back, Miss Vanessa," Addy told her, and continued her story like a fairy tale. "Old Comtesse didn't want anyone to know. She was very angry that you'd been hurt and your grandmother, too. She thought of you as her very own grandchild. You could have planned murder, and she would have sat there nodding her head and giving you more ideas for mischief-making. Not that you needed any." Vanessa, her eyes closing, listened to Addy's muttering. "Convent— hmph! School for hoydens more like! Ah, but you'll not let them marry you off to an old sobersides, my beauty. She taught you too well to get your own way."

The girl was almost asleep. "He was so sure he could have me for the asking," she murmured. "I shall lead him a merry dance just as Madame said." She yawned. "And Addy, he wasn't old at all. He was young and handsome . . . very handsome. . . ."

With great tenderness Addy covered the sleeping girl and placed a pillow under her head. As she left the room, she frowned thoughtfully. The only Vinton who fit that description was Gwenyth's brother, Sylvester Vinton. She must be getting old. She had forgotten that the old lord had died.

So he wanted to marry Miss Vanessa, did he? There would be trouble ahead when those two met. The old Comtesse may have been right when she said young

Vanessa's life would read like a romantic novel, full of adventure until she found her one true love! Well, she for one would help all she could, the way she had promised the old lady, knowing she'd never see her again. As if she wouldn't have, anyway! The girl had the wind behind her now, Lord keep her. She would sail on until she reached a sheltered harbor. "Please, Lord, may it be soon," she prayed. "I'm an old woman and I'd like to see her happy before I go."

Although Melcourt's headache was still very much with him the next morning, he presented himself at the Rose and Garter, determined to identify the inhabitant of the corner room. My lord, not being dull-witted, was not overwhelmed with surprise to discover that the elusive guest had been none other than Miss Vanessa Charldon who, innkeeper Plunkett assured him, was "a mere slip of a girl and she'd pay no heed to anything said that night after such a rough crossin' and I'm mortal sorry that me missus put her in that room. So tired out she was that she never left her room the whole of the morning," the innkeeper said in response to further questioning, "and as for the rest of the day, me lord, I couldn't say, not being there to see."

Plunkett, then, would be unable to help trace the lady's movements. "What of the stableboys?" the Earl inquired.

"I'll be happy to oblige by asking among them, but that little lady was looking so poorly, me lord, that me wife Betsy sent for Addy—her that was Miss Charldon's nurse."

"And did she come?"

"So the missus tells it, y'lordship. Would ye want to be asking any questions o' her?"

"I think not, Plunkett. Just the stableboys, if you please. . . . And Plunkett, I believe this belongs to you. . . ."

Innkeeper Plunkett had wondered why the Earl was carrying a lantern, but he would never ask. He excused himself from the Earl's presence with considerable haste and much puzzlement. He returned with equal alacrity, even more puzzled, and with information that seemed to satisfy my lord, who left the inn, his good humor restored, almost forgetting the pain in his head.

On this same morning, not too many miles distant, Andrew Charldon contemplated his breakfast with his usual attention. A young man of some twenty-nine summers, his placid face reflected an air of extreme youthfulness that his concern with food did not belie. He was engaged in placing thin fingers of toast in his egg cup when Vanessa entered the room. As she shut the door behind her, Andrew looked up.

"Good morning, Vanessa," he said, and returned to his self-appointed task as if it had been last night and not eight years ago that he had last seen her. The entrance of the butler with fresh toast limited Vanessa to a greeting in kind, but as Bassett left the room, she turned to her brother with a militant glint in her eye.

"Is that all you are going to say to me? Good morning?"

"Well? Would you have me say, good night? It *is* morning." Andrew's eyes were focused on Vanessa's head, and it occurred to her that perhaps her wig was askew. His next words wiped the thought from her

44

mind. "Don't be unreasonable, Vanessa. Didn't you sleep well? One sometimes doesn't after a long trip."

"Then you do recall that I've been away!" she commented, suddenly stiffening as something about the way Andrew held himself reminded her of their father. The resemblance was fleeting, gone even as he moved and began to cut fresh strips of toast to add to the gelatinous mass already in the egg cup. Vanessa swallowed hard, promising herself a solitary breakfast in her room if this was the sight that would greet her each morning.

"Thank you, Bassett, that will be all," she said in relief as the servant's appearance with her coffee tore her eyes from Andrew's egg cup. She went through the ritual of adding cream and sugar, then sipped the beverage, not really tasting it.

"Well?"

Andrew's voice came as a shock and she almost jumped.

"You wanted to say something to me," he said, "but you stopped when Bassett came in. What was it?"

"Nothing," she scowled. There was no use asking if he had missed her. In his own way, she thought, he must be as selfish as their father. For all he had looked at her, she could have been dressed in sackcloth and ashes, and he would not have noticed.

Andrew pushed his plate away, glanced at Vanessa, and shuddered. "Don't work yourself into a fit, Firetop! If you are going to see Father this morning, change that attire. You'll get short shrift from him if you go in looking like a cross between a lump of suet and somebody's poor relation."

Vanessa, who had indeed spent the better part of an

45

hour trying to make herself as unattractive as a lump of suet, was not about to undo her handiwork. She was so pleased with its results, in fact, that she missed her brother's next remark and had to ask him to repeat it.

"I said that it's bad enough Father has already prepared a welcoming speech for you without your planning to shock him too."

"What do you mean?"

"I found an underlined copy of *King Lear* in the library," Andrew announced, forestalling further response from his sister by raising his hand. "I'm sure Father left it, Vanessa, for he used some of the phrases when he spoke to me. It was almost a deathbed scene, if you can picture it. He began with 'A man more sinned against than sinning' and went on to filial ingratitude. I had to cover my eyes when he said he'd married Miranda to provide a mother's tender care for his ungrateful daughter."

Vanessa snickered in derision.

"Then he moaned that all the trouble he'd had with his sister had been your fault too, ever since Aunt Edgerton called Miranda an impertinent trollop."

"She didn't!"

"She most certainly did! For that matter, she's called her a lot worse in the past eight years, but I can't see how he can lay that at your door."

"I must say that my memories of Aunt Edgerton were none too pleasant, but now I'm looking forward to seeing her again. I think I'll be more appreciative of her finer qualities; her regard for the truth makes her of sterling worth."

"Gammon, Vanessa. She don't tell the truth for its own sake, but just to put people out of countenance. She can't be trusted any more than father."

"He wants something from me, Andrew," Vanessa said, secure in the knowledge that her father would not have expended ten shillings, let alone ten guineas, to get her home had there not been something in it for him. "What will he say to me?"

"Something about his being a kind old father or that a thankless child is sharper than a serpent's tooth, I imagine. *That* passage was underlined twice," Andrew answered.

"That's not what I mean. What are his plans for me? Do you know, Andrew?"

Andrew either would not or could not tell her what was expected of her. Vanessa had hoped to know by now. Perhaps, if she prompted her father . . .

In a matter of minutes a very proud and reserved Vanessa Charldon stood silently before her father, waiting for him to initiate the conversation. Neither thought it strange that no embrace or endearment was exchanged.

Sir Lucius cleared his throat, patently embarrassed. "My very good child. It's wonderful to have you home again. As you can see," he gestured distastefully toward an array of medicaments at his bedside, "I do not enjoy the best of health."

Vanessa's silence forced him to continue, making him say more than he had intended. "Had I known of the danger, I would have sent for you earlier. I may be weak and foolish, but not so foolish that I should knowingly endanger your life."

47

With a voice as chill as her blank features, she answered him, "The Comte de St. Varres expects there will be further disturbances, and he felt he could no longer protect me. I had no choice, or I should not have inflicted myself on you."

He winced and wished he could have spared himself this distressing interview with such a dowdy, lumpish creature.

"I thought it better for you to go to your mother's family. It was her wish that you be educated at a convent, else I should never have sent you away. Believe me, my child, I did it for your own good."

"Will that be all, sir?"

"Cruel, cruel, to be so cold to your old, kind father who gave you all . . ." Sir Lucius placed one hand in the general vicinity of his heart while with the other he poured a prudent measure of brandy and sipped it for its restorative qualities, using the time to gather his wits.

Vanessa stood with her head bowed in pretended humility, recalling Andrew's warning. "Will that be all, sir?" she repeated, rousing Sir Lucius from his reverie.

"What's that? Oh, yes, of course . . . I'm rather tired." He closed his eyes as she turned to leave. "And . . . hmm . . . Vanessa?"

"Yes, sir?"

"I will ask Andrew to discuss something with you. I find I have quite tired myself. Andrew will convey my wishes to you."

Once again she turned to leave and heard him mutter something. "Sir?"

"Nothing, child, nothing."

Vanessa's face was tight with anger as she left the room. "Whey-faced frump" he'd called her. She couldn't face Andrew now; she was too angry with him, with their father, with herself for allowing them to place her in such a position. She was no fool, no Cordelia offering good for evil, and she said as much to Andrew when he later revealed their father's plan.

"I'm no asset to be married off to the highest bidder," she cried as she paced from one end of the library to the other.

"I don't say you are, Vanessa. Do you think I pay any heed to Father?"

Quite thoughtfully, she compared this shabby room with the library at Shelburne Park. Her lip curled in contempt. No wonder her father needed money. It only remained to find out exactly why the Earl was interested in her.

"You are advising me to marry the Earl, are you not?"

"For your own sake," he responded, ignoring her skeptical look as he sprawled on the sofa. "Sylvester is young, wealthy, and of good family. What more can you want?"

"What does he want with me?"

"He's my best fried—and he's Gwenyth's brother."

"Gwenyth! But she's your wife!"

"Of course, noddy. Can't she be both?"

Vanessa ignored his insult. "She hates me."

"Not at all."

"She thinks I'm not good enough for her brother."

Andrew grinned. "Don't blame her. I sat opposite you at breakfast, remember?"

49

Vanessa stopped pacing and threw herself into a chair.

"That's the chair with the weak leg, Vanessa. Careful!"

"Maybe it will collapse, and I'll break my neck. That should suit your wife." Her voice had a rasping quality that grated on his nerves. "When I saw her at dinner last night, she made it very obvious she had no use for me. No doubt she waited up half the night for you to come home. She wanted to tell you how commonplace your sister is."

"Commonplace? No! She caught me this morning and told me you were beyond belief. . . . And you are." He stood and held out his hand for hers, wishing she would confide in him. "Doing it much too brown, my girl. You can't have changed that much—even after eight years in a convent. At breakfast your face was lumpy on one side, now it's the other, and that monstrous wig you're wearing keeps slipping." He looked her dumpy figure up and down as she allowed him to help her up. "I'm no peagoose, Vanessa." Giving a sudden guileless smile, he confided, "And anyway, Addy told me you weren't a total antidote."

"Oh, did she? I'll thank her to keep her comments to herself—and you too, Andrew. Not a word to your friend Melcourt. I would keep my secrets."

CHAPTER SIX

The secrets Vanessa Charldon wished to keep were in danger of being discovered by the Earl. Since the morning he had spoken with Plunkett at the Rose and Garter, he had been as sure of the identity of his attacker as it was possible to be. It only remained to receive confirmation from his mother, Lady Presteign. Or perhaps Richard Cosway, the miniaturist, could tell him about the locket he had found. Inside was a sample of Cosway's unmistakable style. What was more, the man never flattered, and he never forgot a face. The girl had such a lovely face too. Melcourt did not give a thought to the man whose likeness occupied the other side of the locket. He had plans, and the sooner he left for town, the faster these plans could be set in motion.

The Earl's visit to her ladyship in London was not by any means unusual, although one of the younger footmen so far forgot himself as to remark that no buck of his lordship's stamp traveled to town just to pass the time of day with his mother, when he had seen her not three weeks ago. This, too, was what Lady Presteign thought when, on returning to her town house, she was informed that the Earl had arrived and, finding her from home, had gone out to seek some amusement of his own. She had a strong suspicion that her son's presence in town had its roots in the past—not the far-distant past, but in November, to be precise.

At that time, on a fine evening not too long after the opening of Parliament, Lady Presteign had attended a dinner given by William Pitt's niece, Lady Hester Stanhope. Since Pitt seldom appeared at social functions these troubled days, Lady Presteign had been pleasantly surprised to find herself seated beside him. A longtime acquaintance of her ladyship, the Prime Minister had not hesitated to share his concern over the vulnerability of the Channel coast.

"Do you really believe there is a danger?" she had asked.

"Not at this time, although it is always wise to be prepared." He toyed with his wineglass. "Melcourt's family seat—in Dorset, is it not?" he queried, knowing full well it was. "On the coast?"

"Dorset, yes, and on the coast, but no one could land there. I can't think of many places where a small boat would find safe harbor."

Very gently, Pitt then turned the conversation to Shelburne Park. He professed great interest in that area of Dorset—in Shelburne in particular—and frankly admitted that it was of prime importance to the country to have the use of it—but in secret.

Feeling flattered that he reposed such confidence in her powers of discretion, Lady Presteign suggested that her son was the very person the Prime Minister should approach for information. Even as she spoke, a plan began to take shape in Lady Presteign's head, a plan so outrageous that it might very well succeed.

"Perhaps Melcourt could do more than obtain information for you," she told Pitt. "There is a chance, a slim chance, that he could secure the property. I need scarcely tell you that it all depends on your approach," Lady Presteign hinted.

Pitt did not need to be warned that his request should be couched in terms of patriotism, not politics, my lord Melcourt being a Whig.

"I shall be delighted, dear lady, to appeal to Melcourt, but I can't help wondering what you have in mind for your son. I somehow feel—please don't think me ungrateful—I feel as though you were using me to further a plan of your own."

She laughed and responded, "How very astute you are! But surely you will not deny me my own schemes if they do not conflict with yours?"

He bowed. "As I, too, must keep secrets from the one I would help most, I cannot quarrel with you, dear Lady Presteign. I realize more each day how fortunate I am to have your friendship."

"Politically or socially, sir?" she inquired with amusement.

"Both, my lady, both," he admitted with a smile on his pleasant face. "You have a great deal of influence at Court as well as in the diplomatic circles, you know. You could make or break a minister."

Her ladyship, realizing that Mr. Pitt was referring to his uneasy relationship with the King, merely smiled and turned to the man sitting on her right, who was waiting to claim her attention.

Not until the dinner party had long been a memory

in most minds did Lady Presteign wonder if perhaps her meeting with Pitt had been engineered by the master statesman. He had very likely known that Vanessa Charldon was not only her goddaughter but also the owner of Shelburne Park. It was a case of the manipulator being manipulated, she thought with a grimace. She did not like feeling that she had been outwitted, but she felt she could put up with it if it would accomplish her purpose.

Now, months later, she waited for her son to return, for one more stitch to be taken in the tapestry which would release her goddaughter Vanessa from the toils of her father and, perhaps, gain a wife for her demanding son.

"Mother, Benson said you were in your sitting room, but you shouldn't have waited for me," the object of her thoughts said as he bent to kiss her. She had not heard the door open and was jolted out of her daydream.

"Nonsense! I've only now returned from the Duchess of Severn's rout—a shocking bore, I assure you. I should relish a little excitement now. Come to my room, and you can tell me your news."

He sat at the edge of her bed for a thoughtful minute. She did not force the pace, realizing that he was consolidating his thoughts.

"I had a very—disquieting—interview with Sir Lucius."

His mother raised her brows in silent encouragement, but the Earl was too absorbed in his own thoughts to notice.

"Did he agree to sell Shelburne Park?" she prompted.

"No. It seems that the property does not belong to him but is held in trust, with a further inheritance of sixty thousand pounds, for his daughter."

"Well, then, I suppose you shall have to rent the property, although it would not serve Mr. Pitt's purpose half so well," she mused.

He gave a short laugh that was patently not indicative of amusement. "Mr. Pitt won't have to compromise, Mother, since Sir Lucius tells me it is impossible, under the terms of the will, for anyone to rent the Shelburne property."

"It seems a strange will. Did he explain it to you—or just say no?"

"He explained it to me clearly, and I felt he took a perverse delight in doing so. The estate remains in trust for his daughter until she marries. At that time it becomes the possession of her husband, who cannot sell it unless there is no issue within ten years of the marriage."

He stood, walked to the fireplace, then returned to the bed and looked down at his mother.

"The will cannot be set aside, Sir Lucius assures me," he told her dryly. "He attempted that some years ago when he found himself in straitened circumstances. He also made it clear that if I wanted the property badly enough, he would be pleased to welcome me as his son-in-law. Then he had the effrontery to say that you would be pleased, as you and his first wife had intended this."

"That was too bad of him." Lady Presteign frowned. "I hope you didn't insult him."

"No one could insult Sir Lucius when the smell of money is in the air."

"Don't be vulgar, Sylvester!" his mother almost snapped.

He laughed and bent to kiss her still unwrinkled cheek.

"I didn't offend him, love. I merely told him it was something which required a great deal of thought, as the idea of marriage hadn't been paramount in my mind. We then agreed on the importance of having an heir, and I took my leave with a promise to see him after talking with you—something I've put off for too long."

"Sit down, Sylvester. I can't speak with you if you tower over me. . . . There, now we can talk," she said as he returned to her side.

"You do know something about this betrothal, then, don't you, Mother?"

"Yes," she admitted. "Vanessa's mother and I were friends. We came out the same year and often visited back and forth, even after we married. Sir Lucius had not yet dissipated his fortune, you see, and even you will have to admit that the Charldon lineage is impeccable. He's a different man since his first wife died."

"I don't see what this has to do with—"

"Wait! When your sister Gwenyth was born, we planned that someday she and Andrew would marry. Later, when Vanessa was born, we made similar plans for the two of you, including a formal betrothal."

"It was true, then, what Sir Lucius told me."

"You sound shocked."

"I had no idea."

"Of course not. How could you, after all? The first Lady Charldon died the year after Vanessa was born, and although I was—am—the child's godmother, Lucius and I mutually agreed not to continue the connection. He had not been very friendly before your father died, and after I remarried, I wanted none of his toadeating."

"Yet Gwenyth and Andrew met because I brought him home from school with me on the long vacations."

"So they did, my son. They fell in love and decided to marry, without any assistance from me. I did not mention their childhood betrothal until quite recently."

The Earl smiled wryly. "You always encouraged me to have Andrew come home with me."

"Yes, I know. I'm sorry I was never able to do something for his sister, but she was such a baby. . . . The one time I tried, I was put in my place."

She told her son of the reception she had received from Sir Lucius on the occasion of her visit on behalf of her goddaughter.

"I was not able to see her before she was sent away. I lost track of her then, I'm sorry to say, and your inheriting the title so unexpectedly drove everything out of my mind at the time."

"Sir Lucius may have thought he was rid of her, for until I told him I was interested in Shelburne Park he was not happy about her imminent return to England, necessitated by the dangerous political situation in France. I believe he did everything he could to speed her return after that."

"Vanessa should have left France years ago. For that matter, she should have remained in England. But, Sylvester, now that she is returning, isn't there something that can be done to help the poor child?"

"Now, Mother." He raised his hand in protest. "You know me better than to think I would marry a little schoolgirl because we were betrothed when she was in the cradle."

"Of course you need not marry the child, Sylvester. There must be some way we could get Lucius to allow her to come on a visit." She looked at her son, her blue eyes crinkled at the corners. "There is a way," she said speculatively.

"Go on," he told her, laughing. "I am sure you have planned admirably."

"Well, yes, I believe I have. Call on Sir Lucius; let him know that you're not unwilling to meet the terms of the will if you and Miss Charldon will suit. Naturally after you've met her, I too must see her, and I'll be unable to leave London at that time. Lucius will be forced to send her to me for a prolonged visit. Once Vanessa is with me, I doubt that her father will push too hard for her return. As her godmother I shall present her at Court and, like as not, she will i   e a good match before the year is out. She is a Charldon, after all, and a considerable heiress, if one remembers that will."

Her bright eyes twinkled. "Sylvester! If Lucius thinks there is a chance you might offer for Vanessa, no doubt he will permit you to investigate things at Shelburne. No one will be surprised if you take an interest in an estate that might someday be yours, for you're known in the district as a careful landlord. You could redeem your promise to Pitt."

He stood suddenly, frowning. "It might work at that," he told her. The blue eyes that were so like his mother's were troubled as he reviewed the salient points of her proposal.

"Above all, I'll be relieved to rid myself of this obligation to Pitt. It all seemed so trivial at the time. And if having the child with you will make you happy, you shall have her."

"Thank you, my son."

Not many minutes later he left the room, promising to see her in the morning. As he had told her, he was not without doubts as to the wisdom of the course he was contemplating. He would have to return to Melcourt immediately, and it was not a trip he would enjoy. He would show his mother the miniature in the morning; perhaps she could tell him about it. She had a wide circle of acquaintants. It was too bad Lord Presteign was from home; it would have been good to talk it over with him before he rushed headlong into one of his mother's schemes.

As he entered his bedroom, his valet thought he heard the Earl mutter something about "getting it over with," but beyond saying that they would be leaving London on the morrow, his lordship addressed no further remarks to him.

Lady Presteign was more than satisfied with her plan. She had reasons for suggesting to Pitt that he approach Sylvester and ask his help. She knew Sylvester's cynicism did not involve patriotism. It was directed, rather, at women. And no wonder, for they threw themselves at him, the fools. Unmarried, married, it mattered not a whit to them. The latest and most determined was Lady Charldon, Sir Lucius's wife. Not that Sylvester had not encouraged her at first, for Miranda was a tall, handsome baggage. Her sullen mouth and sultry black eyes, with their be-damned-to-you expression, enticed many men, but she wanted Sylvester Vinton. Rumor had it that he left the Charldon town house at very unusual hours. The Earl did not tell his mother all his problems, but she knew when he was troubled, and had her own sources of information besides.

His marriage—especially to her own stepdaughter—would keep Miranda away from Sylvester. A mother-in-law in amorous pursuit of her son-in-law would be ridiculed. Laughter was the only weapon Miranda feared. If Vanessa Charldon turned out to be a pretty child, with even half her mother's vitality . . . All she could do was provide the setting; everything else would be up to Miss Charldon. Miranda's boldness, she knew, was more appealing to her son than the fainting, giggling young misses whose shrewd mamas were looking for a catch. If Vanessa had the sense to resist him, his interest would be piqued. She must have a serious talk with her goddaughter. Those simpering girls had fawned over Melcourt since he was eighteen and by the time he inherited the title, their mothers had joined in the pursuit. He had been avoiding them ever since. She could understand how diffi-cult it was for a young man to be courted and pursued wherever he went. The only peace he had was with the lightskirts he took under his protection or the fast young matrons of his acquaintance whose husbands turned a blind eye toward their *affaires* because they were busily pursuing their own interests.

Lady Presteign closed her eyes and resolutely put

her plans from her. She slept, dreamlessly, while her son found his thoughts returning to the locket he had been clutching when he recovered from the blow on his head.

CHAPTER SEVEN

Vanessa had been home little more than a week and already she had begun to show her true colors—at least to her brother. Andrew had taken her aside to tell her that their father had written to Melcourt, informing him she was home. Nothing could have been more deceptively mild than the inception of that interview, but by the time it had concluded, Andrew was ready to swear that his sister was no longer possessed by the personal demon that had encouraged her youthful aberrations. It occurred to him that she had probably driven the poor devil out of his mind.

"For the life of me, I can't guess why you're outraged at the idea of marriage to the Earl. It's a frightfully advantageous match," he did not hesitate to tell her. "After all, ain't Melcourt ready to make a large settlement immediately things are arranged? If you can't like the idea, resign yourself to it. You have no choice."

"Father's gamed everything away, hasn't he?" Vanessa asked with muted savagery in her tones.

He nodded, unable to reply.

"And now I'm to be sold to the highest bidder so he can continue his profligacy. I'm thankful that Shelburne has been spared his blighting touch."

Something in his expression caused her to cry out in alarm. "Not that too? How is it possible? It was left to me—in trust until I marry. . . . How did he manage it this time?"

Andrew was silent and very unhappy, searching in vain for words. Suddenly a tidal wave of rage overpowered his sister.

"Out with it or I'll cut your heart out!"

Her brother gazed at her in wonder. "Still have that fiendish temper, don't you, Vanessa?" he said with a queer kind of pride. "And after all that time in a convent?"

"I don't mean to tell you anything, Brother dear," she told him haughtily. Then suddenly the storm was over, and he basked in the brilliance of her smile. "You are a dear brother, you know, Andrew. I don't mean to be unkind, but just think of my position." She sighed. "All right. Tell me, if you must."

Andrew looked at her warily. "Melcourt called on father, said he was interested in Shelburne. Did you know that at one time the Earls of Melcourt owned Shelburne? Must have gamed it away—dash it all, Vanessa—sorry. I didn't mean . . . Melcourt is so eager to acquire the property that even the terms of the will don't seem to throw him off."

Vanessa's eyes flashed at that, but she said nothing.

"Father's right, Vanessa. Our own mother wanted this. Don't look so shocked! You were naught but a baby when you and Melcourt—Sylvester Vinton, then—were betrothed. His mother'd be pleased to see her son settled. She doesn't at all care for Miranda or the bit of muslin he has in his keeping. As a married man he'd have to be more discreet."

His sister's ringing laugh startled him. "What's that?" He realized what he had said and spoke peevishly. "I say, Vanessa, what was that convent place like, anyway?"

"Andrew, you're so naive." She stopped herself from determining if he and her father really did not know the world had fallen quite apart, for it was probably no use.

"In France I was taught to dress, dance, flirt, and converse," she told him, neglecting to mention that it was not in any convent that she had acquired those accomplishments, along with other, less feminine attributes that were necessary for survival.

"Melcourt will be astonished. He thought—we all thought—you'd be taught to keep your eyes down and your mouth shut, besides embroidery, harp playing, and all that female folderol."

Her eyes shot daggers at him, which puzzled him enough to make him ask what he had said to anger her. He was even more startled when she snapped that he was not at all the one who had made her angry.

"I'm not the smartest fellow in the world, little one, but I do know you're up to something. No girl goes about dressed as you do unless she has good reasons.

Addy promised you were a beauty, and I respect her judgment."

"As you said, I know how to keep my mouth shut, Andrew, which is more than I can say for some people."

"If it's not to be Melcourt, you'd best do something about your looks, my girl, although, as I told you, I don't think you have a choice."

"Andrew?" She smiled sweetly. "You won't say anything to Melcourt, will you? About my looks, you know. Here I am, not home a week, and fighting with you. My favorite brother too," she told him mournfully.

"I promise not to say a word to Melcourt. If you do marry him, you just might lead him a merry dance. I hope you do. It's been the other way for years." He had to laugh at the thought of his friend, that nonpareil, Sylvester Vinton, Earl of Melcourt, about to meet his match in a mere slip of a girl.

Sir Lucius, totally ignorant as to the fiery nature of the daughter he had accepted into the bosom of his family, spent an anxious morning attempting to reconcile his wife to the presence of her stepdaughter. His many assurances as to Vanessa's docility made Miranda shudder.

"I'd rather she were a fiend out of hell. She lowers her eyes every time I speak with her, and I imagine that a man would put her entirely out of countenance. My friends would laugh if I were to be a chaperone— and to such a milk-and-water lump!" She added what she thought a clinching argument. "Even your horse-faced daughter-in-law, Gwenyth, agrees with me!

64

Couldn't you laugh? Finally Gwenyth herself has found a suit upon which we can agree and that, in itself, is noteworthy indeed." Lines of discontent etched around her mouth, making her appear older than her years. "At any rate we are promised to the Darlingtons."

Sir Lucius was adamant this time. Melcourt had sent word that he would call at Charldon Manor, and he needed the support of all the Charldons. A man did not like to lose his daughter once he had found her, he told his wife piously, concluding the discussion. Miranda turned up her eyes and proceeded to write a letter of apology to Louisa Darlington. This latest conflict might prove more entertaining than spending a week with her husband and the Darlingtons' set. In any case, Sylvester could not avoid her.

While awaiting the arrival of the Earl, Vanessa took the opportunity of asking questions about him, much to the amusement of her stepmother.

"He likes everything you are not, my girl," Miranda took pleasure in telling her. "He'd rather take a lusty milkmaid than a whey-faced milksop."

Vanessa raised her carefully applied mouse-skin brows. "I'm happy to see that you're taking an interest in the dairy. It's been long neglected, I suspect."

"You needn't play the haughty miss with me, Vanessa Charldon," scornfully continued Lady Charldon. "You'd like nothing better than to trap him into marriage. You and every little fool on the Marriage Mart. But he has no use for any of you. You are the very type he abhors: the *jeune fille de bonne famille*," she mimicked cruelly. "He wants passion, not passivity."

"Your French is delightful!" Miss Charldon answered in over-obvious admiration. "Perhaps he has had his use of you and your full-blown—ah—passion and will find me restful and soothing."

Miranda, who had stiffened to attention during part of her stepdaughter's seemingly ingenuous remark, relaxed visibly. She expressed honest surprise. "Melcourt? Oh, my heavens! You'd bore him in a week! In a day!"

"Methinks the—lady—doth protest too much," Vanessa quoted softly.

Except for a slight flush, Miranda showed no sign that Vanessa's comments had rankled. "If you wish to think so, I'll not attempt to disillusion you. Melcourt will do a far better job. As it is, I've said too much."

Watching Lady Charldon's hasty retreat, Vanessa was very pleased with herself. Miranda, the ninny-hammer, would think she was trying to attract Melcourt, while she was actually using every weapon to repel him. She hated him! How lucky she had been to discover his perfidious scheme before she met him. When Sylvester Vinton came to call, she would be quite prepared to play her role. Only why did she feel like crying? What was it she had said to Addy, about how part of her said "Sit quietly, don't say anything; make yourself as dull and ugly as you can," and the other part answered, "Show them how beautiful and fascinating you can be." What if he thought her dull and uninteresting no matter how she looked? Decide for yourself, Addy had said. How could she say what she wanted, when she didn't know, herself? There was only one place where she felt at home, and that place was forbidden to her. Barring that, she would spend her time with the horses. At least with them she knew where she stood; if they didn't like you, they bit. They didn't pretend.

"I say, Charldon, isn't that your gray?"

"Quite possibly, Fitz," answered a resigned Andrew, knowing full well who was backing the horse.

The third horseman frowned. "Who is the lad in the saddle, Andrew? Surely not one of the grooms?"

"No doubt it's the—er—new stableboy," he replied reluctantly.

"You take it calmly, my dear fellow. That gray is a devil."

"Ah, but see, Sylvester, what a pretty seat the fellow has," broke in Fitzwilliams.

"Hang it all, man, that's a five-foot wall he's putting the brute to!"

Mr. Charldon held his breath with the others as the rider seemed to lift the horse over the wall.

"Oh, my word," breathed Fitz, "what an elegant piece of horsemanship. The boy must have wrists of steel. I'd like to see him on your bay, Sylvester. It would be a grand show."

Melcourt's grunt was noncommittal. Mr. Charldon chose to answer for him. "Don't be an ass, Fitz. You know Melcourt don't let anyone ride that Titan brute."

"Come along, Fitz," the Earl interposed coolly. "We must allow Andrew to go his way or my sister will be quite put out."

"You'll be in the same position before long," his friend retorted.

"So that's the way the wind blows," Fitzwilliams remarked as they took their leave of Andrew. "At the risk of a setdown, Melcourt, I must tell you that all your friends will be very happy to see you shackled."

They let their horses drop to a walk.

"Far be it from me to give you a setdown, Fitz. You probably wouldn't know it if you did receive one. But I gather you are referring to Miranda Charldon." At the other's nod he continued, "You have no need to worry, dear boy. I have no real interest in Miranda. Never had, for that matter," his lordship said in an expansive mood.

Fitzwilliams, surprised and gratified that his attempt to lecture had been so cordially received, confided, "I'm thankful for that. She's the most rapacious female of my acquaintance. Terrifies me, you know."

The Earl's rangy chestnut sidled impatiently. As he nudged his horse's neck with the butt of his whip, he pointed out, "It's only that she's bored. People do quite reckless things when they're bored."

"Quite," his irrepressible friend remarked meaningfully, his eyes twinkling.

The Earl laughed good-naturedly at the sally, and Lord Fitzwilliams, seeing he was still in his friend's good graces despite the explicit remarks, turned the conversation to the merits of the yearling they had seen in a three-furlong sprint that morning. Both gentlemen decided it was a potential Derby winner, although Fitzwilliams declared that the Charldon stables had a few new acquisitions that would gladden the eye of his friend.

"Don't know where or how he got 'em. Not on the market, you know. Not polite to ask," he replied to Melcourt's query.

"I had no idea that would be of concern to you," his friend said blandly.

Lord Melcourt sat easily in the saddle as they rode on silently. After a moment Fitzwilliams said severely, "With that setdown, Sylvester, I don't suppose you'd want to join me for dinner this week?"

"Dear boy, I take it back."

Much mollified, his guard down, Lord Fitzwilliams mumbled some platitude intended to reassure his friend.

"You do know a setdown when you hear one," said my lord, thrusting home.

CHAPTER EIGHT

The Earl of Melcourt, preparing to dispatch a note to Sir Lucius, indicating the time of his call, caught sight of the locket he had found under his hand after his encounter with the mysterious visitor at Shelburne Hall. Frowning, he opened it and once more studied the two faces portrayed within. Surely it was a trick of the miniaturist, but how disconcerting it was to see how they looked at each other. The girl was beautiful and, his mother had said, very much like the first Lady Charldon, who had been an acclaimed beauty.

He would have liked to learn more, but Cosway's Oxford Street studio had been closed. He snapped the locket shut and immediately rang for a footman.

With the morrow's visit to Charldon Manor he intended to entice a very special guest into his net. My lord looked once more at the jeweled ornament. Yes, he was positive that the person who had lost it would do anything, up to and perhaps including murder, to ensure its return. He had every intention of turning that to his own advantage, although it might help if he knew what she had in mind.

"Good lord, Vanessa, it's stifling in here," her brother said as he entered the drawing room.

"Yes, it is," she answered cheerfully as she worked at the embroidery frame.

"Must we have this huge fire? I shall perish of the heat."

Miss Charldon winced as she stabbed herself with the unfamiliar needle, sucked the blood from her injured finger, and answered without raising her eyes from her work. "The fire is most necessary, Andrew."

"Good God! Is that your Aunt Clemency's old embroidery frame? I haven't seen it in years. She wouldn't even take it with her when she left because of you."

"It is her old frame, indeed." Vanessa had a pleasant expression on her face, but Andrew was of a suspicious nature where his sister was concerned.

"What are you up to, Firetop? Not hanging another dead mouse on there, are you?"

"I am merely occupying myself as any convent-bred young lady does. And I implore you, do not call me

Firetop. It sounds so . . . indelicate." Miss Charldon appeared pleased with her choice of words.

"You're quizzing me!"

"Not at all. But you will oblige me, won't you?" she added with deceptive sweetness.

"Of course, of course," he answered hastily. "If I don't, lord only knows what you might do."

"Exactly!" She was composure itself.

"Horrid brat!"

"Yes, sir."

"How I'd like to strangle you!"

The entrance of the Earl of Melcourt on the heels of the butler prevented Miss Charldon from replying in an appropriate manner.

"Good to see you, Sylvester," said Mr. Charldon with heartfelt relief. One could not tell, after all, what his sister would say or do. "May I make known to you my sister?"

The tall young man bowed before the young woman who, very *jeune fille* in chaste white muslin, swept him an equally ceremonious curtsy. In answer to her barely mumbled, "Pray, my lord, be seated," he selected a chair that enabled him to observe her at a respectful distance.

She lowered her eyes to the hearth, and my lord watched her with seeming indifference. If not for his mother's assurance that the miniature was undoubtedly a portrait of Miss Charldon, since it looked so like her mother, he would never have believed it to be the same girl as this sallow, dumpy creature. Whatever she had done to herself, it was not going to put him off. His mother would be disappointed, and as she had pointed out, except for the childhood betrothal, which could be terminated by either party, neither of them was under obligation since no notice had been published in the *Gazette*. He stifled a yawn.

Not usually first to initiate a conversation, the Earl, out of sheer mischief, ventured an opener designed to lure Miss Charldon into betraying herself.

"I have been given to understand that you have been in France for over eight years."

"Yes, my lord," she responded woodenly.

"You were in a convent, I believe."

She looked down at her clasped hands. "My . . . Father . . . wished it."

His eyes gleamed at her evasive answer. She was no fool, then; her masquerade had a purpose. Perhaps this would not prove to be so boring, after all.

The silence grated on their ears, but neither Miss Charldon nor the Earl attempted to assay any further conversation, until Andrew cleared his throat in a loud and significant manner.

"Perhaps my sister would care to walk in the gallery; it's rather stifling in here."

"Oh, no, I am quite cold." She managed a convincing shiver.

"May I get your shawl?"

She declined his offer most politely, but the Earl was determined to get her off by herself to pursue a question paramount in his mind. Although she resisted his maneuvering, the other member of the party, realizing his superfluity—and remembering his father's instructions—excused himself from their presence.

My Lord Melcourt was in no hurry to break the uncomfortable silence that settled on the room with the departure of Mr. Andrew Charldon. When he did speak, it was not of politics or of the sudden warmth of the weather, but of a most unusual object which had chanced to fall into his possession.

Miss Charldon, her interest piqued, turned her eyes from a print of Eclipse winning the Derby in 1791, which was not only out of place in the faded elegance of the drawing room, but also did not quite cover the darker square of yellow silk where something larger had once hung. Dismissing from her thoughts the probable worth of the missing canvas and its undoubted fate, she was moved to express her pleasure in seeing such an article as my lord described and was barely able to conceal her disappointment at his failure to have brought with him such an elegant piece of workmanship. With her permission he would dispatch a servant to ask his man to remove it from the mantel in his room where it had reposed since coming into his possession.

For a brief moment it crossed Vanessa's mind that he might be planning something sinister, then she put the idea from her with impatience. If a ruse, she thought, it was too crude, but even so she would not rise to the bait. With a desperate glint in her eyes she declined his offer in favor of his lordship placing the article in her hand at a future date. She was relieved of the need to sustain further conversation by the entrance of the Earl's sister and Lady Miranda Charldon, harmoniously allied, for the first time, in the cause of preventing a match between the brother of the one and the stepdaughter of the other.

Always an early riser, Vanessa was up with the sun. She brushed her raggedly cut hair into some sem-

73

blance of order and promptly covered it with an unbecoming wig of nondescript color and ancient vintage. She was beginning to deplore her mottled complexion and the cut and color of her own hair.

"A good rubbing with some lemon is what you need to get the rest of that stain off, Miss Vanessa," said Addy. "Covering your face with that white chalk makes you look like raw dough."

"I shall not need it, nor this, too long," she said as she flicked a frizzled curl in disdain. "Unless he is deranged, the Earl will never make an offer for me. By tomorrow he should be well on his way to London—or so I have been informed by my stepmother."

"His lordship is a very handsome man—and wealthy too."

"Handsome is as handsome does," Vanessa said flippantly, "and as for his wealth . . . pooh! He thinks women will fall into his hands like ripe plums!"

She leaned closer to the mirror and adjusted her mouse-skin eyebrows. With a brush dipped into a small pot of color, she further shadowed her face, disguising elegantly high cheekbones.

"An Incomparable! That's what I am," said Vanessa and went into peals of laughter as she saw Addy's face reflected in the glass.

"A crooked nose too?"

"Gilding the lily, Addy dear," managed Vanessa, struggling to regain her composure.

"Right now, Miss Vanessa Francesca Charldon, 'tis a turnip you're like, not a ripe plum, and don't you forget it."

"It is dreadful, isn't it?" she responded with evident satisfaction. She looked carefully at Addy, who was

74

not sharing her enjoyment. "You never address me by my full name unless I've done something wrong," Vanessa commented in a flat little voice.

"Miss, what good has it done you to make yourself so plain—so ugly? The Earl won't likely offer for you now, and if he doesn't, who will? What's to become of you, I don't know, Miss Vanessa, getting yourself all tangled up in lies and such."

"It's only a game, after all. I promise you I'll end it when we get to town. Do you think I want Miranda and Gwenyth to see me neither fish nor fowl? They would be so—amused. 'The poor thing had to dye her hair—and her skin, my dear!—quite ghastly,'" she mimicked. "So far as they know, I was in a convent before coming back to England. They're not interested in me except as food for gossip, so why should I bring myself to their notice any more than necessary?"

Addy continued her grumbling as she helped Vanessa with the buttons on the tight sleeves of her dark riding habit.

"It's not right for a young girl to be so bitter, child. You would be very happy with a nice young husband and children of your own."

"I wonder," she reflected, an errant thought of the Earl flitting across her mind. Then, quickly, as though to avoid further consideration of Addy's remarks, she asked if more of Lady Charldon's discarded clothes had been altered for her.

"Yes, Miss Vanessa, but it doesn't seem right, you wearing other people's castoffs when they're decked out like I don't know what . . . and don't think you're gettin' away with changing the subject."

"Don't nag," said Vanessa, setting her chin obsti-

75

nately. "When I am good and ready to show them all, I will, but not a minute sooner. I shall astound them all. And that will mean new clothes, hairdressers—nothing I can get here. I would rather be ugly and surprise everyone with the change than be a freak. Dazzle or nothing, say I," she concluded flippantly.

Addy sighed and almost capitulated. When Miss Charldon was in a willful mood, it never paid to argue. Even so, she risked a final word. "Who are you planning to dazzle, Miss Vanessa?" she ventured tentatively.

Vanessa controlled her peppery temper with great fortitude, gave her former nurse an affectionate peck on the cheek, and picked up her gloves, hat, and riding crop.

"Ask at the stables if anyone has found your pendant, miss," said Addy. "I noticed just today that it was gone. I'm surprised you didn't realize it."

"Oh, but I did! I think I know where I lost it, Addy. That's why I'm going to pay my respects to my Gypsy friends. Perhaps Zeriza can help me."

"With her crystal ball, miss?" Addy said with obvious disapproval.

"You'll make some excuse for me to the family, I know. I imagine they will be happy to dispense with my presence from their dinner table," she said blithely, ignoring Addy's last remark. "I would not for the world deprive them of their chance to bemoan my return."

"Miss Vanessa! You should not!"

"Don't shake your head. For eight years of my life they didn't care whether I was living or dead. You know it's true, Addy, although I do acquit my brother

76

of such strong emotions; he didn't even spare me a thought! And as for me, I learned not to cry myself to sleep at night."

Miss Charldon did not give Addy a chance to say another word. Further talk wouldn't help, nor would the tears she said she had learned to stop. She must avoid thinking of anything but the pendant. She must get it back before he found the miniatures concealed within. She knew just where she had been when she had felt the tug at her neck. Melcourt's outflung hand must have brushed against the pendant as he fell. It would not have taken much to snap the fine links of the chain. It was foolish to wish that it still lay in the room at Shelburne Hall. Melcourt had taken it with him, apparently hoping it would lead him to its owner. No matter what, she must get it back . . . tonight . . . even if she had to go herself.

CHAPTER NINE

"Good morning, Miss Charldon. What a pleasant surprise to find you up so early." The Earl scrutinized her horse without seeming to spare a glance for herself.

"Early, my lord? I've been up for hours," she gushed. "Why, at the convent we had to be up and dressed before dawn. Then we . . . Is anything amiss, sir?" she inquired anxiously, seeing the pained expression on his face.

He stared at her, bemused, and, realizing she was waiting for an answer, replied hastily, "No, my child, but I fear I keep you from some errand."

"Are you going in my direction, my lord? If you are, I'd appreciate your company." She leaned forward confidingly. "My stepmama tells me there are bad men about."

"I'm sorry that my engagement with your brother prevents me from accompanying you. I'm sure your groom will provide ample protection," he said deliberately, summing up the waiting menial, "although I assure you you have nothing to fear." He bowed politely. "The loss is mine."

Vanessa raised her hand to her mouth and tittered. The Earl winced, then continued, "Ah, Miss Charldon. You must forgive me, but that enchanting pendant I described to you . . ."

"The pendant, my lord?"

"I've quite forgotten to remove it from the mantel-shelf. Perhaps you would receive me tomorrow so we may examine the workmanship together." His bait was too crude by half for her to bite, thought the Earl, disgusted with his approach. His only excuse was that he had been thrown off by her attire this morning.

"I'll be delighted, my lord," exclaimed Miss Charldon, evincing not the slightest suspicion of the Earl's motives. It had just occurred to her that the loss of her locket could have warped her judgment. There was a distinct possibility that Melcourt was baiting a trap for her. What he knew, how he knew, if he knew, she could not conjecture, but any attempt to take her locket tonight might place her in a precarious position, although it might be worth it, just to get the better of him.

Miss Charldon ventured a question of her own. "Are you dining with us, my lord?"

"Why, no, Miss Charldon. Andrew and I are promised to Fitzwilliams and, as usual, I expect we'll be quite late. I think we will make our own appointment for tomorrow afternoon."

A snare in truth, thought Miss Vanessa Charldon as she watched the Earl canter along the elm-lined drive. She congratulated herself on the brilliance of her insight. She was sure her own crafty nature would be more than a match for anything he had in mind. She had bested him in their first encounter—why not again?

The gilding of the lily, as described by Miss Charldon, and his lordship's "Doing it a bit too much, my girl," as he took his leave of her, referred to the same straight, sculptured little nose. At least it had looked small and straight yesterday as Miss Charldon repeatedly returned her spectacles to the bridge of the one feature his discerning eye found she had in common with the girl in the miniature. Today that nose was decidedly crooked and the lump that had disfigured her right cheek and jaw was now swelling the left!

Shown into the yellow drawing room overlooking the rose garden, a rather bleak prospect at this time of year, the Earl was quickly joined by Lady Charldon, who had been on the lookout for him since very early that morning. She was none too pleased when his lordship, once he had dealt with the weather, spoke exclusively of Miss Charldon.

"I didn't know you held my stepdaughter in such great esteem," Lady Charldon said with a humorless smile on her lips.

"Not at all, Miranda. You of all people should know she's too pale and quiet for my tastes. On the few occasions she did speak, her eyes were downcast. She's so meek and timid she trembles when I'm near her."

Miranda laughed throatily. "I told her a convent-bred miss was not in your style, but she would have it that I was jealous. In fact, she all but accused me of lying."

"She did, did she?"

"She told me that the qualities a man looked for in a mistress would be scarcely suitable in a wife."

The Earl's look of amused interest encouraged her to go on. " 'In a *mariage de convenance*,' " Miranda imitated, " 'the wife must be prepared to look the other way. She must expect to bear children and be content to stay at home to raise them.' Or so she instructed me."

"She might be right, you know. Brought up in France, she must be used to this type of arrangement. But tell me, what other worldly wisdom did the chit see fit to impart?"

"She was quite smug about it, Sylvester. She said that men of your stamp were in the habit of devoting themselves to their *chères amies* and riotous companions. You would find her a restful wife, not expecting to hang on your sleeve and not devoting her attentions to a lover when you required her."

"Are you sure you're not bamming me?" he laughed.

"I don't wonder you think that, Sylvester." Miranda frowned. "I was thinking . . . You never met her before, did you?"

"No, she was not at my sister's wedding, I believe."

"She was being punished for some reason or another. She was always being punished. That time it may have been for tying a dead mouse to her Aunt Clemency's embroidery frame." Miranda shuddered. "I saw her only once before Lucius rid himself of her. It took two of them to pull her off me. Revolting little creature!"

"The mouse?" he asked, his eyebrow at an impossible height.

"You've not heard a word I've said," accused Lady Charldon irrationally.

"Nonsense, Miranda. I was wondering about the convent. It is a shame they took all that deviltry out of her."

"That's not what you intended saying."

The Earl ignored her pouting expression and asked, "How long did you say she was there? In the convent, I mean."

"Let me think . . . Eight years. Yes, I'm sure that's right." She thought a moment longer. "I am sure, for she left the year Andrew and Gwenyth were wed, and her grandmother arranged that she be placed in some convent—I forget the name." She laughed. "Not that Lucius ever paid, my dear. He wouldn't dream of offending the de St. Varres family by offering money. Very ill bred he'd think himself if he did so."

"Curious—about your stepdaughter, I mean."

"More than just curious, I'd say, for I don't believe she's acquired even one accomplishment. But at least someone has prevailed upon her to cover that horrid brown complexion. It's either too much sun or my predecessor played dear Lucius false with a wandering Gypsy—of which there are plenty in the neighborhood."

"Andrew does seem to have inherited all the looks in the family, Miranda, my sweet. But be generous! Surely you can find some point of resemblance?"

"So here you are, you two," Gwenyth interrupted, offering her cheek for her brother's kiss. "Were you talking about the Firetop, Miranda?" In her agitated way she didn't pause to give the other time to answer. "Someday I'll tell you a very amusing story about her."

"My dear Gwenyth, I don't think anything connected with that girl could possibly be amusing."

"It is rather pathetic to have Andrew's little devil turn out to be such a tame rabbit. She was one of the Charldon secrets until Andrew offered for me."

"If you two are planning to talk about my stepdaughter, you shall have to excuse me," said Miranda. "My interest in the subject has been exhausted."

Gwenyth's watery blue eyes followed Miranda Charldon as she left the room.

The Earl laughed. "She can't abide the child, can she?"

"I don't blame her. From what I've heard, Vanessa was unreasonably nasty to her, and Miranda's not the forbearing type."

"The stories may have been exaggerated."

"Perhaps . . ." She shrugged her narrow shoulders in a singularly graceless fashion.

"Gwenyth, if you have something to tell me, please

don't hint. I think you should know that if I can possibly bring myself to offer for the chit, I will."

"She's a rabbit caught in a trap, Sylvester. Her father will give her no chance to refuse your offer, and I could wish you something better for a wife."

"Rabbits are good breeders, my dear sister, a much desired quality in a wife."

"Rabbits breed their own kind, brother dear." Mrs. Charldon's sweet smile had a fine edge as she awaited his reaction.

"And if the father is . . . a tiger? The dominant strain would be inherited."

"A rabbit mate with a tiger? It would be wondrous to see," she retorted.

"Then you think she'll try to refuse my offer?"

"Ho! Caught you in the quick that time, Sylvester Vinton. Could your interest be piqued? And by that ugly little sheep?"

"Not at all, Gwen. It just might make things more difficult than I thought they'd be. Now, before you add any other animals to your descriptive remarks about the future Countess of Melcourt, I suggest we join the others."

She fumed but allowed him to escort her to the small dining room, where Miranda and Andrew were beginning to wonder what was keeping them.

"It certainly wasn't anything my brother told me; he's never confided in me," Gwenyth said, answering Miranda's question.

"He confides in no one," said Lady Charldon, making a surprisingly shrewd assessment of the man who sat on her right.

"Ah, but I inspire confidences," said the Earl, showing his teeth in a wicked smile. "I have it in my power to tell half the peeresses in the realm what the other half are wearing to the Royal Wedding. They would be well paid out since their lack of conversation has caused me to suffer unbearable ennui since Malmesbury left Brunswick in December."

"Have you news of Princess Caroline, Sylvester? We were sure that the Princess's party would follow close behind Lord Malmesbury. Has there been any change in plan?"

"No change, Gwenyth, merely a delay because of the dangers of the war with France."

"Yet others manage to cross in safety," Andrew pointed out while helping himself to a generous portion of asparagus.

"Dear Vanessa was very fortunate," said Lady Charldon. "I'd like to know how she managed to get here while the Princess still waits on the other side of the Channel."

"We English are an enterprising people," the Earl drawled, putting an end to her speculation.

Although Lady Charldon could not care less what the servants thought—if she gave them credit for thought at all—she was nevertheless sensitive to her guest's mood. Until the servants could be dismissed, she remained within the bounds of the Earl's sense of propriety by turning the conversation to the unusually hard winter they had endured.

"Lord, yes, just hasn't it been cold?" Andrew said, picking up the conversational ball with something he felt safe. "Scores of birds have fallen from every tree—stone dead." Andrew cleared his throat. "And if the ladies will pardon me, I must tell you that they're saying in town that there are more people dead of cold this winter than died during the plague."

"Really, Andrew, we're not so delicate as you fear," his wife said impatiently before turning to her brother for news of what she considered important. "Rumor has it that the Duke of York's been made Commander-in-Chief at the Horse Guards."

"For once, rumor has it right," the Earl answered. "York's a fine administrator and he'll give them what they need—organization."

"Aren't you switching your loyalty from the Prince?" Lady Charldon wanted to know.

"There's no question of my loyalty involved. I admire a man who plans to do away with selling commissions to juveniles. There'll be no prestige or discipline among the officers so long as commissions can be bought for schoolboys. York's going to demand the return of all commissions given to captains under twelve and lieutenant-colonels under twenty. If anyone can put a stop to political interference in discipline and promotion, he can."

"Lucius's friend, Lord Gresham, would agree with you if he heard you. He's a great admirer of York and no doubt he will be spending more time at the Horse Guards than ever. Lucius will be very disappointed to lose a card-playing crony.

"You and the others may go, Bassett. I'll ring if we need you," said Lady Charldon, perceiving that everyone had been served.

As the butler left with his retinue, conversation returned to more personal matters, and the Earl, pursuing an apparently idle thought, asked, "Andrew, do you think that gray a fitting mount for your sister?"

Andrew opened his mouth, prepared to reply.

"If he doesn't care, why should you bother your head over it?" Lady Miranda Charldon snapped.

Mr. Charldon turned in her direction. He was again about to speak when his wife forestalled him.

"Miranda, you're just angry because you can't back the brute."

Lady Charldon faced them in stony silence.

"Did you really attempt it?" queried my lord, addressing her in an amused drawl.

"She couldn't get near him," related his sister with glee, momentarily forgetting both her die-away air and her newly established truce with Miranda.

From beneath his lazily lowered eyelids the Earl risked an intent glance at Andrew, who sat staring at his plate with a pained expression on his face.

"Do you see how it is, Melcourt?" Mr. Charldon lifted his eyes to his friend.

"Ladies," intoned the Earl, "please excuse me while I help my brother-in-law bear up under his anguish, or he'll be completely unmanned."

CHAPTER TEN

As the Earl and Mr. Charldon were about to leave the house for the stables, Andrew received word that Cliffe, his father's agent, had arrived and was even now with Sir Lucius.

"Go on, Andrew," urged Melcourt. "I know how concerned you've been. I too would like to know if there's anything further on that other matter—at Shelburne."

This oblique reference to a rather perturbing situation distressed Andrew still further, yet he managed to reassure his friend and speed him to the stables even as he hurried away.

The Earl watched Andrew disappear into the house and thought of the likely possibility of his marriage to his friend's sister. The idea was not quite so distasteful as it had been previously. Without a doubt he would like to learn a little more about the elusive Miss Charldon.

As he sauntered toward the large, well-kept building that housed the Charldon horses, he was forced to give way to a wildly plunging gray gelding led by two stableboys under the direction of a middle-aged groom.

"Miss Charldon—where is she?" the Earl inquired peremptorily of the groom, who had accompanied Vanessa Charldon on her ride that very morning.

"She be at the Gypsy camp an' up to somethin', no doubt, beggin' 'ee pardon, me lord."

"You left her there?"

"Aye, me lord. But if 'ee be thinkin' that I left Miss without her horse, no, me lord, though 'tis no wonder that 'ee think it. Them two geldings be full brothers but never broke to a double harness. No, me lord, Miss Vanessa has Hannibal with her. Maybe she'll find what it were she lost. She had us all but turn the yard and stables upside down a-lookin' for some gimcrack, then sudden-like she tells us to never mind 'cause she knows where it is. Then she says she'll visit them heathens anon—though I can swear she's not been to their camp, and they'd never steal anything o' hers."

The Earl stored that bit of information in his mind for future deliberation. Meeting this garrulous fellow was an unexpected bit of luck of which the Earl was ready to take full advantage.

"That gray is no fit mount for a girl. I'm surprised that Mr. Charldon has not refused his permission."

"Lord love 'ee, me lord, but Mr. Andrew has nowt to say on it. 'Tis Miss Vanessa's horse, sent on from France afore she come home-along," he said in the soft speech of the locals. The man hesitated. "Beggin' 'ee pardon, me lord, if 'ee be wantin' to see t'other cattle Miss sent home, it were proud I'd be to show 'ee."

"Thank you, Bolton; if you speak well of them, it's a true recommendation."

The groom, beaming at the Earl's praise, uttered a few suitably deferential words as he led the way into the building.

"The empty stall on this side were for Charlemagne, twin to the one Miss rode this morning, me lord."

Seeing the Earl's frown and attributing it to anxiety, the groom ventured to relieve the Earl's mind. "There's nowt to worry 'ee, me lord; Miss Vanessa was always wi' them Gypsies when she were little."

"You put my worries quite to rest, Bolton. Perhaps you can tell me about Miss Charldon and her— friends."

The man didn't need much encouragement to tell the story. His lordship was going to marry Miss Vanessa, everybody knew that; of course he wanted to hear all about her.

The history related by the groom was what Lord Melcourt's mother had led him to suspect. "And after her grandfather died, it were no wonder Miss spent her time in the kitchens and stables, where she were always welcome. Why, she even tried runnin' away wi' the Gypsies more'n once, me lord, but they always brought her back. That's why we be so friendly wi' them hereabouts, law or no law."

He risked a foxy glance at the Earl, who was the local magistrate, but Melcourt made no comment, merely inclining his head, indicating approval, as the talkative old fellow rambled on.

"Well, me lord, I always thought Miss were too wild, even for them, they bein' that anxious to return her. But they admired her spirit so much, they adopted her. And Miss don't forget her friends," he concluded. "For all her wild ways, she be a true lady."

By the time the groom had exhausted the subject of Miss Charldon's unfortunate childhood, they had reached the far end of the stables.

"Magnificent," breathed the Earl, dropping both quizzing glass and affectation at the sight of a striking black stallion of some sixteen hands.

"Miss calls him Orion. And here, me lord, are Persephone, Psyche, and Cassandra, lovely ladies all. And in this end stall be Nimrod."

The Earl looked at the yearling with appreciation. "I warrant, Bolton, that nothing like this has been seen in the county for many a year."

"Him'll put 'em all to shame, me lord."

"Was that Miss Charldon on the gray yesterday?" the Earl asked casually.

"'Ee saw her then, me lord? Her ladyship near fainted no sooner she saw Miss Vanessa's riding clothes." Bolton chuckled.

"Breeches?" murmured the Earl inquiringly. "I shouldn't wonder," he continued in response to the other's nod. "Thank you, Bolton. Good day."

The groom pocketed the generous tip he received, touched his cap, and watched the tall young nobleman stride away.

Andrew, coming from the house, was pleased to find his friend still there.

"I've been examining the horses," called Melcourt. "Beauties, Andrew."

"Ain't they, though. . . . Especially that little one, Nimrod. Bred that 'un herself. Selected the dam and the sire. Arranged everything. None of the females you and I know could do that." He laughed reminiscently. "Miranda told her it wasn't all the thing, then

90

Vanessa said Miranda shouldn't expect her to act like a ninnyhammer because . . ."

"Go on, Andrew. You intrigue me," the Earl prompted.

"I don't quite remember. You could ask Gwenyth; she was there." He grinned. "You know your sister. She remembers every setdown given to Miranda."

"She started to tell me something, but it can wait, dear fellow, for I find that something has come up I must attend to."

Andrew was puzzled. What could possibly have occurred to occasion such erratic behavior on the part of his friend? His curiosity remained unsatisfied, for the Earl returned to his home without divulging his reason for canceling his dinner engagement.

"You can usually depend on his lordship to stick to his plans," said the Earl's valet to Parker as he imparted the news that the master would be dining at home.

"Since we became involved with Mr. Pitt, Chester, we can never be certain of our engagements," returned the butler.

The Earl, however, had not noticed any problem created by his decision. In fact, had he been told that his sudden change of plan would cause a catastrophic disturbance in the nether regions of his home, Melcourt would have received the news with raised brow and quizzing glass.

After dashing off an apology for breaking his dinner engagement on such short notice, he had handed it to his valet. "See that this note gets to Lord Fitzwilliams right away, Pringle. I'll be dining at home tonight."

The message sent to the kitchens had been duly received by the chef, who had been making inroads on the cooking spirits. The excitable Gallic creature brandished an empty bottle at an apprentice to hurry him in his task of killing two pullets for his lordship's dinner. The assistant chopping the onions for the sauce began to work faster. In a few minutes the kitchens were humming with furious activity.

Unaware and totally unconcerned with all this stir in the bowels of Melcourt Castle, the Earl made his way up the stairs to prepare for his expected visitor. Vanessa knew where he kept the locket; he had told her himself only this morning at the same time that he had informed her he would be at Fitzwilliams's for dinner. He did not think she would ignore such a tempting invitation.

Lengthening shadows made their way across the room, warning of the fast approach of night, but the Earl, seemingly engrossed in thought, did not notice. If Miss Charldon knew of the passage into Shelburne, he told himself, she would doubtless know of the one into this room.

The panel beside the mantel began to move, and in a flash the Earl had flattened himself against the wall, a convenient candelabrum in hand. He had thought she would be too impatient to wait another day, but had she come alone? Seeing the mysterious visitor glide into the room, Melcourt lay down his impromptu weapon and resumed his usual lazy pose.

"Good evening," he said. "What luck I chanced to be at home to receive you." The Earl's soft, silky tones were much more frightening to the intruder than any string of oaths. Melcourt reached out a long arm and released a catch, allowing the panel to slide shut.

The figure stumbled, recovered, her full cloak swirling about her, and then, without turning around, made a mad dash for the door. Not appearing to move with undue haste, the Earl reached the door first and, with a graceful bow, cut off her exit.

"Surely you're not planning to leave so soon? You've just arrived. I insist that you accept my hospitality."

Vanessa watched as the Earl turned in a deliberate manner and proceeded to engage the lock on the door.

"Not that I don't trust you, my girl, but the sight of a woman fleeing from my room would no doubt startle the underfootman at the bottom of the stairs."

A tart remark was bitten off midsentence, but Melcourt understood the gist of it and answered with equanimity, "Ah, but you see my—er—henchman is new to his position and has yet to accustom himself to my dissolute ways."

He walked toward her, extending his hand. "I'm being a neglectful host; let me take your cloak."

Vanessa held it more tightly about her and pulled the hood close, hiding her face.

"If you wish to continue with the farce, it is all one to me," the Earl drawled. "However, I'm sure you'll discover it quite impossible to eat dinner while your hands are engaged in trying to conceal your identity— although it is most unnecessary, my dear Miss Charldon."

Vanessa hesitated, not knowing whether to laugh or cry. Chancing a timid question which Melcourt ignored, she answered the question herself: He meant

93

to keep her there! For a moment a chill uncertainty swept over her, leaving her confused, apprehensive, and unable to move. With a tremendous effort she tried to throw off the apathy that could prove her undoing. Forgetting that you are never so easily fooled as when you try to fool someone else, she berated herself scornfully. Chicken-hearted, that's what she was. What could he do, after all? If she couldn't outwit him, it wouldn't be for want of trying.

Restlessly pacing back and forth like a tethered goat baiting a trap, Vanessa was unconscious of the Earl's scrutiny, merely registering with part of her mind that he was busying himself with a decanter. He did not press her to speak or to accept the wine he poured for her, merely placing it on the tray.

"Won't you be seated, Miss Charldon?" he asked politely.

She simpered, then, realizing that in the dimness he would not see the silly smirk upon her face, she giggled nervously. But the laugh got away from her, and she bit it back before it became a sob. "I shouldn't be here, my lord," she trilled, forcing playfulness into her voice.

"I'm aware of that. Nonetheless it is fatiguing to watch you wear out my Aubusson."

Vanessa half uttered something, recalled herself to the part she had decided to play, and sat down in the proffered chair, pushing her hood away from her face. In the faint light she was a pale blur as seen from the chair he had selected.

"How came you, then, to be here, if, as you say, you know better?" Melcourt asked, wondering what manner of story Miss Charldon would contrive.

"I merely suspected there was a passage, my lord; I did not know where it would lead, but until today I had never explored it. You needn't be harsh with me, my lord," she sniveled. "You can imagine I was shocked speechless at seeing you."

"I'm sure you were," he agreed sympathetically. "Since I am here, however, I'd like to take advantage of your presence."

She looked at him hurriedly, but the firelight offered him the same protection it did her. His next words almost made her wish his intentions were not quite so honorable.

"I realize this is not the place for a proposal of marriage, but neither of us seems to care much for the conventions."

"And what makes you think that, my lord?" Vanessa asked, ignoring the first part of his declaration.

"Why, your very presence here, Miss Charldon."

"Oh, that!" She shrugged, the hood of the cloak sliding unheeded to her shoulders. "I could not care less about that."

"Do you then make a practice of calling upon men in their bedchambers?"

"The point is, my lord, had I known the passage would lead me to you, I wouldn't have come."

"On the contrary. The point is that I am here—and you are too."

"No one knows!"

"Wrong again, Miss Charldon. You know, I know, and, in about fifteen minutes when I escort you into the dining room, my servants will know too."

"Since I will not say a word of this to anyone and you say your servants know how to keep their mouths

95

shut, I can only suspect your intentions, my lord. And I must say that it is bad of you to take such advantage." Her voice ran on. "I am very sensible of the honor you do me, my lord, but we would not suit. I would not fit in your circle. I am very meek and shy, and I know I have no style at all." She jumped to her feet, punctuated her little speech with a curtsy, and sat down as hastily as she had risen.

It had been a totally unbelievable, angry speech and one he ignored, except for her reference to his close-mouthed servants. It was as he had thought. Miss Charldon had been his assailant at Shelburne Hall. No other woman of his acquaintance would have been capable of that. Unfortunately she had heard enough to account him the veriest coxcomb and would not succumb to his practiced address. To have her father force the alliance upon her was no light step to take, but there was no choice at this point.

The Earl excused himself on some flimsy pretext, but Vanessa did not seem to be aware of what he said. Appearing not the least worried, she turned a cheerful face to him. If he was surprised at her acceptance of her position, he did not show it. He took her hand and placed a kiss on the upturned palm.

"Ten minutes," he said, and departed.

The sound of the door closing behind the Earl wrenched Vanessa's quivering nerves into immediate action. Flying to the window, she thrust it open, looked out, and then, satisfied, slid out on the narrow ledge, her face to the rough stone.

From a vantage point in the library, the Earl was able to keep his eyes upon the open doorway as he signed, sealed, and arranged for the early delivery of a note. Expecting Vanessa to charge down the stairs at any moment, he quickly removed a large pendant from a skillfully concealed wall safe, and strode purposefully up the stairs, wondering if she would cry and plead, or if she would try to gull him, or if she would tell him the truth. He frowned. He could be wrong. Perhaps she was no more than she seemed to be: a foolish, giggling, empty-headed chit. He did not think so, and when he opened the door on an apparently empty room, he knew he was right.

Seeing the open window, he recalled the last time he had chased after Miss Charldon. He was on to her, the little vixen, and he'd be damned if he would give her another crack at him.

The room was too quiet, almost eerily so, Melcourt decided, watching for some telltale movement of the draperies. Warily, he stepped to the window and moved the portieres to the side. Finding nothing, he forced himself to look at the ground, dreading what he might find. There was no sign of her. Momentarily, the Earl was confounded. Then it hit him. The little devil! There was only one other way he knew to leave the room and that could have proved disastrous. Perhaps it was just as well she had made good her escape. If he had found her, he might have been obliged to put an end to her game, although he had been tempted, just for a moment, to take advantage of the situation.

Meanwhile he was deriving a great deal of amusement from the unpredictable, unconventional, and decidedly captivating little minx.

CHAPTER ELEVEN

"Praise be the Lord!" Addy intoned fervently. "It was real worried I was this morning with you staying overnight with them Gypsies." She helped the girl remove her riding coat. "Was your Gypsy friend able to help you get the locket?"

"No! Damn that Sylvester Vinton!" Her hand swept clean the top of the dressing table, smashing the powder box into the wall, where it upended and left a chalky white trail as it fell to the floor.

Addy was patently shocked. Miss Vanessa's temper was always peppery, but she'd not had a tantrum in years. Knowing she would eventually be told the story, the elderly woman kept silent as she helped Vanessa change from her severe, almost masculine attire, to a simple white muslin that had obviously been made for a bigger woman. Aside from a tightening of her lips, Addy showed no sign of disapproval.

Watching her former nurse's grim expression reflected in the tall mirror, Vanessa was tempted to fabricate a story that would satisfy the servant's sense of propriety. However, she, having as much experience of Addy as Addy had of her, thought the better of it and admitted the woman into her confidence.

It was well that she did, for Addy took it rather better than she had supposed. She alternately laughed and shivered in the right places, yet kept a very keen watch on the artless face of the girl.

"I know what his intentions would've been if you'd let him see you as you really are, and you wouldn't have escaped him so easily. You're far more beautiful than your mama was. And how those Frenchies could've mistaken you for a man with such a bosom as you have is more than I can see!"

Vanessa, who had blushed at Addy's observation, now paled. "Oh, Addy! The locket! He has surely found it. What if he opens it?" Her voice sounded panic-stricken even to her own ears.

"Tush, child. And what if he does? If he's a gentleman, he'll return it without a word. From what you say, he already knows you've been trying to flummox him. You can always think up some story to tell him, since you're so good at fairy tales."

Not at all abashed, Miss Charldon gave this her careful consideration. "But I forget," Addy went on. "First thing this morning a letter came from the Earl. Your father read it and sent for you, but I told him you'd had a restless night and shouldn't be disturbed. You'd better see him now, my honey."

Vanessa turned a piteous face toward the older woman. "From the Earl! Do you think . . . ? Is he going to ask for my hand?"

"Oh, my honey, my precious lamb, I don't know. And I don't think you yourself know what it is you're wanting."

* * *

As though walking in her sleep, Vanessa drifted from her father's sitting room, the door closing silently behind her. The interview had been painful. Pleas, threats, and recriminations had left her father unmoved. His last words echoed in her ears: "You will accept the Earl's suit, Daughter, for I'll not change my mind. If you prove exceptionably obstinate, I will engage to find another husband for you . . . General Dalrymple—or perhaps Lord Gresham . . . who won't care if you say yes or no."

Vanessa knew she had no choice, yet she hated herself for her cowardice. How could she bear the thought of General Dalrymple, who had been old when she was a child—or worse, Lord Gresham, who had slobbered all over her hand on the night of her seventeenth birthday, when Raoul and Jeanne had taken her to the Paris Opera. Vanessa shuddered, remembering the other times she had seen him and how he always made her flesh crawl.

She must not think of that now, she told herself. She had promised to see the Earl and would reserve her final answer until then. If he was his usual hateful, sneering self, she might still find the courage to refuse him. But last night he had not sneered. Last night, if she had waited for him, he would not have been hateful. The locket had been only an excuse, she realized, an excuse to see him, be near him.

It was strange; she hardly knew him, yet . . . She should not have been afraid of what he might do. There must be worse things in the world, after all. At least she would have been wanted and safe in his arms, if only for a while. To belong to him, body and soul . . . no, she must not think that way, for that only led to weakness and she must be strong: strong enough to resist the urge to accept Melcourt as a husband no matter what his reason for proposing. She would have to fight her own feelings. She could not let herself be sold—bartered as if she were some inanimate thing, incapable of emotion. Sometimes it seemed as if she could not fight any longer. How exhausted she was. Like a bird futilely beating its wings against the bars of a cage, she was trapped.

"Miss Charldon, will you take a turn in the garden with me?" the Earl asked kindly.

He was startled by the depth of despair in the tear-filled blue-violet eyes she turned to him. Not waiting for her to answer, he took her unresisting, cold hand in his big warm one and led her from the chill, somber drawing room, through the doors, and into the warmth of the sun-drenched garden. The sudden brightness forced Vanessa to blink, sending a tear coursing, unnoticed, down her cheek.

She was unconscious of his scrutiny as they walked beneath lofty, newly leafed branches to a stone bench at the base of an ancient oak. Sitting at Vanessa's side, still holding her icy hand, the Earl felt a strange stirring in his heart. What a lovely thing she must be, if Cosway's miniature was true to life. He would like to see what she looked like without the disfiguring padding his experienced eyes discerned. The thought was suddenly exciting.

"Miss Charldon . . . Vanessa . . . Your father has given me leave to address you."

"Yes, my lord?"

"Will you do me the honor of becoming my wife?"

101

The forlorn little creature before him betrayed her agitation by wringing her hands.

"Do you indeed wish to marry me, my lord?"

"Without a doubt." He knew he was in earnest now.

"If you waited until I was of age, I would find some way of selling Shelburne Hall."

"Absolutely out of the question."

"I don't know what to do."

"Marry me."

He sought to recapture her hand, but thought better of it when she said, "But you can't wish to marry someone who doesn't wish to marry you."

She was desperate, was she? He might have known she would be compelled to accept his suit. If he withdrew it now, life would be made even more unbearable for her. Her grief demanded an outlet, yet he knew her pride would not permit her to break down before him. A good, strong, healthy anger was preferable to the sick despondency mirrored in her eyes.

"It is quite refreshing to find someone who professes disdain. I hate women to fawn over me."

"You are insufferable!" She sprang up as though finding his proximity distasteful.

"And since you are not desirous of hanging on my arm," he continued with a bow as he got to his feet, "we shall deal famously. The best marriages, you know, begin with a little aversion."

"I warn you, my lord, I shall be a most unwilling bride," Miss Charldon said with all the dignity she could muster.

He surveyed her through his quizzing glass. "That will be most stimulating to my jaded appetites, my dear. I shall press for an immediate ceremony before your sentiments change, as I'm sure they will."

"Never!"

He had flung a challenge, and she had accepted. Her extraordinary eyes flashed bolts of lightning at him that even her ridiculous eyeglasses could not disguise.

Seeming not to care that he was driving her into a fury, he drew her toward him. "Shall I make you melt in my arms, little icicle? I can, you know."

For a moment her knees felt weak. Was this how he made them feel, the women who craved his love? How dared he treat her like one of them? She swung at him in sudden anger, but he caught her fist in his open palm.

"Your swing is too wide, and you've left yourself defenseless. I shall teach you better when we are wed," he told her with a laugh.

"I'll do my best to make you miserable," she warned as she wrenched herself from his grasp and ran toward the house.

The Earl of Melcourt, happy that Miss Charldon seemed to be in better spirits, followed at a more leisurely pace, enjoying the unseasonable warmth of the day. He was not in the least perturbed that his proposal had been accepted in so irregular a fashion.

While Addy tried to calm her hot-tempered mistress, the Earl was closeted with a beaming Sir Lucius.

"Yes, yes, of course, the wedding must be as soon as possible. Ah, it is good to know my daughter will not be alone when I pass on."

103

At another time the Earl might have been amused to find that the existence of a brother, several aunts, and numerous cousins had been forgotten, but now he was eager to settle his affairs.

"My mother will sponsor Miss Charldon's coming out, and naturally she will come to stay at Mount Street as soon as possible."

Sir Lucius's expression clearly indicated his surprise.

"No one will remark if Miss Charldon is invited to make her debut under the aegis of her godmother," the Earl pressed on urbanely.

"I had quite forgot. It has been some years, you know, since . . ." Sir Lucius's voice trailed off in feigned embarrassment.

"So I've been given to understand, sir," the Earl confirmed blandly.

"I think, my boy, that this will answer. I was wondering if my wife should not handle the whole, but if, as you say, your mother means to take charge, my mind is relieved. And now, about the wedding?"

"I believe, sir, that all can be safely left in the care of my mother," the Earl put in smoothly. "As Miss Charldon's godmother, she will make the announcements and send her off in proper style."

"Good, good. I'm delighted. Now, if there is anything . . ."

"Nothing at all, Sir Lucius. My mother will see to everything."

Sir Lucius leaned back against his pillows as his future son-in-law departed. With a gusty sigh of satisfaction he decided that perhaps his daughter was not as worthless as he had believed. Not only would he have his debts paid, but there would be a generous settlement, and he would be saved the expense of a come-out and the wedding itself—to say nothing of the bride clothes and other gewgaws so dear to female hearts.

He was feeling better already. No doubt he should be well enough to return to London after the money was in his hands.

That night, for the first time in years, Sir Lucius was not visited by the nightmare figures of creditors chasing him down St. James's Street and through the sacred portals of White's. In his dreams he filled his pockets as he went from one gaming hall to the next, winning with every turn of the cards. The next morning, he spent each waking moment savoring his good fortune.

His daughter was not so lucky. Balked, baffled, and frustrated, Vanessa watched the preparations being made for her trip to London. There was no way she could stop them, unless she were suddenly to contract a serious ailment. This being hardly likely, she assumed an indifferent attitude, which did not fool her maid.

Addy, while complaining bitterly about the unseemly haste, secretly blessed the Earl for removing her mistress from the gloomy Manor. Although she could not say so for sure, she suspected he was responsible for the militant sparkle that had completely replaced the defeat in Vanessa's eyes.

CHAPTER TWELVE

Through long acquaintance Addy had intimate knowledge of Miss Charldon's dangerous moods and was able to recognize an impending crisis. She could do nothing, however, but mutter an appeal to the Deity to ward off disaster as she wrapped the furs in silver tissue, placed them in their allotted boxes, and directed the maids about their tasks. She finally packed everything herself for, as she grumbled to the understanding housekeeper, "Like as not these empty-headed country girls would do it all wrong, and then I'd only have to undo all their mistakes and begin again."

"Lady Presteign won't let Miss be seen in them rubbishy made-overs," the housekeeper said with benevolent condescension. "The Earl's mother, you know, is ever so fashionable."

"Then it will be up to Lady Presteign to dress her suitably," answered Addy matter-of-factly.

"That's a mercy. Happen she won't look nearly so ill-favored." Realizing that this time she had gone too far, the housekeeper amended hastily, "I don't mean to say Miss is a complete disaster, exactly, but she is a very plain-featured and retiring young lady."

The housekeeper made several similarly uncomplimentary remarks relating to Miss Charldon's lumpish figure and unfortunate lack of any claim to beauty. Addy, who had allowed her fellow domestic's previous slights to pass unchallenged, now gave her to understand that Miss was of such awe-inspiring beauty that a famous artist had once begged her to pose for him. The name of this personage effectively silenced as well as bewildered the housekeeper, for even below stairs they had heard the name. Lady Charldon and Sir Lucius had had a real ripper over a painting she wanted done on ivory by Cosway.

"There," Addy sighed as she folded the last remodeled garment and placed it in the trunk. "Now all that remains is to have it taken out with the others."

The housekeeper informed the butler, and he in turn directed two footmen to tie it to the rear of the ancient traveling carriage.

A dressing case and a bandbox containing the articles she would need on her journey did not occupy much space, and since Vanessa and Addy were the only passengers in the vehicle, there was room to spare as they set off for London.

The trip, noteworthy only in its tedium, was broken once at an establishment that earned Addy's scorn for its unaired sheets, although it provided a respectable dinner for the weary travelers.

Vanessa had spent the day staring, unseeing, out of the coach window, and now she tossed the night away, torn between high-flown schemes of revenge upon her would-be seducer, Sylvester Vinton, Earl of Melcourt, and reflections on the amusements London society had to offer. Her companion, imagining all sorts of ills arising from the poor housekeeping of the landlord's wife, passed a no more restful night. So it was that early morning found them again on their way and, due to their propitious start, the old-fashioned carriage rumbled over London's cobblestone roads and pulled up in front of the Presteign town house well before dark.

Benson, Lady Presteign's elderly butler, had kept his staff on the watch for Miss Charldon since noon. Now, perceiving the antiquated equipage and its even more ancient coachman, he sent one of his minions to inform her ladyship that Miss Charldon had arrived, and indicated to another that the double doors of the house should be thrown open in welcome. A gawky lad jumped from the box and ran to let down the carriage steps; a footman hurried out to open the mud-bespattered door, brushing aside the youth in shabby green livery. He was followed by Benson, who handed Miss Charldon out personally, showing her how very welcome she was. Vanessa followed him into the house, Addy close behind, leaving the footman to deal with the trunk and assorted pieces of baggage they had brought with them.

The elegant simplicity of the black and white marble flooring of the entryway was lost on Vanessa, who had been steeling herself toward this moment. She followed the butler up the magnificent staircase to a drawing room on the first floor, where Lady Presteign, embroidery abandoned, greeted her with outstretched arms.

Vanessa felt her stiffness vanish before the warm smile and engaging manner of her godmother, and she returned the other's kiss with sincerity. As she took a closer look at Lady Presteign, her heart seemed to contract; the piercing blue eyes that looked on her so kindly were the eyes of the Earl of Melcourt! So much for forgetting that this tall, slender woman was his mother. The resemblance was overwhelming!

Noticing the strained look on Vanessa's face and correctly attributing it to her striking likeness to Sylvester, Lady Presteign declared, "There, child, I daresay you will be frightened of me, but let's not talk of that now, for I'm sure you will be glad of a bath and your bed. And while you are having your dinner on a tray in your room, I shall have a word with Addy."

"It's very kind of your ladyship to remember me," Addy replied as Lady Presteign accompanied them up the stairs to the next floor and placed Vanessa in the hands of her own abigail, with instructions to see that Miss Charldon had a hot bath and went right to bed.

Lady Presteign patted Vanessa's hand. "Go on, my dear; I'll be up in an hour. We can chat then." She hesitated. "That is, if you don't mind."

"Oh, no, my lady. I am looking forward to talking with you," she replied in all sincerity. She watched Lady Presteign leave the room; her eyes were troubled, and she wondered if she would think of the Earl every time she saw his mother. And she had thought to get away from him! He seemed to be haunting her.

Lady Presteign enjoyed her talk with Addy, learning from the old woman some very interesting things about Vanessa's reaction to Melcourt. She was quite cheered to hear that, far from being indifferent, the girl practically became a spitting, clawing wildcat at the very mention of his name. Even accounting for the probable exaggeration that Addy included to enlarge on the drama of her narrative, it was encouraging. She left the old woman in the care of Mrs. Benson, the housekeeper, and, noticing the hour had flown, tapped on Vanessa's door, entering at the sound of her voice.

"Addy and I had a most interesting coze." She closed the door behind her and approached the bed, where Vanessa, fresh from her bath, waited expectantly.

"I have just now left her in the care of my housekeeper," Lady Presteign continued, seating herself at the edge of the bed and taking possession of Vanessa's hand. "She is getting old, my dear, and we must see that she gets her rest."

"An enterprising undertaking, my lady."

"Not if we see that she returns to Charldon Manor. I believe we should engage a younger maid for you, Vanessa. It is too much to expect Addy to wait up for you and attend you at all hours."

Vanessa was stricken. "I did not think! I am so accustomed to having her there. . . . But you are right," she said firmly. "Town life is more demanding than country life, and Addy can attend me when I return home." Having made up her mind, there was nothing more for Vanessa to do but tell Addy. She said as much to Lady Presteign.

"I have suggested it to her, child, and she is quite agreeable. She wished me to tell you she will be returning to the Manor with the coach very early in the morning. I took the liberty of telling her you would not mind if she slips into your room and wakes you before she leaves. It is all right, is it not?" Lady Presteign sighed with relief at Vanessa's nod. "Good! I sent her to bed—she looked exhausted. Do you wish me to send around to the stables in your name with a message for your coachman? It might be wise to tell him that Addy will be returning with him and that he is to take it in very easy stages."

"You are very thoughtful, my lady."

"Surely you can call me Aunt Margaret. I am your godmother, after all."

"Not if you do not mind, my . . . Aunt Margaret," she corrected herself.

"That is much better. It makes it far easier to talk if you think of me as your godmother and not as Melcourt's mother."

Delicate color touched Vanessa's face as Lady Presteign regarded her appraisingly. "Although you have found my likeness to my son so startling, you are not as like your mother as the miniature led me to believe."

"The locket! Then he did open it. I had no idea," she said by way of explanation.

"It was very naughty of him to deceive you, but then Sylvester is the greatest tease, my dear. One should never take him too seriously."

Vanessa would not have characterized him quite that way, but she had no wish to embarrass his mother.

"I daresay he has been rather overbearing and highhanded with you. I warned him not to, you know, for I remembered that red hair of yours, although it is strangely two-tone now," she said with a humorous quirk of her brow.

"He doesn't know, Aunt Margaret," Vanessa said diffidently. "I was wearing a wig."

"Not the one you were wearing when you arrived here?"

Vanessa nodded.

"Oh, dear! Well, you must tell me all about it. I'd quite like to see that son of mine fooled for once."

"Oh, you are kind!"

"Nonsense, child. Just call it my prying mind, to be sure."

Lady Presteign's avowed curiosity and lively sense of humor was indulged by her goddaughter and shortly the two were exchanging confidences.

"And how do you feel about Melcourt?" Lady Presteign asked. "If you do not wish to tell me, I shall understand, dear," she continued when Vanessa seemed to hesitate.

"It's not that. . . . It's just . . . He thinks I'm of no more value than a piece of furniture," she finally blurted.

"Isn't that what you wanted?"

"Yes! And that's what I cannot understand. I think I've changed my mind!"

"In that case, it will help that you are very lovely, much more beautiful than the miniature led me to expect, which is surprising, for Cosway is not known to err in that direction."

A rosy blush suffused Vanessa's face as she admitted, "It is not my likeness."

"No?" Lady Presteign did not seem surprised at all. "To tell the truth, I thought not—because of your hair, my dear," she said in reply to Vanessa's questioning look. "It must be a study of your Cousin Jeanne. I had

heard that she was the very image of your mother."
She was thoughtful. "Am I correct in supposing the
man to be her husband?"

Vanessa verified her godmother's conjecture and
further offered a brief recital of the journey in which
Raoul de St. Varres had played so prominent a role
and of the events which had led to her return to England. A fleeting glance at the girl's artless countenance assured Lady Presteign that her devotion to her
cousin's husband was no more than one would bestow
upon a dear brother or young uncle.

"We will not tell Melcourt anything about Raoul.
You did say his name is Raoul, did you not?"

Vanessa nodded, perplexed.

"It will do Melcourt no harm to be unsure of you,"
my lady told her by way of an answer.

"Why would he care? He doesn't love me. He is
marrying me for Shelburne Park, so why should my
past concern him? Or is it that his wife must be above
reproach? No! Don't tell me." She made a wry face. "I
have answered my own question."

"Has Melcourt not told you of my little scheme?"

"He said nothing beyond asking me to marry him,"
Vanessa said, mentally crossing her fingers. Whatever
else he had said was not for his mother's ears.

Lady Presteign was pleased at Vanessa's disclosure.
It was not by chance that he had neglected to divulge
their plan. If she was not mistaken, and she was sure
that she was not, he could be no more indifferent to
Vanessa than she was to him.

"Then I do not have to marry Melcourt after all,"
she said after Lady Presteign revealed the plan her
inventive mind had conceived.

"No, my child, not unless you and he decide you will suit—as indeed I hope you shall."

"I am sorry to disappoint you, ma'am, but that will never happen." Vanessa's voice was firm.

"Do you find my son so distasteful then, my dear?" she queried gently.

Vanessa found herself struggling for words.

"Do not imagine that you injure my feelings, child, for I have found myself out of patience with Sylvester time out of mind. But I must tell you . . . explain to you . . . I don't quite know how . . . Gentlemen do not have the sensitivity or delicacy of mind that would cause them to refrain from trying to fix their interests with one type of female at the same time they make an offer for a young lady. They think we are blind to the folly committed in the name of love.

"I believe you understand what I mean, and I will say no more, for I too have not been happy with a connection that can lead only to scandal and sorrow for all who are concerned."

Lady Presteign placed a kiss on her goddaughter's open brow. She thought Vanessa's candor refreshing; no sly boots this, up to every rig and row in town. Her antagonism was merely a form of self-preservation. Sylvester would find her defiance provocative and enchanting. Trust him to storm the citadel and carry off the prize. It was a ticklish situation, and she supposed she must not become entangled in their battle.

"By the bye, Vanessa, I think you can safely dispense with the wig. We will have Clébèrt do something with your hair. One can almost warm one's hands at its fire," my lady continued appreciatively. "I know Sylvester has no idea. . . . If he had seen you like

114

this, he would have wished to carry you off on his saddlebow or whatever it is that one is thrown across."

Vanessa's eyes twinkled. "Addy has it upon the authority of our housekeeper that you are very tonnish, ma'am, and an authority on the Polite World."

"Vile girl. You don't believe me now, but you will see."

Lady Presteign did not trouble to hide her smile as she said good night. She left a sorely troubled girl behind her, however, one who felt that being a reigning beauty would bring nothing but trouble upon her fiery head, men being such vain creatures and no one to defend her honor. She would have to be at her wit's end before accepting Melcourt as her champion, although it would serve him right if he were shot in a duel. She would sooner shoot him herself, if it came to that, she concluded angrily.

Vanessa decided it was all a farrago of nonsense in her godmother's mind and dwelled upon the warmth of her reception in the fashionable London house. How surprised she had been to be welcomed as if she had been a dear daughter. She had not known what to exepct from the woman who must pass judgment on her as the Earl of Melcourt's future wife. She had, in all truth, been hoping that Lady Presteign would not approve of the match, but all her hopes had become ashes at their meeting, only to rise phoenixlike when her godmother revealed her strategy. If only the Earl had explained before she left for London! It would have made her so much easier in her mind if she had known the truth.

"I don't trust him," she said out loud as she snuggled between the smooth satin sheets.

Her last conscious thought was that Melcourt probably had a plan all his own, which she would discover in good time. She hoped it did not concern her.

The morning fog had lifted before the ladies left their rooms.

"A perfect day for visiting the shops," suggested Lady Presteign over breakfast, "if you think you are quite up to it."

Vanessa, drinking her coffee and eyeing Lady Presteign's close-fitting *pierrot* jacket and full gathered skirt of russet velvet, assured her that she had recovered from her trip and was looking forward to seeing Bond Street for the first time.

"You shall look and buy to your heart's content, my love, for my husband spoils me dreadfully, you must know, and encourages me to indulge my every whim. No, no," she said when Vanessa showed signs of wishing to interrupt her. "My lord is always a little disappointed on his return if I have not spent all he has given me. You know," she confided, "I believe he feels he must make it up to me for not taking me with him, although I have assured him I would far rather wait for him in London than travel with him on those diplomatic missions. Won't you make us both happy by accepting whatever I can give you?"

Vanessa pushed the half-eaten toast aside. "It would be ungracious in me to refuse, dear Aunt," she whispered in a choked voice.

"Then it is all settled. We will be off immediately

Clébèrt leaves. He is the most fashionable coiffeur in London and not without reason."

"Do you not think we should put our trip off until tomorrow? If your Clébèrt is to do something with my hair, nothing short of a miracle will help him to leave here before evening."

"Nonsense. The man is a genius with the scissors, as you will see directly," Vanessa was told as the butler announced that the hairdresser was waiting above stairs for Miss Charldon.

A hour later, studying the results of the coiffeur's manipulations, Vanessa was forced to admit he deserved his reputation for the way he had salvaged her sadly shorn locks.

At his direction she turned her head this way and that before the glass. The fire in the grate was no whit warmer than the burnished ringlets that covered her head and framed a face as exquisite as the fabled Helen's, or so Clébèrt would have her believe.

"You were right, dear Aunt," Vanessa said after Clébèrt had left. "The man is a wonder. Now at least I can go about London without feeling conspicuous."

Lady Presteign had to laugh.

"Child, you but have to glance in your looking glass to see there is no help for that."

She could see that Vanessa seemed puzzled. "If it is anonymity you want, you should not have the eyes, complexion, and figure you have. Don't think for one moment that Clébèrt was not serious in his way. You have everyone convinced you are a dowdy, covent-educated young lady, but you cannot hide forever," Lady Presteign said philosophically. "Be yourself, and you will take all London by storm!"

117

Margaret Presteign could have hugged herself with joy. Vanessa was beautiful, unassuming, and delightful. No man would be able to resist this darling. It was better than she could have expected—and better than her son deserved. If he wanted to claim Vanessa, he would have to hurry before someone else snatched her up.

CHAPTER THIRTEEN

"How do you feel, dear?"

"Like an early Christian martyr about to be thrown to the lions," pronounced Vanessa gloomily as she prepared to pay her first social call since coming to town.

"I shan't let your Aunt Edgerton eat you, child, if that's what is worrying you," Lady Presteign promised with some amusement as they entered the Edgerton town house.

"I never would have recognized you, Vanessa," said Lady Edgerton as she offered her cheek for her niece's salute, "yet I am sure that I see a family resemblance."

"I am sure we all can, Mother," interceded a stocky young lady little older than Miss Charldon. "Only in Cousin Vanessa's case the red hair is quite undeniable. I'm your Cousin Meg," she explained, giving Va-

118

nessa a peck on the cheek. "If anyone had ever told me that a redhead could have a complexion and eyes like yours, I should have called him a liar; you are certainly not what I have been led to expect."

"Pay no heed to our Meg," said her brother Philip. "Whatever enters her head leaves it by way of her tongue so swiftly that it's no wonder she is empty-headed."

Philip's sadly maligned sister wrinkled her freckled nose at him but he had turned to Vanessa. "Do you find yourself still in need of my support, dear Cousin?" he asked, a smile lighting his cool, blond good looks as he took Vanessa's hand. "I said you would be safe in the bosom of your family. There's no need to be afraid of Mother; however Meg, here, is a different matter: she's been frothing at the mouth since I told her that I'd met you this morning."

"It wasn't fair of you to be the first to meet our cousin," Meg said mournfully.

"Oh, no, you don't. You can't lay it at my door. I asked you to come riding with me this morning, but you said you were too tired." Philip looked at her mockingly. "*Lazy* is the word I would have used."

"That's too bad of you, Philip! If you had told me you were planning to ride with Andrew and Vanessa, I would have come with you." Meg's chin was thrust out in a most defiant manner, and Philip, noticing signs of impending warfare, groaned.

"I told you it was merely a chance encounter, Meg. You tell her, Vanessa. Nothing that I say will convince her."

"Truly, Meg, neither Andrew nor I had the least intention of riding this morning," said Vanessa. "In fact,

119

I was surprised to see him. To be honest . . ." she broke off.

"By all means let us be honest," interjected Meg tartly, waiting for Vanessa to come to the point. It did not escape her notice that her companions were studiously avoiding each other's eyes. "Odious, horrid creatures—both," cried Meg somewhat incoherently as she flounced off, only to be restrained by Philip's hand on her arm.

"Peace, little hothead, and we'll tell you," he said.

"Don't tease yourself," she retorted testily.

"Listen here, Meg. Either you want to know or you don't," and Philip turned as if to leave.

"If ever anyone was bacon-brained . . . Of course I want to know," hissed Meg. "You just took too long to tell me."

"Tell her, Vanessa. I can't."

"Oh, Meg. I thought I should die laughing," Vanessa chortled. "Andrew told us he had to escape after Gwenyth trailed her sleeve in his coffee. He said it always signals a bad day when she does that—and I thought to myself 'How like the Abbé Chappe's semaphore she is.'"

Strange choking noises came from Philip while Meg looked considerably puzzled. "Explain *semaphore* please," she asked.

"I can't, child. I shall disgrace myself," her brother gasped.

"You, Vanessa?"

"It's a signal device—an upright post with movable arms," managed Vanessa before snorting inelegantly.

"Oh ho! Very like, now that I see her," agreed Meg, making a rude sound as she observed some little activity at the door. Watching her mother sail forth to greet the new arrivals, she continued, "It is fascinating to watch Gwenyth, now you've cleared up the mystery, Vanessa. I used to think she resembled a seagull flapping its wings, but now I see she is just like that Abbé fellow's signal posts—watch the right hand flutter just so. Aha! That means she will be floating our way. . . . Why, Gwen dear," Meg continued in the same breath, "how are you? I haven't seen you in ages."

"Not since yesterday, at any rate," came the notably breathless reply as Gwenyth glided into the room. "How are you, Philip? You haven't been near us since Christmas. Have you met Vanessa yet? I see that my mother is here but where . . ." Gwenyth's fluttering soprano climbed into the upper registers as she looked closely at the lovely young woman sandwiched between the Edgertons. "Oh!" she breathed. "Vanessa? Vanessa, is it really you? Oh, my, this does change everything, doesn't it? And Andrew knew; why didn't he tell me? And all these weeks I thought . . . and Sylvester too . . . my own brother . . ." She trailed off, a dazed yet delighted expression on her face.

"You can be sure that my brother is no better," Meg told her wryly. "He met Vanessa today and didn't tell me a thing about her. Brothers, fie!" she chuckled. "What we poor sisters must put up with for the sake of our families!"

"You won't give up, will you, Meg?" Philip asked, more amused than annoyed, but Lady Edgerton thought it time to step in.

"Children, stop squabbling! You are not in the schoolroom now, so do stop behaving as if you were."

"That is quite your fault, ma'am, for addressing us

121

in that manner," lovingly admonished her irrepressible daughter. "By so doing, you imply to us, as well as to the rest of the world, that we are not fully grown." She turned her large brown eyes to Vanessa. "Do you not think that right, Cousin?"

"Aunt, how can I not answer such an appeal? I am not heartless, you know."

"It would be better if you were, my dear niece; being heartless is an asset when you contemplate marriage to a rake."

Vanessa felt herself flush.

"How like I am to mother, do you not think, Cousin?" said Meg. "But I assure you we mean no harm by it." She looked at her sympathetically.

Vanessa was afraid to commit herself and looked toward her godmother, who rose to the occasion nobly. "I feared people might link Vanessa's name with Sylvester's, forgetting that I am her godmother. We shall have to employ Philip's services as an escort until Vanessa makes herself known as a desirable partner. Even if Sylvester was in town and could be prevailed upon to dance attendance on a debutante, it would not be in order now."

Much relieved at hearing that Melcourt had not pledged himself to the marital state, Lady Edgerton rolled her eyes speakingly at her daughter before placing her son at the disposal of Lady Presteign. Meg, as much because she liked Vanessa as because she wished to avoid her mother's heavy-handed matchmaking, attached herself to the pair with an offer to play propriety, which caused everyone to laugh, except for Lady Edgerton who sat with a slightly dazed look contemplating the worth of a marriage between her son and her niece.

Seated at Vanessa's side in the returning carriage, Lady Presteign felt eminently satisfied with the day's outing.

"How do you feel now, dear?" she asked as she settled herself against the soft gray upholstery.

"Somewhat mauled, but not missing any parts, thank you," Vanessa admitted with a sigh.

Decidedly mauled, nodded Lady Presteign in silent agreement and, to keep up Vanessa's flagging spirits, she indulged in one delightfully ungracious remark after another, one of which likened Lady Edgerton to a well-fed cat planning a leisurely assault on an unsuspecting canary. "Although quite unlike the creature in the story, her prospective victim is protected by someone well able to take care of his own."

"Surely Aunt Edgerton does not really suspect . . .?"

"No, for if she did the news would be all over town in a matter of days. I pray your father does not reveal his hopes to either of his sisters."

"Have no fear on that score, dear ma'am," her companion chuckled, "for he has never liked either of them above half, and I have no doubt but that the passage of years has merely strengthened his persuasion."

Lady Presteign's rich laughter filled the carriage. "How can a daughter so undervalue that most worthy parent? And as for Gwenyth, why you have obviously made a conquest there, a complete about-face until one realizes she expects you to put Miranda's nose out of joint."

"I have been treated to several of Gwenyth's little speeches, so do not think to spare my feelings—she did not seem to think I had any. Her catalog of aspirants to the position of Countess of Melcourt, along with their sundry virtues, was dinned into my ears several times a day at Charldon Manor. Miss Wrexham did not have enough beauty of countenance to please him, Miss Seymour would bore him with her missish ways, Lady Sophia was not lively enough for his tastes, and I was no more than a dowdy, lumpish Miss Prunes and Prisms, which would cause them to say in the clubs that Melcourt has lost his fortune and has taken that way to repair it."

"Gwenyth to the life, my dear. Heaven knows I have tried to give her more polish, but I have failed. At least I succeeded with one of my children; Sylvester has never alarmed me—although of late I have been inclined to think him a trifle too reserved," Lady Presteign added virtuously, not looking at Vanessa, who thought, herself, that the Earl was considerably less staid than his mother painted him. After all, Lady Presteign's viewpoint was based strictly upon a mother's experience, while hers was . . . different.

Lady Presteign tilted her head and examined the interior of the carriage as though searching for a solution to the problem the Earl presented. "I have decided you need an opportunity to try your hand with the other sex. It might be wise to begin with your Cousin Philip. If I'm not mistaken, he is already quite *épris*. I don't believe you will find our young men too difficult to manage, although you are used to the more conventional ways of the French."

"Do you truly think so?" quavered her goddaughter,

whose life in France had been anything but conventional.

"Yes, child, and you must remember that the English, in general, are very different from the French, although," she concluded, a frown ridging her brow, "a rake's a rake in any country."

CHAPTER FOURTEEN

With Melcourt absent from town, Lady Presteign invited the Honorable Philip Edgerton to complete her party of six for Miss Burney's new play.

The evening began well; Andrew and Gwenyth had been surprisingly on time, and Philip's appearance had followed on the heels of Sir Geoffrey Helmsford's introduction to Vanessa.

"To what do we owe your lady's prompt arrival, Andrew?" whispered his sister in an aside as they were about to go in to dinner.

"Miranda," said Andrew, not one to waste words.

"And just when did our charming stepmother arrive?" she ventured, knowing that Miranda was not apt to travel without a personable male as escort.

"This afternoon," came Andrew's blunt answer, and he turned away as Philip claimed Vanessa for his dinner partner.

She smiled vaguely at Philip as she wondered if her father had found his pockets enough recovered to appear in town, or if Miranda had had another companion on the journey. Gwenyth, after greeting Vanessa, had been strangely silent, leaving Vanessa to suspect they were to be once again at daggers drawn. She hoped not.

A pleasant dinner behind them and expectations of a delightful evening ahead of them, Lady Presteign's guests took their seats minutes prior to the raising of the curtain on *Edwy and Elgiva.* Several ladies and gentlemen in nearby boxes exchanged bows with members of their party as they settled themselves to view the tragedy. As all agreed later, it was a tragedy that no one had seen fit to explain to Miss Burney that the cry of "Bring in the Bishop" was highly inappropriate to the tone of her play. The gentlemen were quick to share their amusement with the ladies and ripples of laughter elsewhere in the theater made it obvious that others were enlightening their companions.

Sir Geoffrey chuckled heartily. "Bishop is a punch, Miss Charldon, not an ecclesiastic, and while one can't expect a writer of Miss Burney's refinement to be familiar with tavern language, I'm sure that many of her associates have asked a waiter to bring in the bishop when they thirsted for spirits, not the spiritual."

Vanessa's response must have pleased him, although, for the life of her, she did not know what she had said; even as Sir Geoffrey leaned back in his chair, a rumble of laughter still coming from his big frame, her attention was claimed by the occupants of a box on the opposite side of the theater. They had just arrived, and as the curtain was lowered, Melcourt could be seen solicitously bending over Lady Charldon as she arranged her skirts. As he straightened, he seemed to stare directly at Vanessa: he turned to say something to Miranda, who, after a moment of hesitation, nodded, arose from her seat, and left the box with the Earl.

"They're coming here, Mother," Gwenyth whispered, then, turning to Vanessa, "Oh, this is better than the play. Wait until Miranda sees you! She'll have a fit! And Sylvester!"

"Gwenyth, dear, do try for a trifle more self-control," said Lady Presteign, eyeing her daughter with increasing displeasure. Andrew, who usually found little to say, now said less than ever and patted his wife's hands.

Vanessa did not wish to see Melcourt and prevailed upon Philip to walk with her in the corridor, neatly avoiding the other couple by returning just as the curtain went up on the second act. Her eyes focused on the box across the way, and it was almost a repeat of what had gone before, except that this time Melcourt pulled his chair close enough to Miranda for their shoulders to brush.

Throughout the whole of this act Vanessa kept her eyes on them, ready to bolt if they showed signs of leaving their seats. When the curtain came down, there was some desultory applause, followed by a flurry of activity in the theater. Momentarily, Philip attracted her attention, but she did not really hear what he said. Not wishing to offend him, she turned her head, intending to ask him to repeat himself, but

127

found that Sir Geoffrey had responded in her stead and had everyone listening to his lively commentary.

Vanessa looked across the theater. There was Miranda. The seat next to her was occupied by a woman, and there were three men in evening clothes conversing behind them. Of Melcourt there was no sign.

"Philip," Vanessa began, but it was too late.

"Twice in one night, Sylvester? And to what do I owe the honor?" his mother twitted him.

"Why, to your very lovely goddaughter, ma'am." His eyes swept Vanessa with approval and lingered on her fiery curls. "A stroll in the corridor, Miss Charldon? You must tell me how you go on since last I saw you."

Philip stood, uncertain of what to do. "Good evening, Edgerton," the Earl said, dismissing the younger man with an affable nod. His hand on Vanessa's arm brooked no refusal, and she hastily swallowed her angry words until they had left the others.

"Must you always have your own way?" she hissed.

"Not now, child," he cautioned, throwing her a warning glance. "A dragon in purple velvet is about to descend on us.

"Good evening, Lady Edgerton."

Thus prepared, Vanessa turned with remarkable composure and watched her aunt bear down upon them.

"Good evening, Aunt."

"Good evening, Vanessa, Melcourt," she replied in response to their greeting and then proceeded to address herself exclusively to the Earl. "I'm happy to see you've decided to support your mother. Her home has been filled with marriageable young females protest-

128

ing undying friendship for Vanessa—but all awaiting your return to town."

"And your daughter, Meg, keeping them company while young Philip deputizes for me?"

"Ha! If you think to put me to the blush, you're mistaken, my lord. You will excuse me? I have a few choice bits of news for your mother; she is seldom as well informed as you." She inclined her head the correct amount to signify dismissal and entered the Presteign box.

"Attack and retreat," said the Earl, an engaging smile on his face. Looking up at him, Vanessa felt her heart give a sudden lurch and her stomach sink to a level somewhere near her knees. "What's the matter, kitten?" he asked.

"N . . . nothing." She bent her head and recovered herself admirably.

His fingers flicked her red-gold curls. "I was about to ask my mother who that red-haired charmer was, but then I saw your eyes."

Those same blue-violet eyes looked up at him, framed by incredibly long lashes that threw pools of shadow on her cheeks.

"Somehow I hadn't pictured you with red hair."

"Are you pleased, my lord?" she asked demurely.

"It explains a lot, my little termagant," he told her dryly, "but yes, I do like it."

A flush touched her cheeks and he, amused by the sudden rush of heat to her face, relieved her of her dainty fan and waved it in a cooling motion.

"I'm sorry if my words have caused you any embarrassment."

"One would think you had more to do, my lord, than concern yourself with old wives' tales about people with red hair," she retorted, and tried to regain the fan, which he held just beyond her reach.

"I'd like to concern myself with one particular red-haired person," the Earl told her lazily. He leaned his shoulders against the wall, flashed a quick look up and down the corridor, and then grinned at her. "The more I see you, the more lost to propriety I become . . . and right now you look good enough to eat. If the curtain was not about to go up, I would kiss you right here, but in a minute this corridor will be filled with very inquisitive people returning to their own boxes. I'll have to remedy this soon. You are promised to Lady Bellingham, are you not?" He did not wait for an answer but went on abruptly, "I will look for you there." So saying, he returned her fan and escorted her to the box, she seething and speechless with fury, he blandly wishing the company a good night.

The Earl had noticed the mutinous expression on Miss Charldon's lovely face and reading it to mean she would not attend the rout, he did not waste time attempting to track her down at Lady Bellingham's, but instead, tired and not at all pleased with the way his day had gone, he presented himself at the Presteign town house.

He exchanged a few pleasantries with the elderly butler as he handed his coat, hat, and cane to the footmen stationed at the door, and tossed his gloves onto a marquetry table. Then, in pursuit of his quarry, he asked whether Miss Charldon had retired for the evening.

"I will inquire, my lord." The butler signaled one of the lackeys, who promptly disappeared below stairs.

"Oh, and Benson . . . I had to cancel my dinner engagement this evening . . ."

"Certainly, my lord." The very dignified butler smiled warmly. "Something sustaining?"

"And Mrs. Benson, how is she?" asked the Earl after agreeing that yes, indeed, he needed something sustaining.

"As well as can be expected, my lord—getting on in years and after me to retire."

"Things wouldn't be the same without the Bensons," the Earl told him, patting the old man's shoulder.

"You're very kind, my lord."

"If there are any jam tarts, Benson . . ."

"You leave it to Mrs. Benson, my lord; she'll know just what you like . . . and, my lord, she baked the jam tarts fresh this morning."

"I picked the right day," the Earl declared with a smile. "I shall be in the Jade Room," he threw back over his shoulder as he ascended the stairs.

The Jade Room, long the family's favorite gathering place, housed Lord Presteign's magnificent collection of oriental *objets d'art.* Opposite the glass-enclosed teak cases, which occupied one wall, was a white marble fireplace, its delicate green veining enhanced by pale green silk walls. Matching draperies framed long windows at either end of the room. The furniture was comfortable, as befitted the use to which the room had been put; it was also elegant, one piece a handsome inlaid cardtable. Seated here, Lord and Lady Presteign had played at Speculation with her two young children. Here, too, Lord Presteign had taught his stepson the pitfalls of chess, and later the intricacies of piquet (and the dangers of other games that had proved the undoing of many a young man) before bringing him to the attention of the fashionable world. Several doors led off to various rooms, one of which was Vanessa's sitting room, and it was this which opened as her maid reported that Miss had retired for the night.

Melcourt was not satisfied with this answer and sent the girl back to her mistress, apologizing for the inconvenience (not meaning a word of it) but requesting a few moments of her time. A bare minute later the girl returned and delivered Miss Charldon's regrets. Something about the maid's flustered appearance caused the Earl to smile to himself.

"Girl—what is your name?"

"Iris, your lordship," she identified herself with a curtsy.

"Iris, tell Miss Charldon that if she is not here in two minutes, I shall come in and get her."

With another curtsy and a harried expression on her face, Iris left to do the Earl's bidding. She hesitated at the doorway, looked back, and, seeing the timepiece in his hand, picked up her skirts and ran to her mistress.

Vanessa had thrown off her clothes and had been about to slip into bed when her maid returned with the Earl's ultimatum. Ignoring Iris's frantic screech, she stormed into the Jade Room, prepared to do battle.

"How dare you!" she exploded.

Melcourt verified the time, replaced his watch, and allowed his eyes to travel from curling pink toes to tousled red curls. "Apparently my message worked," he drawled, blandly ignoring her anger. "I said two minutes? It is well under that, and here you are—although"—he raised one quizzical brow—"I did not expect you in such *déshabillé*."

Anger gone, she flushed, suddenly aware of the revealing picture she presented in her thin lawn nightdress. She wanted to cover herself with her hands, but her pride would not allow it. She would have retreated then, but his hand reached out to stop her.

Melcourt stepped past her through the doorway. "Bring a robe for your mistress, Iris, and something for her feet."

The girl bolted from the room, anxious to carry out his orders and determined not to leave her mistress alone for a second longer than necessary. On her return he took the robe and looked down at the young maid, not unkindly. "That will be all, Iris. You need have no fear for your mistress. I shall not keep her from her bed for too long."

Fears of quite the opposite intention on his lordship's part receded, although Iris gave Miss Charldon a troubled look.

Vanessa, her composure worn thin, turned to her maid. "Oh, go to bed, do, Iris. I'm entirely safe with his lordship."

Hearing the scarcely veiled impatience in her mistress's voice, Iris almost fled from the room, wondering what her ladyship would say and deciding to place her problem in the butler's very capable hands.

"My apologies," said Melcourt smoothly. "I thought you were hoaxing me. I did not realize you had retired."

Vanessa looked over her shoulder as he held the robe for her, an imp of mischief in her eyes. "I had not retired," she chuckled. "I thought you might not be above coming into my room to check."

"It did occur to me," he grinned, suddenly not tired anymore, "but this was much more—rewarding."

"You mean—revealing."

"That too." His eyes were on her full young breasts.

"Wretched creature. At least, if we marry, you shall know what it is you are getting."

The Earl had to admire her quick recovery but was not above another gibe. "Not 'if.' Do you think there is any doubt in my mind after seeing you tonight?"

"Good night, my lord."

"Don't freeze up on me. I did not mean to embarrass you any further, child. It is just that you are so damned beautiful . . ." He held out his hand. "Don't go, please. Won't you share my supper? I shall be on my best behavior."

She hesitated, a smile lurking in the depths of her eyes. "You cannot mean that, my lord."

"Why not?" He was his haughty, arrogant self again.

"At this hour of the night, my lord, the strain attendant upon such unaccustomed conduct would surely play havoc with your digestion."

"Come here, sauce box." Once again, he held out his hand, and this time she allowed her fingers to rest in his.

"The servants . . . I'm sure Iris went running to Benson."

134

"A rubber or two of piquet? That should convince him everything is in order."

With a tremulous smile Vanessa allowed the Earl to lead her to the cardtable.

CHAPTER FIFTEEN

Highly irregular was what Benson thought as he relieved a flunky of a well-laden tray at the door. He would have brought himself to say something to that effect but for the fact that Miss Charldon showed no signs of alarm but was, instead, seated at the cardtable, engaged in a hand of piquet with his lordship.

The Earl looked up with a smile as the butler entered. "Let me give you a hand with that, Benson. It looks enough to feed an army." He pulled up a side table for the tray. "Ummm . . . Jam tarts, indeed! Be sure to thank Mrs. Benson for me. We will serve ourselves," he said, dismissing the butler.

As Benson left, Vanessa turned to Melcourt in wonder. "You are two different people, my lord. I never thought to see you so considerate of a servant. No . . . *considerate* is the wrong word to choose, for I have never seen you less than considerate—in regard to servants, that is. The word I am looking for is a warmer one—*kind*."

The Earl filled their wineglasses and then looked up. "In all the years I have known Benson, he has never been other than kind; should I, then, be less than that to him, now that he is an old man and I no longer a scruffy schoolboy?"

"Scruffy, my lord?" She accepted a glass from him.

"Decidedly scruffy. And as for your accusation that I am two different people, what can I say to *you,* Miss Charldon, a past mistress of disguise?"

This time Vanessa refused to be baited. "You could offer me one of your tarts, Melcourt, and may I tell you, you must rate high with Mrs. Benson. She chased me from the kitchen this morning before she took the tarts from the oven. 'Spoil your appetite,' she said, but I can see now that she was saving them for you."

"So you are the thief who has been at my private stock! You have upset the staff no end. Mrs. Benson has been accusing them of pilfering and, when they denied even touching the tarts, she accused me of sneaking around and playing off my tricks on her, as she calls it—something she has not mentioned since the last time I asked her to marry me."

"You didn't!" she gurgled.

"I most certainly did! You see, Mother has always said that Mrs. Benson had a lighter hand with pies and cakes than the cook, so I, a chubby and determined four-year-old, asked for said hand."

"And did she accept?"

"Conditionally. I was to ask permission of Benson. I recall her being much broken up and covering her face with a towel, but she managed to send me off to Benson before her feelings got the better of her."

"And he?" she urged.

"We came to a gentlemen's agreement, since he declared he would not like to lose her—for which he begged my pardon, but, being a right 'un, promised me that all jam tarts Mrs. Benson made would be mine. And that is why, my dear Miss Charldon, from that day to this, the Bensons and I regard all jam tarts as my exclusive property."

"What a delightful story. How I wish I had known you then!"

"Considering that you didn't make your appearance until some years later, it would have been well nigh impossible, my dear. Incidentally, she was the first and last woman I offered for, until I met you."

"And the first and last time you failed to get the woman you wanted until . . ." She left the sentence unfinished.

"You are being deliberately provocative, Vanessa," the Earl said, looking up from the plate he was preparing for her.

"Most likely." She sighed sharply. "It is something I cannot seem to help when I am with you," Vanessa confessed ruefully.

"I am encouraged, child."

"I shall have a bit of the ham, Melcourt," said Miss Charldon, pointedly ignoring the Earl's last remark.

"Just because you thought it necessary to plead the headache was no reason to give up your dinner."

"Oh, did your mother tell you I was not well?" she asked innocently as she surveyed the tempting morsels he had set in front of her. "I did so want to go to Lady Bellingham's rout. Was it a sad crush?"

"My mother did not tell me—I did not see her—and I never intended going to Lady Bellingham's rout," the Earl said as he skillfully moved the plate out of Vanessa's reach. "Why should I waste my time looking for you there when you made it evident you would not be attending?"

"Put the plate back and give me another jam tart. I promise not to throw anything at you, Melcourt."

He kept a wary eye on her as he began to work his way through a rosy, succulent slice of ham.

"It is perfectly vile of you to sit there stuffing yourself when my stomach is growling." She raised her eyes to his. "I promised."

"So you did." He smiled and returned the dish along with a second jam tart. "Peace offering," he indicated as she attacked the food with relish, and he watched her demolish the ham and bite into one of the tarts.

"You have a very strange opinion of me if you think I would waste such good food by throwing it— when I'm so hungry," she said mockingly as soon as she was able to talk.

He had to laugh. With warmth and approval in his voice he remarked, "Just when I think I know what you are going to say, you say something completely unexpected."

"That's part of my charm," she pointed out impudently, licking jam from her fingers.

"By God, I think it is!" he said with some force.

"Fiddle! I was only funning; I am not so vain as all that."

"No, you are not vain, although you have every right to be, Vanessa."

"The last game was yours, I believe," Vanessa stated, uncomfortable at the turn the conversation had taken.

Melcourt realized how ill at ease she was at his obvious admiration. It was hard for him to drag his eyes from her. As she took time over her discard, she felt him looking at her and rebuked him for not attending to the game.

"I am justly admonished, child. I require a wager to make me play in earnest."

"Name it, then, Melcourt."

"You first, Vanessa."

"A ride behind your grays—with the reins in my hands," came her answer with scarcely a pause.

His eyelids hiding his piercing blue gaze, he considered her for a moment, then nodded.

"And you?" she prompted.

"Let us play first."

Vanessa scolded him roundly, letting him know in very definite terms how she felt about such a scheme. "For who knows what stakes you might name, and I should be honor bound to pay up."

"Quite so," he responded, not at all abashed. "You are not very trusting."

"Quite so," returned Vanessa. "Name your stakes, if you will."

"And if I say 'a kiss'?"

"And if you do?"

Her blue-violet eyes sparkled in enjoyment as she fenced with him. There was an answering flame as his eyes swept over her.

"A kiss then it is, Vanessa," he said deliberately.

The game, played now in earnest, fell to the Earl on all counts. Vanessa, on her mettle, played cautiously, but as Melcourt proceeded to pile up the points, she sacrificed chance after chance of scoring, allowing him to win one trick after the other. It was the final hand. The Earl discarded but two of the cards dealt to him.

Vanessa hesitated over her discard and elected to exchange three cards. She played well, she thought, but the cards had seemed to fall to him. At one point she had barely managed to spoil his pique, but he was winning.

He moved a wineglass closer to her and filled it as well as his own. Vanessa's hand reached out automatically, as she frowned over her cards.

"A point of forty-eight," he called.

"Your point is good, my lord," said his opponent.

"And my quarte?"

"That too."

He refilled his glass with the heady red wine, but hesitated before filling Vanessa's glass only halfway. She smiled at him, pleased at his thoughtfulness.

"I want you in full possession of your senses as I collect my winnings," he remarked as he prepared to declare, "A quatorze of fourteen points."

"There too, my lord. And I with a trio of nines. I am well and truly undone."

"Will you pay your losses now, or shall we settle at a future date?"

She looked at him shyly, surprised that he had left her a graceful way out. "I will pay now, if you please." It was the veriest whisper.

He stood and came around to her side of the table. With a smile he held out his hands to help her from her seat and very slowly, her hands in his, she was drawn so close to him that she could feel the heat of his body. Her eyes remained fastened on his face as his arms reached out to encircle her.

"Wicked, wicked children!" accused Lady Presteign as she opened the door. "How could you leave me to that dreadful Serena Bellingham when I would have longed to spend a quiet evening with my family?" Her voice faltered as she entered the room.

The Earl stepped toward his mother, screening Vanessa and allowing her time to compose herself.

Lady Presteign prattled on in a way most unlike her own, talking of the rout and the people who had been there, until the Earl said, "We've left you some ham, though if you stayed to supper at Lady Bellingham's, it is not likely that you will be hungry."

Lady Presteign groaned. "You are so right, Sylvester. One could wish that Serena Bellingham's taste extended more to aesthetics. Her decorations were a veritable assault on the eyes—and the music!

"Vanessa, child, you were quite wise. If you did not have the headache before, you would have it now—as I have—and I am going straight to my bed. Good night, children; do not stay up too long."

Lady Presteign kissed each of them, ignoring Vanessa's guilty look, and left the room as suddenly as she had entered it.

"Good night, Vanessa."

"Good night?" She was startled.

"Sleep well, child. You will be ready tomorrow afternoon? I do not like to keep my horses waiting."

"Your horses, my lord?" she echoed dazedly.

"You did say you wished to handle the reins, did you not?" he asked with considerable amusement.

"But you won, my lord."

He took her unresisting hands in his. "Let us say, rather, that we are both winners." He raised her hands to his lips and kissed first one and then the other.

Long after he had departed, Vanessa lay in bed wondering if all gamblers had the same burning desire to pay their debts as she had. Somehow she doubted it.

A letter arrived with Vanessa's morning chocolate. Ignoring the cup, she instead devoured the letter, only to scowl and throw it onto the tray, obstinately refusing to reveal any distress. She was more perturbed at the overwhelming depth of her disappointment than at Melcourt's cancellation of their drive. Common sense told her that some important business must have come up, causing him to change his plans. It was too bad that that same common sense could not raise her spirits.

"Take it away," she sighed, pushing at the tray.

"The letter, miss, or the chocolate?"

"Both . . . No! Wait, Iris . . . just the chocolate."

The maid speedily returned to the kitchen with the rejected beverage. Cook, sampling it, declared Miss Charldon to be sickening for something. And so it seemed later that day when Vanessa sat and picked at her dinner with no more relish than a lovesick canary—an observation made by the second footman, causing considerable speculation in the servants' dining room, since everyone from Benson down to the tiniest tweeny knew the Earl had been playing cards with Miss until one o'clock in the morning. It was also known that a messenger in the Earl's livery had delivered a letter for Miss Charldon at a very early hour that morning.

Iris sat quietly and allowed the servants' wild theories of love and marriage to fly about her head. The maids looked at her enviously; not only had she been elevated to a position of importance by becoming personal maid to Miss Charldon, but if there was a wedding, Iris would outrank them all, including her ladyship's own abigail, earls rating higher than mere barons. Cook, the Bensons, and Lady Presteign's personal maid nodded to each other, approving Iris's reticence in the presence of the lower servants and, by prior agreement, extended to her an invitation to take tea in the privacy of the housekeeper's parlor the following day.

Although she knew she could not ignore what was tantamount to a royal command, Iris planned to divulge to her fellow servants only what was common knowledge: that Miss had received a letter from the Earl and that later in the morning the Edgertons had taken her up in their carriage. Only she was aware that Miss had returned from her outing in a raging tantrum, shouting for the letter she had received that morning and tearing it to shreds as she muttered something about perfidious wretches, broken promises, designing hussies, and double-faced libertines. Immediately thereupon Miss Charldon had become violently ill, but had been determined to come down to dinner, her lack of appetite thus giving rise to flights of fancy in the servants' hall.

Somehow Iris pieced together that Miss had seen Lady Charldon driving with the Earl. She shook her

143

head and thought it a pity that Miss was letting her feelings run away with her. She rather wished Miss would use some common sense, unconsciously echoing what Vanessa had told herself only that morning.

CHAPTER SIXTEEN

During the course of the next few weeks, Vanessa, to her intense relief (as she frequently assured herself), saw little of the Earl. At the musicales, balls, and card parties that they both attended, he was invariably giving his support to the Prince of Wales; on the few occasions he called at Mount Street, she was promised to her Edgerton cousins. Mornings were spent walking in Green Park or driving in Hyde Park with occasional forays to London's most fashionable shops to augment a depleted stocking or glove box. Afternoons were devoted to such varied pursuits as watching a review of the Light Horse Volunteers on Wimbledon Common and riding in Rotten Row.

On his way to spar a few rounds at Mendoza's, the Earl was fortunate to see the elusive Miss Charldon come out of Ackermann's Repository of Arts, accompanied by the Edgertons. He pulled up, and they made their way to his curricle, Meg asking in her pert way how he had escaped from the Prince who, they had heard, did not let him or Lord Malmesbury out of his sight.

"Or is it that you and Malmesbury do not dare let the Prince out of your sight?" she asked with an undercurrent of laughter in her voice.

"I had it from Lady Jersey," broke in Philip, "that after one look at Princess Caroline, the Prince told Malmesbury to get him a glass of brandy. And then she said the Prince jumped on a horse and galloped all the way to Richmond, just to pass Mrs. Fitzherbert's house."

"It's true enough," the Earl said with a grim expression on his face. "It was to be expected with such a bride—and I am sure Lady Jersey has described the Princess's personal habits in full. She never misses a chance to be malicious, and this time there is no need to be inventive."

Meg spoke next. "She told Mother she had it from an excellent source that you were considering marriage, so do not ask me for a dance, should you be at Lady Harwood's tonight; I should not like anyone to wonder if you were looking in my direction for a bride," Meg said candidly.

Her brother had a fit of coughing, and Miss Charldon, who had not put herself forward after her initial greeting, hurriedly looked for her handkerchief, while the Earl displayed a remarkably unperturbed mien.

"I like you well enough, Melcourt," said Meg. "In fact, one of the nicest things about you is that nothing I say ever fazes you. Unlike those two, now"—she motioned toward her companions—"you didn't bat an eye. But don't think, in spite of my liking for you, that I wish you for a husband, no matter what my mother plans. I shudder every time I think of setting foot in Melcourt Castle."

"My sister is an avid reader of Mrs. Radcliffe's novels, my lord," intervened Philip hastily.

"Much you know," Meg said darkly. "I heard Mother tell Father only last night that she would like to see me the lady of Melcourt Castle no matter how many women haunt its bedrooms." Her eyes flew wide as her words seemed to echo in her ears. "Oh!"

Philip grinned maliciously and the Earl's shout of laughter was quickly turned into a strangled cough as Vanessa's eyes met his. She turned away deliberately, her lip curled in disdain.

"Our Meg is nothing if not direct," choked Philip. "Hear all, tell all."

"Say no more, Philip, or I'll reveal Mother's latest scheme for you!" Meg looked from him to Vanessa and back again.

Philip, usually a self-possessed young man, felt himself flush as Melcourt regarded him quizzically. Philip had been persistent in his attentions to Vanessa, albeit she was his cousin. He looked Melcourt in the eye and thrust out his chin.

The volatile Meg, once saying what was on her mind, turned to Vanessa and rapidly lost herself in discussing the undoubted merits of a celestial blue gauze as opposed to a bronze satin. Vanessa was aware that the Earl's eyes followed her as she disappeared with Meg into the interior of a highly recommended silk warehouse.

It was fortunate that he had been left alone with young Edgerton, thought Melcourt. He had to be set straight: The emergence of yet another suitor for Vanessa's hand would only complicate matters.

"You are in a position to do me a great service, Edgerton," he said, "by keeping your eye on my . . . on Miss Charldon when I'm from town."

Only now did Philip recall Vanessa's unusual silence. He hoped she had not been embarrassed by anything his scatterbrained sister had said.

"You have decided on your bride, then, my lord? I see there was more than just a grain of truth in Lady Jersey's gossip."

"There usually is," the Earl said sardonically. "That's what makes her so confounded objectionable. I need not tell you that there is to be no announcement at present?"

The younger man grinned. "When there is, I hope you will let my mother be the first to know, my lord. She had it all arranged: Vanessa for me and Meg for you.

"Our Meg will be relieved, at any rate," he continued, "and as for me, I believe I would have had no chance with Vanessa. The relationship is too close for her father to approve, despite my mother's wishes," Philip pointed out.

Melcourt's face was unreadable as he considered how little difference it would make to Vanessa's father, provided he got his price. It fair set his teeth on edge.

The Earl's parting from the others was polite but abrupt. As Philip bundled the ladies into their vehicle and saw to the disposition of their purchases, Melcourt wished them all a good day and drove down the

Strand, intending to work off some of his ill feeling at Mendoza's Lyceum of Boxing.

How he could spare a thought for the Prince and Caroline of Brunswick was beyond him when his own plans for Vanessa Charldon might be upset by her father's return to London. If he could stall Sir Lucius until next week . . . Perhaps his threat to marry Vanessa off to Gresham was merely a ploy. Gresham's pockets had been to let for years; it would be impossible for him to pay Sir Lucius's debts and manage the settlement too. Yet, oddly enough, Gresham had had plenty of the ready at Lady Archer's the other night.

A round or two with Daniel Mendoza should chase the blue devils from his mind and place things in their proper perspective. In his mind he rehearsed all the things he wished he could tell Vanessa, beginning with that night in the Jade Room. He had promised that she could drive his grays, but on returning to his house in Berkeley Square, a message from the Prime Minister had awaited him. In the morning he had sent a hasty note to her, canceling their drive. Later that day, as a tacit apology and a token of his esteem, he had chosen an exquisite gold and sapphire spray of flowers at Rundell and Bridge, the jewelers. He had been on the point of leaving the establishment when an inner door had opened and out had stormed Miranda Charldon, followed by the Bridge half of Rundell and Bridge, looking very well pleased with himself. Miranda, having come by hackney coach, had asked to be driven home. She had hung upon his arm, and as he had helped her into his curricle, Vanessa and her cousins had driven past. He could well imagine the interpretation Vanessa had put on it . . . and this time he was innocent.

Damn Miranda! Damn Pitt and the French! For that matter, damn the Dutch as well. They had lost Amsterdam. The Dutch fleet, except for a few small ships, had been captured by the French. French cavalry advancing across the frozen Zuider Zee had surprised the ice-bound Dutch battleships. With the collapse of the Netherlands, the entire continental coastline facing England belonged to the enemy.

"I have no illusions about the Grand Alliance, my lord," Pitt had explained on that morning several weeks ago. "We are in grave danger of losing our remaining allies to the French. Information is what we need. I must know the names of the officials who are being bribed by the French and how much it will cost to buy them back. If we do not succeed in this, we may very well find ourselves standing alone against all of Europe."

"And what can I do to help, sir?" Melcourt had asked, almost dreading an answer.

"Many of my agents have disappeared. . . . This time I want you to arrange for my—friends—to be delivered to ships of the Channel fleet—at night, and in secret. No one else will know, not the land officers, not the Preventives."

No one else would know, agreed Melcourt in silence, provided Pitt did not linger too long over his port. As he had left Downing Street, Melcourt had realized that he was getting in deeper and deeper. What had begun as a favor to Pitt had now involved him in irregular activities. If he was not careful, the man would talk him into becoming a spy too.

Perhaps it was just as well that Vanessa had seen him with Miranda later that day. At least she would not be looking for him in the next week or so; he must be free to disappear at will.

The eighteenth day of April had come and gone, leaving all London in sympathy with one or the other of the royal couple whose wedding tour had begun and ended in mutual aversion. By and large the common people supported the Princess, while the *haut ton* espoused the cause of the Prince. In the fashionable houses the latest vagary of the unhappy pair was discussed with coffee, tea, champagne, and the morning chocolate.

Miss Margaret Edgerton, being received in her cousin's bedchamber, wondered if the Prince would be present at Lady Presteign's ball the following night, for he was still hanging on Melcourt's arm. "And so is Miranda," she continued. "I cannot picture Melcourt playing the injured husband, but would you not love to see him marry someone who would lead him a merry dance?"

"I have never given it thought," responded Vanessa in an offhand manner.

"I'll go bail you haven't," Meg retorted crudely. "I don't know what schemes you have in your pretty head, but he is not the man to play them off on."

Vanessa looked at her cousin with mock concern. "A very astute gentleman you would say, Coz?"

"He has been avoiding matchmaking mamas—mine included—for well nigh a decade," Meg asserted coolly.

"That does argue a certain wiliness. But astuteness? I will reserve my judgment."

"As you will, child. It is you, after all, who is to cross swords with him. I don't envy you."

"Not even a little, Meg?"

"La, no!" that lady declared breezily. "He would never put up with my fits and starts, nor I with his assorted strumpets. . . . Oh, lud, now I've done it!" she exclaimed mournfully. "Gone and opened my mouth and let the wrong thing come out, as usual."

Impulsively she embraced the stricken girl. "Pay me no heed. All that was before he met you."

Vanessa turned to the looking glass and attempted without success to set her hands to improving the arrangement of her hair.

"Here! You're ruining it. Let me." Taking up brush and comb to repair the damage caused by her cousin's shaking hands, Meg watched Vanessa's reflection and suffered a rare twinge of conscience. "Philip told me he suspected an understanding between you and Melcourt from something the Earl said. I did not believe him until now. It was a cruel way for me to find out: you hide your feelings well."

"Do I?" She laughed, and her laughter caught in her throat. Just last week at Lady Jersey's, she had seen him enter with the Prince, only to leave soon after. It had been such a dreadful crush that he might not have known she was there. By the end of the long, dull evening Vanessa realized that she missed the anticipation and excitement of verbally fencing with the Earl. There was a vitality about him that made everyone else seem insipid.

151

"Vanessa, do you not wish to marry him?"

"Truly, Meg, I do not know," Vanessa shrugged. "I do not think my wishes will count for much. All I know is that my white satin shoes are ruined, and I have danced holes through my last pair of silk stockings," she finished lightly.

"Your new conquest stepped on my toes last night. I thought I should need new feet."

"Gresham? He is a horrid man, is he not? I have been trying to avoid him all week." Vanessa tied her bonnet and adjusted the ribbons, which matched her azure-blue zephyr pelisse. "At least my dances are all taken for tomorrow night; he will not be able to ruin my slippers." She led the way down the stairs. "He may be your father's friend, Meg, but the man positively slobbers over me."

"And why do you think I need new gloves, Vanessa? I think he quite dotes on me too," Meg giggled. She was still laughing as they left the house and entered the carriage.

"Oh, Meg, do you think he'll offer for you?" Vanessa gurgled.

"For me? Not likely. I am not the heiress—you are!"

For some inexplicable reason a *frisson* of terror rippled along Vanessa's nerves, yet she was able to reply with a certain insouciance, "You are nonsensical, Meg."

"Of course!" her cousin said cordially, sitting back and enjoying the drive.

CHAPTER SEVENTEEN

The long-awaited day of Lady Presteign's ball dawned bright and clear, and the entire household was up betimes, polishing and repolishing what they had twice polished the day before. The red carpet, attested free of the hated moth as recently as last week, lay at the side of the entry, awaiting final placement for the monumental unrolling.

Cooks, lackeys, baker's assistants, and housemaids (in addition to anyone else who could manage to create an errand within the ballroom area) were all prepared to tell the workmen how to go on, but Lady Presteign would brook interference from no one. She knew exactly what she wanted, and it was into a garden of blue and gold that my lady entered on the arm of her son.

Not many hours ago, as she had enjoined Vanessa to lie upon her bed and rest, she had wondered if her son would be on hand to take the Duchess of Steign into dinner while she took the arm of His Grace. There had been no need to worry about anything after all. A fine supper had been prepared by her chef and his underlings: the pastries had arrived from Gunter's, the wine was on ice, and her son had arrived in good time to help greet her first guests. Now, standing in the floral-domed ballroom, she felt the satisfaction, known to every noteworthy hostess, that accompanies a successful party.

As pleased with her goddaughter's appearance as with her other arrangements, Lady Presteign knew that the most critical of matrons could not fault the dressing of Vanessa's curls or the simple elegance of her white satin gown. She was far and away the most beautiful female present. What was Sylvester thinking to allow her to avoid him these past weeks? And to accept without a murmur that her dance card was filled? It was not like him. If only they would cease their childish games, her satisfaction would be complete.

The ballroom was alive with people and gay with flowers and music, but Vanessa had eyes for only one person. She had not seen him for several days, in fact had purposely dodged him, but it made no difference. No other man existed for her. She tried not to admit his attraction. She told herself that his tall, magnificent body, handsome features, and laughing, mocking eyes did not thrill her; she told herself she was as indifferent to his smiles as she was to his sneers. But she was indifferent to neither. She was attracted, against her will, to a man who lusted after other women, one of them her father's wife.

Vanessa told herself she was a fool, but she could not help the way she felt. She could, however, keep him and everyone else from knowing what was in her heart. No matter how it hurt her, no matter how she longed for his love, she must hide her feelings or lose

154

all respect for herself. Only as an equal would she face him, never as a supplicant.

Perhaps at another time, another place, she and Miranda would have vied for his affection, but not now, not here, where everyone from the Prince down to the scrubbiest scullery maid watched avidly for just such a diversion.

She heard it on all sides; they did not even trouble to lower their voices while discussing her, her father, her father's wife, and the wife's lover.

"Shameless!" gasped a turbaned dowager with delight as the Earl of Melcourt joined Miranda.

"Melcourt always preferred an adept mistress to a virgin who is not fly to the time of day," laughed another.

"He might consider that her wealth more than makes up for a lack of expertise. In fact, most men would consider that an advantage," the first speaker was moved to say.

Vanessa wanted to run from the room but some strange force compelled her to listen to their scathing commentary.

"You must know Melcourt has ever preferred the sophisticate to the *jeune fille*."

"Miranda will not let him go in a hurry—and to her own stepdaughter? . . . What do you think, Helen?" she asked the third member of the party, who had been quietly watching the couple.

"If that is not the boldest piece I ever saw. I warrant Melcourt pays her dressmaker's bills, for Lucius never bought that rig for her. I pity the little Charldon if Sylvester Vinton takes her to wife. She will pay heavily for the privilege of calling herself 'Countess.'"

"If Sir Lucius has sold her to Melcourt, be sure he has sold her dear" was the final comment before the promise of an extravagant collation invited their attention.

With a barely murmured excuse to the young man at her side, Vanessa left the ballroom and walked out onto the deserted balcony. The beauty of the night was lost on her. Her agitated thoughts dwelled upon what she had overheard, and she did not realize that she was no longer alone until she heart a slight cough. She turned toward the shadowy figure and was enraged at herself for feeling a sharp pang of disappointment.

"Good evening, Miss Charldon. I pray I am not intruding."

"Not at all, Lord Gresham. I merely felt in need of a breath of air," replied Vanessa, polite despite her unease.

"It is a sad crush, is it not?"

She did not feel his question required an answer and turned to go, but he caught her hand and fondled it. "What is your hurry, my dear?" His voice was insinuating, as was his manner, but she forced herself to endure his loathsome touch. She had never been alone with him and did not quite know what to expect, but he was received everywhere. Perhaps this feeling of revulsion was unwarranted and unjust.

"I bear a message from your father," he said.

Vanessa waited in silence. When he saw that she was not going to speak, Lord Gresham cleared his throat several times.

"I—ahem—have written to Sir Lucius telling him how taken I was with you, my beauty."

Vanessa blanched and struggled to release herself as his hand grazed her breast, but he was stronger than she.

"No, no, my dear. Hear me out. Your father has stipulated that he wants you to marry, and he gave me permission to address myself to you, provided your affections were not already engaged."

His grip on her hand tightened, and he pulled her closer to him. "I can tell that you are pure and innocent—untouched by these young coxcombs who know nothing of teaching a young girl about love." Moisture collected at the corners of his loose lips. He was unpleasantly close, and Vanessa tried once more to recover possession of her hand.

"You are mistaken, Lord Gresham." Her voice was as coolly impersonal as she could possibly make it, although he set her teeth on edge. "My engagement to the Earl of Melcourt is to be announced tonight."

She pulled away from the portly libertine and almost ran into the noisy ballroom.

There was Melcourt, with Miranda on his arm. No doubt he was taking her in to supper. Vanessa did not hesitate an instant. Hastening her steps, she caught up with them before they could leave the room.

"Ah, there you are, Sylvester! I am sure Miranda will excuse you." She gave Miranda a slight proprietary smile and then ignored her as she drew the Earl to one side. "Do you think our engagement should be announced tonight? It was necessary for me to inform Lord Gresham just a moment ago."

He noticed the bright splash of color on her cheeks and the rapid beat of the pulse at the base of her throat. Melcourt's eyes searched for and found Lord

Gresham standing at the balcony window, and his eyes narrowed just a fraction before he bowed and kissed Vanessa's trembling hand.

"Are you sure you prefer me to yon gallant?" He could not resist the gibe.

Vanessa looked around quickly, but no one else had heard.

"You knew?" she hissed.

"Your father was kind enough to tell me that Gresham would pay handsomely for you," he taunted.

Thinking he was angry with her because his hand had been forced, Vanessa flinched at the cruelty in his voice. His anger, however, was directed not at her, but at the author of this plot which had her staked out as a sacrifice.

Melcourt's wrath had reached its zenith yesterday afternoon and even now, more than twenty-four hours later, it had not abated. A message sent round to him had summoned him to the Charldons' house in St. James's Square. Until then the Earl had not known Sir Lucius to be in town. Interpreting the message to be more command than request, the Earl had called that same afternoon. It was obvious to him that Sir Lucius had more than his arm up his sleeve, for the old devil had been in a suspiciously benign mood.

"I must tell you, my lord, that I have given up all hope of ever seeing news of your engagement to my daughter. I am sure it was all a take-in, but I am not one to hold a grudge. After all, you and your dear mother meant well."

Sir Lucius's boneless hand held out a letter.

"Do you intend to countenance that lecher's suit?"

the Earl asked as he ran his eyes over the closely written lines.

"I have already done so, my lord," replied Sir Lucius, refusing to take offense. "Lord Gresham will not let the grass grow under his feet, my lord, so I suggest you do something now, if you have any intention of wedding my daughter."

Like an angler playing a fish, Sir Lucius had maneuvered them into position. It had been up to Vanessa, then. She had had to choose between him and Gresham. She was no fool. No matter how she wished to spite him, she would not have become the chattel of Lyman Gresham.

Now, watching Vanessa out of the corner of his eye as they approached Lady Presteign, it occurred to the Earl that he was no longer angry. For the first time in more than twenty-four hours—since his confrontation with Sir Lucius yesterday afternoon—he could think about the man without contemplating violence. Perhaps he should thank Sir Lucius for presenting him with a sound reason for an early wedding.

Melcourt bent to his mother's ear. Lady Presteign's smile deepened as she embraced him and then held out her arms to Vanessa. Those of her guests close enough to witness this realized that an event of some significance was about to take place.

"I am so very happy for you. May I share this wonderful news with our friends?" asked Lady Presteign, a suspicious brightness in her eyes.

Vanessa nodded hesitantly as Melcourt's eyes fastened on her. She seemed to be in a dream as she allowed herself to be drawn forward.

At the far end of the room the harsh features of Lyman Gresham twisted in malice. People standing near him shuddered at the naked hatred revealed in his expression, but they pushed forward. Like most things unpleasant, he was soon forgotten.

"Dear, dear friends." The light, sweet tones of Lady Presteign reached Vanessa as if from far away. "I am so very pleased to tell you . . ." The sound of her voice faded, only to return louder, stronger, deeper; it faded and swelled again like the throb of waves on an ocean shore. The floor moved up and down in an unsettling manner, and the air was so heavy that she could hardly breathe. There was an unpleasant metallic taste in her mouth, and she could not rid herself of it, although she tried repeatedly to swallow.

She took one step back, intimidated by the wall of humanity surrounding her, and came up against the warm, strong body of the Earl. Suddenly the floor stilled beneath her feet, and her breathing eased. Everything returned to normal, but she caught only the tail end of Lady Presteign's announcement before the hushed expectancy of the guests gave way to noisy congratulations.

Vanessa felt relieved. The decision had been made, and she would fight no longer. In placing herself in the Earl's hands, she had left the next move to him.

For all the world like a storybook bride, Vanessa acknowledged good wishes and received felicitations at the side of her intended husband. The hand that was placed lightly at her waist was both comforting and disturbing. Under the sound of the congratulatory remarks he teased her and told her outrageous things. A queer new exhilaration filled her; she felt herself unwilling to leave the shelter of his presence.

The Earl looked down at her, aware that she had moved closer to him.

"I feel this is a fairy tale come to life," she confessed in a whisper.

"*Sleeping Beauty,* of course," he mocked.

"Not really. I thought *Beauty and the Beast* most like," she riposted and burst into peals of laughter at his expression.

A quick wit. Able to laugh despite her predicament . . . What other surprises did Vanessa have for him? the Earl wondered.

"Every man is looking at you and wishing me dead," he breathed in her ear.

"And the women cannnot keep their eyes off you."

"I must appeal to their lower instincts."

"For once, my lord, I find it impossible to disagree with you." The expression on her face was demure, but her eyes laughed.

"My one regret is that you seem to have no lower instincts to which I can appeal." He leered at her wickedly. "I must gratify one appetite, at least. Shall we have supper?"

Vanessa had to laugh. How could she be cold and distant to this man, she asked herself as he seated her in the midst of a convivial group of well-wishers.

The plate he set in front of her contained dainties enough to tempt the most elusive appetite for, as he told her in an undertone she could not pretend to misunderstand, "If you intend to resist me, you will need all your strength."

She refused to meet his eyes. "And if I . . . submit?"

"Submit? A rather tame word, don't you think? We shall talk of this again after we are wed."

He felt her stiffen beside him and knew what her next question would be before she voiced it.

"When?"

"In three weeks. Your father wishes us to be married in his house," he explained. "There will be no guests, just family."

"Three weeks," she repeated dazedly. Just when she had reconciled herself to being engaged to him . . . now this . . . this unseemly haste . . . What was she to think? "Three weeks—that is too soon."

"Three weeks," he said once more, firmly dismissing her objections.

CHAPTER EIGHTEEN

It should not be supposed that all things went smoothly for the officially plighted pair. Miss Charldon made it a practice never to be long at home, in case the Earl took it into his head to call, while the Earl himself went often to Hampshire to check the progress of Count Puisaye. The Count, a Breton whose tardiness in supporting the Bourbon cause was made up for by his enthusiasm, was organizing a Royalist army of invasion. Fully armed had sprung the goddess Athena from the head of Zeus; such was not the case with Puisaye's Royalist army. Visions of an *émigré* force had sprung full blown from the giant Breton's head, but England, it seemed, was to supply the arms and ammunition, the uniforms and the money, the transportation to Quiberon peninsula, and so forth and so on.

Pitt, trying to hold together the pitiful remnants of the Grand Alliance by secretly supporting the Royalist cause, was not in concord with the Earl. Candidly informed by Melcourt of the endless bickering and lack of leadership in the Royalist camp, the Prime Minister had responded with a touch of asperity.

"By carrying the war to the enemy, my lord," said Pitt, "we are less likely to suffer an invasion of our own shores."

Melcourt could not deny the worth of such tactics, but, to his mind, the release of French prisoners to augment the Royalist force was not in England's best interests. "The French prisoners of war will do anything to get home," he insisted. "They will promise to fight under the Bourbon flag and will keep their promise—until they land in France. Our soldiers, then, would have two forces with which to contend: one confronting them, one in their midst, and both hostile."

"Yet your own Whig party supports Count Puisaye!"

"Politics be damned! And politicians too!" The Earl was fast losing his temper.

"No doubt, my lord, no doubt. But damned or not, Puisaye's friends control Parliament. Therefore I too am bound to support him."

"You asked me to keep you informed, Prime Minister. For what purpose?"

Pitt leaned forward in his chair and placed his hands flat on the desk. "Come, come, my lord. I do not ignore what you have told me. I will consider it, although I understand that Lord Gresham believes an invasion of France to be a worthwhile undertaking at this time. And he, as you know, is very close to the Bourbon heir-presumptive." He rubbed his hands together with a show of briskness. "Now, business being over, will you join me in a glass of wine?"

A few minutes later Melcourt prepared to leave Downing Street, the wine having done nothing to ease his mind. Pitt congratulated himself on his handling of the situation; the Earl, who viewed with a jaundiced eye anything with which Lord Gresham had to do, kept his doubts to himself. He promised to hold himself in readiness if Pitt should need him again, although he hoped that his usefulness was at an end.

It was a relief to be able to resume the normal pursuits of his life, Melcourt thought as he looked for, and found, Miss Charldon among the dancers at Almack's Assembly Rooms.

Vanessa, who had not expected him to arrive this close to eleven o'clock, the hour at which the doors closed, protested even as he led her off the floor. "My lord, I promised this dance to Lord Fitzwilliams. They are making up the sets."

"I am sure he will excuse us," Melcourt told her. "I have not talked to you for two days. You are out when I call in the morning and in the evenings we are both so busy accepting the congratulations of our friends that we have had no time for ourselves. You have not been trying to eschew my company, have you?"

"N—no. It is just that . . . fittings for my . . . my trousseau have kept me much occupied," she stammered.

He was suddenly contrite. "Forgive me. I was not serious. I have no wish to make you uncomfortable."

Seeing that his confession did just that, he began to speak of their honeymoon, continuing as though not noticing her confusion. "I did not think you would wish to leave town now for an extended period. We would be obliged to cancel so many social engagements."

She looked at him in dismay. "How dreadful, to be sure; of course, whatever you say" were the words she managed to utter.

"May I take you back to my mother? She is concerned you are not getting your rest and hopes you will retire at a good hour. Tomorrow will be a fatiguing day."

Tomorrow! As she walked at Melcourt's side, Vanessa thought how pleasant it would be to sleep through tomorrow, sleep without worrying what would become of her after the ceremony, when she would be delivered to his house along with her trousseau. Was she to become just another of his possessions or—and she shivered—did he have other plans for her? If only she knew. Her mouth quivered. There was no sign of Miranda—of that she must be glad. But after tomorrow—what then? She would never show him she was not . . . indifferent to him. She would not let herself be hurt. The soft fullness of her lips tightened into a straight line.

Vanessa spared no more than a polite inclination of her head as the Earl took his leave after seeing them to Mount Street. Her expression was distracted, he noticed as he bade her a good night. He hoped she would do nothing foolish now that he almost had her safe.

Knowing nothing of the Earl's plans for her, Vanessa spent a restless night, tormented by thoughts of what the next day would bring. As it turned out, once the final words had been spoken, she felt no different than she had before the event.

The wedding took place at the house of the bride's father. Guests spoke of it later as an elegant, if small, piece of business. Vanessa entered the drawing room on the arm of her father. The room seemed long and narrow, an endless tunnel stretching before her as she concentrated on her steps. She could see nothing, no one but the man waiting at the improvised altar. Yet, as if they had been painted on her mind by an old master, she was aware of everyone to the smallest detail.

Aunt Edgerton, in aubergine silk, and her husband, crowlike in black, were on one side; her son, wearing a rich claret color, was on the other. Someone else—Aunt Clemency, perhaps—was dressed in puce and sitting at Philip's other side. The pictures were vivid: Andrew; Gwenyth—the latter in her favorite and most unbecoming bronze-green; Lady Presteign in silver-gray and as well turned out as usual; and Miranda in white satin and silver tissue. Did she not know it was no longer the fashion for guests to wear bridal white? But, then, she was not a guest. She was the mother of the bride. Vanessa laughed soundlessly and without

"My lady?"

"Yes? What is it, Iris?" she asked the maid, who was now moving away from the door.

"My lady, Lady Charldon is below and wishes conversation with you," the maid repeated the footman's message.

"*Merde!* What a morning to oversleep!"

"Do you wish the footman to show her up, my lady, or will you see her downstairs?"

Taking a cursory look around the room, Vanessa decided she had no wish for her stepmother to enter a room so very obviously free of all masculine appointments.

"I'll see her in the morning room, Iris," she told the maid as she made a face at her image in the dressing-table mirror.

True to his word, the Earl returned late that evening. Vanessa felt foolish as she hesitated at his door. She had spent much of her day wishing away the hours—when she had not been contemplating the murder of her stepmother. Just thinking of Miranda's visit that morning turned Vanessa's hands into claws. She derived minor satisfaction by scratching at the door.

"You wished to see me?" Melcourt inquired courteously as he opened the connecting door. As he entered, she matched his steps, one back for each one he took in her direction. Vanessa had been living with him for two weeks and still found herself tongue-tied in his presence, but the amusement in his eyes was not to be borne, and she forced herself to stand her ground.

"My dear stepmother came to call and, finding you

171

from home, requested that I put into your hands a very important letter. She insisted, in her own inimitable fashion, that it was too personal to be left on your desk or in the hands of a servant." Without waiting for him to speak, she turned and swept across the room with unconscious elegance. The sealed letter was removed from the mantel, where it had lain since late morning, and, holding it with the tips of her fingers as though seeking to avoid contamination, she approached him with a hauteur that was not without a suggestion of contempt. The Earl took the white square in his hands and deliberately, methodically tore it to pieces. "I want you to know that I have never . . . cared . . . for Miranda," he said.

She stammered something that made him frown. "Yes, I know, Vanessa. I did see her yesterday but only to make it clear to her that I am married to you. Are you such a little fool that you do not know what game she is playing?"

"And your game, my lord? Have you found your old *poule* insipid? Perhaps that is her complaint." No sooner were the words out of her mouth than she wished she could call them back. She had meant him to translate *poule* as mistress, but perhaps he would think her crude.

He gave a shout of laughter, relieving her mind. "Perhaps. You do mean me to translate *poule* as hen and not anything derogatory to her morals?" He went on, not expecting an answer. "And perhaps I would try a toothsome *poullet* instead of an old hen. Young chicks are more tender. Your job to see to it, I believe; a wife should cater to her husband."

Vanessa watched him warily but he seemed amused

172

by the double entendre. "For a moment I thought you . . . would be insulted," she confessed.

"Not at all," he responded, a twinkle in his eyes. "Your comment was exceedingly well put and quite true in one aspect; no one could mistake your stepmother for a chick."

An involuntary gurgle of laughter escaped her. "Not even in the dark?" She flushed painfully. That was worse than calling Miranda his old mistress.

"My wretched tongue," she apologized, meeting his eyes squarely. "I deserve to have my ears boxed for that."

"Are you boy or girl?" Melcourt was nonplussed; this was a side of Vanessa he had never seen.

"Sometimes one, sometimes the other," she confided.

His quizzing glass was raised to eye level, and she reached out in sudden supplication. "Don't! Please!" There was a tremor in her voice.

"What? Oh, this!" He dropped the glass. "It is only habit."

Vanessa struggled through the explanation she felt was owed to him. "It makes me feel as though I am . . . something . . . " She took a deep breath and finished in a rush, " . . . something not worth crushing." Blue-violet eyes flashed a brief, nervous glance at him, then fell. "I would not want to embarrass you in front of your friends." Her voice rang out in passionate sincerity as she concluded, "If ever I say anything like that again, you have my permission to kick me."

Melcourt stepped forward, made a fist, and, pretending to cuff her on the point of her chin, made her look at him. "Will that do?" he asked.

A shy, flickering smile rewarded him. "You are very kind."

"Kind? I?" He was strangely touched.

"My father and . . . Miranda . . . make me feel inconsequential. I cannot fight all the time. I have been happier here than I could have been with them."

"Then I am happy too."

Vanessa knew he was sincere. She pulled herself together with a certain bravado. "Can we be friends?"

The Earl's hands were on her shoulders, and she shrugged herself away from his touch. "Friends!" she repeated tersely.

"Friends," he conceded and extended his open palm to her. After a moment's hesitation she placed her hand in his, and his warm strong fingers closed about hers for uncounted seconds. Melcourt bowed, placed a light kiss on her hand, then released her. At the door, he turned as if something had just crossed his mind.

"Would you care to ride with me in the morning?"

"I should like it immensely."

"I leave early," he warned.

"I shall be ready."

"Sleep well, then," said the Earl as he closed the door behind him.

This was another Vanessa, as direct as a boy, wholly without coquetry—so different from anything in his experience. She had taken him quite by storm, this strange child-woman who had become his bride. If he did nothing to destroy their newfound friendship, perhaps she would learn to trust him.

Once the door had closed behind the Earl, Vanessa threw herself on the bed, anguished, despairing, smothering her sobs in a pillow. She would never

174

show him by word or deed that she wanted to be more than a casual companion—unless he pursued her. How could she compete with his lightskirts and the noble harlots who dallied with him?

Despising her momentary weakness, Vanessa sniffed, untangled herself from the bedclothes, and bathed her swollen eyes. She must face him on the morrow with a radiant face—and supreme indifference. He had as good as admitted that he was finished with Miranda. She would not make her rival's mistake. My lord enjoyed the chase.

CHAPTER NINETEEN

"Good morning. This is a pleasant surprise. I had thought you still in bed," Melcourt said, seating himself opposite Vanessa at the breakfast table. "Have you had your breakfast?"

"I was waiting for you," she said shyly. She looked up, concerned. "Did you forget—you haven't forgotten asking me to ride with you this morning, have you?"

"I did not forget. I thought perhaps you might have changed your mind."

"Oh." She blinked and fell silent as the servants entered and began to serve.

They spoke of inconsequentials as the Earl ate. Vanessa desired nothing more than toast and coffee, and even this she did not eat, for she was aware of him watching her, and it made her nervous.

"Is anything wrong, my lord?" she asked him, unable to remain silent.

"I am merely admiring your choice of riding habit, my lady," he said as he arose from the table and came to her side.

She stood facing him, at first hesitant, and then, seeming to make up her mind, she asked, "Are we ready to ride?" She appeared eager to return to the easy camaraderie they had found last night, and he clapped her on the shoulder just as if she were a boy. She strove to keep from trembling at his touch and knew that in the future she must avoid even the most casual physical contact with her husband.

The groom held the horses as the Earl and his Countess descended the steps. Melcourt helped her to mount, motioning the groom aside, unheeding her protest that she could manage by herself.

"In the country, perhaps," he said as he smiled up at her and assisted her with the stirrup. She returned his smile and watched in admiration as he swung himself into the saddle.

They had been riding for some minutes when Vanessa spoke. "At what time do you leave for Melcourt Castle?"

"Early tomorrow, I think."

"I see."

This time it was the Earl who broke the silence. "If you have nothing else planned, why not come with me?"

humor. Miranda was gaudy with feathers in her hair, a diamond tiara on her head. New? From Rundell and Bridge? It was much smaller than the one she usually wore. Now, there was a man in blue—Fitzwilliams; Meg, how becoming in her azure gauze. And Melcourt.

Until now it had always been the man, not his clothes that had been outstanding. His satin breeches and coat were the color of old ivory. How unusual! He usually wore blue or black, that much she knew. His waistcoat was of snow-white silk brocade, cut short in the new style. She was aware of every detail of his clothing—but she could not raise her eyes past his cravat to the man himself.

Vanessa felt dragged down by the weight of the veil—an heirloom worn by all Vinton brides. Diamond pins held the Brussels lace to the back of her head and, scarflike, it was wrapped about her bare arms. Hot and cold by turns, she was glad her dress was without sleeves, then sorry it was of too sheer a silk to keep her warm. The sweet-scented lilies she carried made her dizzy, almost ill.

Afraid she would not respond in the proper place, Vanessa listened carefully to the clergyman's every word. In spite of this she did not recall anything of the brief service, or remember making her responses. Yet she must have, for the ring was on her finger. She turned her head as if to admire it and managed to evade her bridegroom's kiss, thus assuaging, for the most part, the uncomfortable climax of the ceremony.

The health of the bride and groom was drunk in champagne; Sir Lucius soon took himself off to his invalid's couch and left his guests. He declared to all that the strain of giving away his daughter had been too much for him. Vanessa thought herself that he would be at White's before the day was much older. As for giving her away, she wondered just how much the man standing beside her—her husband—had paid for her. Given away? No, she had not been given away.

They did not linger at Sir Lucius's bedside, for neither Countess nor Earl had anything to say to the self-styled invalid and quickly repaired to the Earl's town house several squares away. The servants were lined up in the entrance hall to greet them in time-honored tradition. The ritual was soon over and the servants gone about their duties.

Melcourt had dined heartily not many hours before; Vanessa, who had refused her dinner and had no appetite for the refreshments served by a welcoming staff, discovered a rare thirst for the iced champagne that awaited them. Easing her dry throat with several glasses of the cool wine while making a pretense of eating, she somehow found courage to question Melcourt about something that had long troubled her. Vanessa carefully set her glass down so as not to tip it over with a hand grown suddenly unsteady.

"Was it worth so much to you . . . our marriage?" she asked.

"I was not averse to settling your father's debts if I achieved my objective. I never cavil at paying the price of anything I want."

Vanessa leaned forward as the Earl poured the bubbling wine into his glass. When he returned to the sofa, she asked, "Even to marriage? Was Shelburne Park worth marrying me for?" she persisted.

"Would you believe me if I said you are more important to me than Shelburne Park?"

Her shrug was so eloquent of distrust that he winced.

"No?" Melcourt quickly recovered his composure. "Then apparently there is nothing I can say to convince you." He set down his glass. "I know you wish to retire; I will escort you to your room." At the door he bowed with his customary grace. "My room is next door, if you need me," he said and abandoned her to Iris, who quietly prepared her mistress for bed, sensing her usual chatter would not be welcome.

The household settled and the typical after-dark noises came and went, but the door between the bedrooms of the Earl and his Countess remained closed. Cold comfort, indeed, to Vanessa, who had been prepared to deny her husband his rights until his superior strength compelled her surrender. And now, to have him leave like that, without even trying to make love to her! It was not wonderfully reassuring.

She recalled a childish game, almost heard her voice—a little girl's voice—in the solemn words of the ceremony. "If the bee comes to this white rose, everything will be all right." What she had meant by "all right," she did not remember. "If it chooses the yellow, everything will go wrong" went the second part of the magic spell. Aloud, she recited, "If Sylvester comes to me tonight, everything will be all right. If he does not . . ." Her voice died, her hopes with it. "Damn you, Sylvester Vinton! I will be more indifferent even than you," she vowed. She wept into her pillow and fell asleep with the bitter taste of tears upon her lips.

Upon leaving Vanessa, the Earl had congratulated himself on his self-control while deploring its necessity. If he had spent many more minutes with his wife, he would have made passionate love to her, something he did not dare do as yet. He would have to move slowly and carefully if he was to make her love him. He could not convince her that he loved her—not now, when Shelburne was to be kept Pitt's secret. It was damnable what one sometimes had to do for one's country.

"Good morning, my lady," greeted Iris, entering the room and placing Vanessa's morning chocolate on the bedside table, as she had done every morning for the past two weeks. "His lordship said I was to let you sleep as you was tired. He will not be in until late this evening, so you are not to wait for him," she prattled as she opened the curtains on a bright, sunny day and busied herself around the room.

"I am overwhelmed by his lordship's consideration," muttered Vanessa into her cup in a voice too low for the maid to hear. It was all of a piece with his ignoring her, as he had since their wedding, she thought, until a twinge of conscience forced her to admit that Melcourt had not ignored her so much as she had kept out of his way. They usually met at dinner, after which he escorted her to their box at the opera or to see Mrs. Siddons at Drury Lane.

They had kept to themselves lately, in spite of plans to keep up with their social engagements. Their friends had left them much alone too, which would have thrown them upon one another's company had she not taken steps to evade him.

"My lady?"

"Yes? What is it, Iris?" she asked the maid, who was now moving away from the door.

"My lady, Lady Charldon is below and wishes conversation with you," the maid repeated the footman's message.

"*Merde!* What a morning to oversleep!"

"Do you wish the footman to show her up, my lady, or will you see her downstairs?"

Taking a cursory look around the room, Vanessa decided she had no wish for her stepmother to enter a room so very obviously free of all masculine appointments.

"I'll see her in the morning room, Iris," she told the maid as she made a face at her image in the dressing-table mirror.

True to his word, the Earl returned late that evening. Vanessa felt foolish as she hesitated at his door. She had spent much of her day wishing away the hours—when she had not been contemplating the murder of her stepmother. Just thinking of Miranda's visit that morning turned Vanessa's hands into claws. She derived minor satisfaction by scratching at the door.

"You wished to see me?" Melcourt inquired courteously as he opened the connecting door. As he entered, she matched his steps, one back for each one he took in her direction. Vanessa had been living with him for two weeks and still found herself tongue-tied in his presence, but the amusement in his eyes was not to be borne, and she forced herself to stand her ground.

"My dear stepmother came to call and, finding you

171

from home, requested that I put into your hands a very important letter. She insisted, in her own inimitable fashion, that it was too personal to be left on your desk or in the hands of a servant." Without waiting for him to speak, she turned and swept across the room with unconscious elegance. The sealed letter was removed from the mantel, where it had lain since late morning, and, holding it with the tips of her fingers as though seeking to avoid contamination, she approached him with a hauteur that was not without a suggestion of contempt. The Earl took the white square in his hands and deliberately, methodically tore it to pieces. "I want you to know that I have never . . . cared . . . for Miranda," he said.

She stammered something that made him frown. "Yes, I know, Vanessa. I did see her yesterday but only to make it clear to her that I am married to you. Are you such a little fool that you do not know what game she is playing?"

"And your game, my lord? Have you found your old *poule* insipid? Perhaps that is her complaint." No sooner were the words out of her mouth than she wished she could call them back. She had meant him to translate *poule* as mistress, but perhaps he would think her crude.

He gave a shout of laughter, relieving her mind. "Perhaps. You do mean me to translate *poule* as hen and not anything derogatory to her morals?" He went on, not expecting an answer. "And perhaps I would try a toothsome *poullet* instead of an old hen. Young chicks are more tender. Your job to see to it, I believe; a wife should cater to her husband."

Vanessa watched him warily but he seemed amused

by the double entendre. "For a moment I thought you . . . would be insulted," she confessed.

"Not at all," he responded, a twinkle in his eyes. "Your comment was exceedingly well put and quite true in one aspect; no one could mistake your stepmother for a chick."

An involuntary gurgle of laughter escaped her. "Not even in the dark?" She flushed painfully. That was worse than calling Miranda his old mistress.

"My wretched tongue," she apologized, meeting his eyes squarely. "I deserve to have my ears boxed for that."

"Are you boy or girl?" Melcourt was nonplussed; this was a side of Vanessa he had never seen.

"Sometimes one, sometimes the other," she confided.

His quizzing glass was raised to eye level, and she reached out in sudden supplication. "Don't! Please!" There was a tremor in her voice.

"What? Oh, this!" He dropped the glass. "It is only habit."

Vanessa struggled through the explanation she felt was owed to him. "It makes me feel as though I am . . . something . . . " She took a deep breath and finished in a rush, " . . . something not worth crushing." Blue-violet eyes flashed a brief, nervous glance at him, then fell. "I would not want to embarrass you in front of your friends." Her voice rang out in passionate sincerity as she concluded, "If ever I say anything like that again, you have my permission to kick me."

Melcourt stepped forward, made a fist, and, pretending to cuff her on the point of her chin, made her look at him. "Will that do?" he asked.

A shy, flickering smile rewarded him. "You are very kind."

"Kind? I?" He was strangely touched.

"My father and . . . Miranda . . . make me feel inconsequential. I cannot fight all the time. I have been happier here than I could have been with them."

"Then I am happy too."

Vanessa knew he was sincere. She pulled herself together with a certain bravado. "Can we be friends?"

The Earl's hands were on her shoulders, and she shrugged herself away from his touch. "Friends!" she repeated tersely.

"Friends," he conceded and extended his open palm to her. After a moment's hesitation she placed her hand in his, and his warm strong fingers closed about hers for uncounted seconds. Melcourt bowed, placed a light kiss on her hand, then released her. At the door, he turned as if something had just crossed his mind.

"Would you care to ride with me in the morning?"

"I should like it immensely."

"I leave early," he warned.

"I shall be ready."

"Sleep well, then," said the Earl as he closed the door behind him.

This was another Vanessa, as direct as a boy, wholly without coquetry—so different from anything in his experience. She had taken him quite by storm, this strange child-woman who had become his bride. If he did nothing to destroy their newfound friendship, perhaps she would learn to trust him.

Once the door had closed behind the Earl, Vanessa threw herself on the bed, anguished, despairing, smothering her sobs in a pillow. She would never

174

show him by word or deed that she wanted to be more than a casual companion—unless he pursued her. How could she compete with his lightskirts and the noble harlots who dallied with him?

Despising her momentary weakness, Vanessa sniffed, untangled herself from the bedclothes, and bathed her swollen eyes. She must face him on the morrow with a radiant face—and supreme indifference. He had as good as admitted that he was finished with Miranda. She would not make her rival's mistake. My lord enjoyed the chase.

CHAPTER NINETEEN

"Good morning. This is a pleasant surprise. I had thought you still in bed," Melcourt said, seating himself opposite Vanessa at the breakfast table. "Have you had your breakfast?"

"I was waiting for you," she said shyly. She looked up, concerned. "Did you forget—you haven't forgotten asking me to ride with you this morning, have you?"

"I did not forget. I thought perhaps you might have changed your mind."

"Oh." She blinked and fell silent as the servants entered and began to serve.

They spoke of inconsequentials as the Earl ate. Vanessa desired nothing more than toast and coffee, and even this she did not eat, for she was aware of him watching her, and it made her nervous.

"Is anything wrong, my lord?" she asked him, unable to remain silent.

"I am merely admiring your choice of riding habit, my lady," he said as he arose from the table and came to her side.

She stood facing him, at first hesitant, and then, seeming to make up her mind, she asked, "Are we ready to ride?" She appeared eager to return to the easy camaraderie they had found last night, and he clapped her on the shoulder just as if she were a boy. She strove to keep from trembling at his touch and knew that in the future she must avoid even the most casual physical contact with her husband.

The groom held the horses as the Earl and his Countess descended the steps. Melcourt helped her to mount, motioning the groom aside, unheeding her protest that she could manage by herself.

"In the country, perhaps," he said as he smiled up at her and assisted her with the stirrup. She returned his smile and watched in admiration as he swung himself into the saddle.

They had been riding for some minutes when Vanessa spoke. "At what time do you leave for Melcourt Castle?"

"Early tomorrow, I think."

"I see."

This time it was the Earl who broke the silence. "If you have nothing else planned, why not come with me?"

"May I? You are sure you want me?" She sounded surprised.

"I am sure I want you," he answered, a disquieting note in his voice.

Vanessa looked at him from under her lashes, but could tell nothing from his expression. The Earl sensed she was looking at him and turned to her, but she would not meet his eyes.

"Is this indeed Hyde Park, my lord?"

"It is indeed, my lady," he replied with exaggerated formality as they entered the park gate.

Her sudden laugh took him quite by surprise. "I am sorry! I was being vexingly shy again, was I not? I shall try to call you by your given name, if you wish."

"I shall regard that as a pledge," he said gravely, a smile lighting his eyes.

The day was bright and clear, but the balmy spring air gave promise of an advancing summer as the two riders cantered through the park. Too early for members of the *haut ton* to display their modish attire, fashionable conveyances, and high-bred horses, too early even for the nursemaids with their young charges, the almost deserted park proved an irresistible temptation to Vanessa and, throwing a dare over her shoulder, she was away like the wind. His lordship, never one to ignore a challenge, wheeled his horse and raced after his wife, who was galloping over the grass some two lengths ahead. There could be no doubt about it—she rode as if she and the horse were one. She had reached the end of the park when he caught up with her. She laughed and pulled her horse to a walk.

"If I had a better mount, Sylvester, you should never have caught me."

The face she turned toward him was alive with color and excitement. He had an almost uncontrollable desire to sweep her into his arms and make love to her. "You, my dear child, are a sad romp and," he told her with mock severity, suppressing his impulse, "you are patently a bad influence. You will have us both made outcasts by polite society, and we shall be forced to retreat in disgrace to our country estate."

"There is a perfect place for a point-to-point in Shelburne Park, should we be forced to rusticate. Of course, you would ride the famous bay I have heard my brother talk of so much," she said with a glimmer of laughter in her eyes, "and I, one of my own nags. I would give you a run for your money."

Vanessa noticed his mouth twitch in amusement. "You need not feel so superior, Sylvester, for although I have never seen that bay of yours, I can assure you that my cattle are not to be sneezed at."

"Indeed not, my love, but Titan he is named and a Titan he is in fact."

She felt a strange and not unpleasant flutter inside her at his words. She loved the teasing and the endearment he had so carelessly uttered. "There is one horse, at least, he could not best," she retaliated, trying to hide her confusion.

"Where is this paragon, Vanessa?" queried the Earl, pleased to note that his affectionate words had brought a blush to his bride's cheeks.

"In France," she faltered. Her voice was charged with emotion, recalling that she had heard nothing of

Raoul de St. Varres since the night she had left France.

The Earl studied her through half-closed eyes, but she was unaware of his scrutiny. "You have never told me of your escape from France, Vanessa, or why you waited so long to return to your home."

"I traveled by fishing lugger—an exceedingly uneventful trip. As for my return, I defy you to give me one good reason for me to have come back at all," she said lightly.

"Did you not think your family would be concerned?"

She uttered a terse French expletive which elicited a strangled cough from the Earl.

"You speak French," she said accusingly.

"Just a half-dozen words of the same genre, my dear Vanessa. I believe you did not learn that in a convent school."

"I am mortified." But no one could have looked less mortified than she, with a dimple coming and going at the corner of her mouth. "You must keep me in line, I fear, or I shall disgrace you."

Melcourt reached out and grasped the bridle of her mount, bringing both slow-stepping horses to a halt. She looked up at him, uncertain of his intention. He did not leave her long in doubt, for he released the bridle only to take her unresisting hand and raise it to his lips. She shivered and once more felt that mysterious flutter as his mouth touched not her gloved fingers but the sensitive skin on the inside of her wrist.

"We Vintons have always placed the highest confidence in our wives. I am no exception," he said simply.

With a different kind of shiver this time, Vanessa withdrew her hand. "I hope you will not regret it," she replied.

Upon their return to Berkeley Square my lord and my lady parted to prepare for their forthcoming journey. Vanessa spent a delightful hour going through her wardrobe with her maid, deciding upon the clothes she would need during her stay in Dorset.

"Will that be all, my lady?"

"I am not sure, Iris. Please see to these things, meanwhile."

"Yes, my lady." The maid curtsied, thinking as she went to get the silver tissue to wrap the clothes how lucky she was to have a mistress who believed in using "please" and "thank you" even to her servants.

"A real fine lady, not like some as I could tell you about," she told them in the servants' hall at Melcourt Castle two days later.

The Earl's servants did not need convincing, for they too had been much impressed by his lordship's beautiful young bride. They all deferred, however, to the superior knowledge of Mrs. Clemson, the housekeeper, who had known the present Countess when she was a child.

"Beautiful she is and with a lovely, quiet way about her to be sure, but . . ." and here Mrs. Clemson paused for effect and looked squarely at each member of her avid audience, ". . . but when she was a young girl, it was like she had a fire inside her and a temper I hope you will never see."

"What could our darlin' ladyship do to surprise any of us?" grinned an intrepid footman.

The housekeeper frowned at him. "I'll be telling

you, me lad," she retorted, betraying her provincial extraction. "I saw her take after a groom as worked for the old lord—with a whip."

There was silence. The servants looked a one another uneasily, and the housekeeper, afraid she had said the wrong thing, and too much of it, went on hastily, "Not but what her grandfather said it was well done."

"Comin' it a bit too strong," muttered one of the footmen to an upstairs maid.

Mrs. Clemson glared at him. "His lordship said as how he would have taken a whip to him himself 'cause he didn't hold with horse beating."

"Horse beater, was he? Well, now, that explains it," the footman conceded.

Mrs. Clemson sighed gustily. Already she regretted the impulse that had led her to abandon her dignity and gossip with the lower servants. It had been a very trying day. It was seeing the way Master Sylvester looked at Miss Vanessa and she looked at him, when each thought the other was not watching. Something, she could tell, was not right between them.

"So she has a temper," said Iris. "All redheads do, you know. And she's been ever so kind to me. However she was as a child, she's never lost her temper either at Mount Street or at Berkeley Square. In fact, she's quiet like."

Torn from her thoughts by the maid's spirited defense of her mistress, Mrs. Clemson raised herself from her chair and wished them a good night. Her departure was the signal for the others to leave, and within a short space of time the darkened windows gave evidence that the residents of Melcourt Castle had retired for the night.

There was one exception, however. The Earl, preparing for bed after the long journey, sat rereading the note that had caused him to leave London on such short notice. He was irritated by the presumption of the writer. His promise to Pitt had been redeemed. Shelburne Hall, on the occasion of his marriage, had become his property, as had the highly desirable Vanessa Charldon. Pitt was welcome to use Shelburne for whatever slippery scheme he wished. As for himself, he planned to direct all of his not inconsiderable charm toward winning the confidence of his enchanting young wife.

With an impatient gesture the Earl pushed the letter from him. He would comply with the writer's request this time, but Billy Pitt would have to find someone else to do his work in the future. He snuffed the remaining candles and stretched out in his huge bed, prepared to spend several sleepless hours in contemplation of the enchanting girl in the adjoining room.

Vanessa was beginning to depend on him, he was sure. Tomorrow he would take her riding along the coast. Yes, she would enjoy that, and perhaps a picnic lunch.

He fell asleep, satisfied both with his progress and his plans.

In the depths of her bed, Vanessa stretched languorously as her maid opened the draperies on a beautiful spring morning.

What a wonderful week this had been! The long rides, the solitary picnics and dinners they had shared, had led her to depend on him as she had never depended on anyone. She loved him; she knew now that she must have loved him for a long time. And he loved her too—she was almost sure of it. Tonight, yes, perhaps tonight, he would take her in his arms and kiss her for the first time. She would offer herself not with words—one could not say right out, "I want you to make love to me."

Tonight she would order dinner served in her sitting room, and she would wear a robe of the softest, sheerest silk imaginable. She had never worn it except in the privacy of her bedroom because its caressing sapphire folds clung to her, giving more than just a promise of the lithe form beneath. She would make herself as desirable as any painted courtesan.

CHAPTER TWENTY

"Just one thing more, my lady." Little tendrils of bright red hair were coaxed from the cap of curls about Vanessa's head and were placed like artless question marks on her alabaster forehead. "There! Oh, my lady! How beautiful you look!" said Iris, almost clapping her hands in delight as she stepped back to admire her mistress.

More blue than violet tonight, Vanessa's eyes

seemed the color of the clinging gown she wore. She presented a totally seductive image, of which she remained unconscious even as she gazed into the tall pier glass. All she thought was that she looked so obviously young . . . and unfledged.

By the morning, she assured herself, all that would be different. Would spending just one night with a man be enough to dispel that untouched look or would it take several nights? Something happened between a man and a woman to account for the difference. . . . She was not completely ignorant, but, after all, humans could not be equated with animals.

"When did his lordship return, Iris?" Vanessa asked, becoming acutely aware of voices in the adjoining room.

"While you were in your bath, my lady."

"I see. . . . You may go when you are finished, Iris. I will not be needing you again this evening," she said almost absentmindedly, her attention fixed on the activity on the other side of the communicating door. She could imagine Melcourt changing for dinner and talking to his man as he did so. The sound of the door closing behind Iris was echoed further down the corridor, and Vanessa knew that the Earl was alone even as she was. She stared at the door for several minutes before summoning the courage to knock and then almost wished she had waited, for the door opened suddenly, as if he had been standing very close to it. He looked so big, so overwhelming, as he smiled down at her. He held something in his hand that he tossed onto the little table adjacent to the doorway separating their rooms.

"I missed you, Vanessa," Melcourt said as he came

close. Resting his hands lightly on her silk-clad shoulders, he looked down into her eyes with a burning intensity that released her from the speechlessness that had claimed her as she had stood at the door.

"I have been waiting for you to come home since you said good-bye this morning," she whispered.

"Then you did find it a little lonely without me. Do you realize I have not seen you all day?"

Vanessa relaxed under his hands and let herself sway toward him. His hands slid around her, and he drew her unresisting body imperceptibly closer to him.

"Do you think you would like to dine up here tonight, Sylvester? I . . . we . . . it will not be necessary to dress for dinner . . ." She blushed at her own temerity, but her eyes met his bravely as she waited for him to show his approval.

Her invitation went through the Earl like a shock. She was almost in his embrace, and she was promising more! Damn his obligations! Groaning inwardly, he told her with apparently unruffled composure, "Vanessa, dear, I should like it above all things, but I cannot possibly, not tonight. I am dining from home."

Melcourt felt her stiffen under his hands and glide away from him with a slight movement of her body. As he looked into her eyes, he knew that she had withdrawn completely. Almost ready to explain, he recalled in time that the secret was not his to divulge.

"Please forgive me," she intoned in a small, wooden voice. "I am not usually this stupid. I do not know what has come over me. I must be very tired."

"No, Vanessa! My dear, I am the one who must ask

forgiveness. I have an . . . engagement . . . I must keep."

"Yes, of course. I understand." She gave him a brilliant smile, then swiftly turned so he would not see that she was blinded by tears.

"Good night," came Melcourt's voice softly, regretfully.

She could not answer. Someone had placed a metal band about her chest and it was so tight she ached for want of breath; her throat felt raw with unshed tears. She sat down at the mirrored dressing table. One does not die of a broken heart, but how wonderful if one could. Stupid! Stupid! He never thought of her at all; it was all a take-in . . . a trick! It was Miranda—always Miranda. It was her letter paper he had tossed aside when she had interrupted him. She would have recognized it anywhere.

The eyes reflected in the looking glass were becoming dark and stormy as anguish gave way to a cold rage, which made all her past tantrums seem mild. She relived every event of the past week, wincing at the thought of the fool she had been and the narrow escape she had had. Vanessa could see clearly what he had in mind. An heir! It was lucky for her that Melcourt was meeting Miranda—probably at Shelburne again. It all fell into place! It was the perfect place for the clandestine meetings of two people whose own homes were not free from prying eyes. She had almost surrendered herself to him! Vanessa shuddered. What a fool he must think her. Everyone but she knew he preferred the sparkle and boldness of Miranda and the many before her. She had been told, but she had refused to accept the truth.

She would show him! If gaiety and brilliance were what he wanted, he would see she had them. She would fight Miranda with her own weapons—and win! She had youth on her side, after all, and Melcourt, by nature a possessive man, was no more immune to the green-eyed beast than any other. It would not be difficult to arouse his jealousy. She could picture it: other men gathered around her in admiration. She had done with being humble. Let him be the one to beg. Then she would laugh. "Oh, how I will laugh," she said aloud, and with the back of her hand wiped away the tears.

The Earl returned to London on the twenty-fifth of June. He had driven himself hard in the three weeks since Vanessa had left him at Melcourt. Much of this time had been spent in nursemaiding the leaders of the "army of invasion" in and around Southhampton: from the Wool House, where French prisoners of war killed time by carving their names and sentiments on the beams, to the Star Inn, where he had been tempted to do the same while waiting for Count Puisaye and the others to stop their bickering. They had sailed, finally, on the seventeenth. It had not been the end of it, however, for three days after this, the Channel fleet had encountered the French and had chased them back to port. Melcourt had enjoyed hearing Admiral Lord Bridport tell of the capture of three of the French ships, but the Admiral's comments had not been so pleasing.

"They knew about the invasion, the four thousand men of the advance guard, and the arms for twenty thousand more! You know what interested the French, my lord! A sweet plum to fall into their hands. Lucky you persuaded Pitt to send us out."

Lucky indeed, thought the Earl, and clenched his teeth, remembering how Gresham had made light of danger from the enemy. Lucky, for the French had been ready and waiting. No doubt, thought the Earl as he entered his town house, he would be hearing from Pitt this evening.

Inquiring as to the direction of her ladyship and being informed merely that she was from home, he changed for dinner and devoted himself to his long-neglected correspondence and a decanter of his favorite brandy with imprudent partiality.

The level of the brandy in the decanter showed that his lordship had made considerable inroads when the butler informed him that her ladyship had just now returned and was changing for dinner.

The Earl thought ironically that three weeks ago he would have been allowed as far as the boudoir, and once more applied himself to the brandy, his eyes turning time and again to the clock on the mantel. Its hands were almost on the dinner hour when Vanessa entered the room.

"Now indeed do I know at how slow a pace time can creep," he said, getting to his feet. He raised her hand to his lips in silent homage as his eyes feasted on her loveliness. Never had he seen her like this—sparkling as the diamonds that swung from her ears, scintillating as those resting on her bosom. Never had he seen her in a gown that showed her to such advantage—and so much of her. Its deep blue color accented the whiteness of her skin, the soft flesh that swelled at the low-cut bodice.

"Why did you not come to my boudoir?" she asked him in an offhand manner.

"I could not bring myself to believe that you would welcome me after the way we parted at Melcourt."

"Nonsense! I was probably in one of my pets. You must really learn to disregard them; they mean nothing." Vanessa's voice was as cool and remote as she was herself. There was studied indifference in her expression as she asked, "Are you dining from home tonight?"

"I thought we would spend this night by ourselves. We have been married for over a month and, as yet"—his arm stole about her and he lowered his voice until it was a caress—"as yet I have not made love to you."

The Earl bent his head until his lips almost touched Vanessa's hair. His remark had been intended to cast her into blushing confusion, but no sooner had he uttered it than he knew that for once he had been mistaken about a woman's feelings.

On her part, Vanessa was angry with herself at the depth of emotion he was able to inspire in her. She turned slightly and let his arm fall from about her shoulders. "I have an engagement tonight."

"One you cannot break?"

"One I have no intention of breaking."

The disappointment he felt did not register in his face or voice: he was coldly sarcastic.

"And who is this paragon you cannot bear to disappoint?"

Melcourt did not wait for an answer. Intoxicated by her beauty as well as by the considerable amount of brandy he had consumed, blinded by desire as well as anger, he crushed her to him and lowered his head to drink dry the honey of her mouth. Vanessa fought him with all her strength, but opposition only inflamed his senses; resistance made him cruel. She was a mad, unsatisfied craving in his blood.

Vanessa wanted to shrink from the savagery of his embrace, but there was no way to escape the maelstrom that whirled her around and around. Deep within her something stirred, and she gave herself up to the warmth of his demanding mouth.

She did not know when he released her, just that he had opened the door and was looking at a letter handed to him by one of the servants. The paper was well known to her, and probably better known to him, she thought as he escorted her to the dining room.

Throughout the long meal Vanessa was conscious of his unceasing watchfulness. She picked at her food and heaved a sigh of relief when the final course had been removed, and she was free to leave him to his port. As she began to rise from her seat, she knew he intended to stop her, and he would have if the butler had not entered to say that Lady Charldon had arrived and was desirous of speaking with his lordship.

Vanessa thought the Earl's surprise well done: a mere flicker of the eyes, a slight raising of his left eyebrow. His eyes sought hers, but she would not meet them.

"Well, my lady?"

"I am sure that you and my stepmother have a great deal to discuss. If you will excuse me?"

As she left, she knew that he would have had the servants say he was from home if she had asked. But she would not humble herself to him. If he wanted

Miranda, let him have her, but *she* would never share him with anyone. He would have to do without a wife until he made up his mind. Meanwhile something would be done to make him realize that other men found his wife attractive. Within the hour she would be flirting with every eligible and not so eligible man at Carlton House. Perhaps he would be there to see that she had become an Incomparable. She hoped so, but she must promise herself that she would not look for him in that revealing way she had.

As she made her way down the curved staircase, Vanessa knew that she surpassed her stepmother in every way, yet she was despondent. Miranda was alone with him while she, his wife, waited for another man. She sighed. She could have been with him. All she had to do was say the word and he would have forgotten Miranda—until the next time. And that was what she was afraid of—the next time, and the next, and the times after that.

She reached the last step as the butler admitted her escort. Vanessa welcomed him with outstretched hands and a dazzling smile. "Fitz!"

"Charming, Lady M. A pleasure to be seen with you. Lucky dog, Melcourt."

Vanessa smiled at him gratefully as he saw her into the carriage. Fitzwilliams always said something to make her feel quite the thing.

"When does Sylvester return, ma'am? The Prince has been asking for him these three weeks past."

"He is back, Fitz. He returned today."

"Then may we look for him at Carlton House tonight?"

"Perhaps. I do not know what his plans are."

Surprised, he said nothing for a moment and then, quickly recovering his composure, let fall a few choice pieces of gossip. "The latest *on dit* is that your stepmother lost her diamond earbobs to Lord Gresham at Lady Buckinghamshire's faro bank the other night, and your father won't redeem 'em."

Vanessa appreciated that Fitzwilliams was trying to entertain her with the latest gems of scandal, but it was not very amusing to imagine her stepmother closeted with Sylvester and asking him to recover her jewels. No doubt she would succeed, Vanessa thought, and remained in a state of silent reflection for the remainder of the drive.

By the time they had pulled up before the imposing door of the Prince's London residence, Vanessa had made up her mind to leave London. There was, after all, nothing to hold her there. The last Wednesday of Almack's short twelve-week season had come and gone. Knockers were being removed from doors in the fashionable section of town; populations of select seaside resorts swelled with an influx of visitors. Yes, London was always thin of company in July.

CHAPTER TWENTY-ONE

With a flourish of the coachman's whip Lady Melcourt's entourage pulled up at the Brighton residence of Lord and Lady Edgerton. One of the outriders sought admittance for her ladyship at the double-paneled front door, while the other helped the Countess descend the steps of her traveling coach. After a surprisingly long wait, during which the outrider hammered repeatedly at the door, it was opened by the butler, the rumpled nature of his neckcloth proclaiming a state of extreme agitation.

"Your ladyship! Thank goodness!" he gasped.

"What has happened, Lawton? Is it my aunt?" Vanessa's sharp tone recalled him to his position even as he ushered her into the hall.

"Her ladyship's taken a fall and hurt her ankle, but she won't let us send for the doctor."

"I see. . . . Her maid is with her, I assume?"

The butler was recovering his dignified demeanor by degrees and swiftly assured the Countess that not only was her ladyship's maid with her, but also the housekeeper, the head chambermaid, and the first parlormaid.

"Send the housekeeper to me, Lawton, and tell my

aunt I shall be in directly. Inform her maid that she is to remain at her ladyship's side and send the others about their business.

"Iris, see to the trunks, and as soon as you are settled, report to me."

Shortly thereafter a plump woman scurried down the steps while the butler followed at a pace more in keeping with his stateliness.

"The sound of your keys tells me you are the housekeeper," Vanessa said in a handsome manner that quite reassured the housekeeper.

"Jukes, your ladyship," the woman puffed, keys swinging against the gray poplin of her dress.

"How bad is my aunt?" Vanessa asked, acknowledging the curtsy with a perfunctory nod.

"Bad, my lady. The ankle is swollen something fierce, but my lady won't let us send for Dr. Cranshaw."

Vanessa made an instantaneous decision. "Lawton, send a footman for the doctor, and then order tea for her ladyship and me.

"Mrs. Jukes, please show my maid to my room and then see that she and my other servants are accommodated and are given some refreshment.

"I can see that we will all have to pitch in and do what we can to make it easier for my aunt." A smile reached her eyes, momentarily easing the worried expression. "I am afraid that I have been barking orders like a general, Lawton."

"Not at all, my lady. And I am sure that I speak for the rest of the staff, my lady, when I say that we are just so thankful that you're here to take charge, what with his lordship still in London and Miss Meg and Master Philip visiting in Hampshire."

Within twenty minutes of her arrival—it being a well-run household—Vanessa and her aunt were sitting over a large pot of tea. Lady Edgerton regarded her ankle with a rueful twist of her lips. "Niece, you have outgeneraled me!" she barked, almost causing Vanessa to upset her cup.

"It runs in the family, Aunt," she retorted just as the doctor was announced.

Lady Edgerton cursed the doctor for a foolish old woman but otherwise suffered his ministrations in silence. Vanessa, who received Dr. Cranshaw's instructions a few minutes later, was dismayed to learn that her aunt would be disabled for the better part of two weeks. "Although I would not tell her that until she's feeling more the thing, my lady. As it is, the pain will be enough for her to deal with. I'll be sending my man around with a draught to relieve the worst of it," he said, peering at her from under grizzled brows.

"Oh, do you think she will need it? Surely a sprain . . ."

"The pain is too severe to be merely a sprain—Oh, no, nothing broken, my lady," he hastened to assure her. "Chipped perhaps, but nothing to worry about except easing her ladyship's discomfort."

The evening proved Dr. Cranshaw to be right, and Lady Edgerton accepted with gratitude the paregoric she usually spurned. She admitted as much to the doctor when she saw him the following afternoon.

"Well, now, my lady, that's a bad sprain you have there—enough to keep you off your feet for the next two weeks."

"How can I? My masquerade!" she moaned, referring to an event that annually drew the *ton* from surrounding watering places. "Whatever shall I do, Vanessa?" she cried, capitulating to the inevitable.

"Do, Aunt? Why nothing, except tell me what it is you feel must be done for your party and then sit back and let me do it."

"There, my lady. Just what the doctor ordered, if I may permit myself a small witticism." The doctor's eyes twinkled from under his shaggy brows as he took his leave. "Good day, my lady, Lady Melcourt. I'm sure I leave my patient in the best of hands."

"Your presence is a comfort, Vanessa," remarked the Countess's matronly relative as she shifted her newly bandaged ankle uncomfortably under the Norwich shawl, which had been put to such plebeian use during the past ten days.

"Very restful," Vanessa scoffed.

"Much more so than my own children," admitted an exasperated Lady Edgerton. "They are at each other constantly for some imagined slight, and while I do not maintain that you are a restful person, you do have other qualities which endear you to me."

Once she had accepted her niece's betrothal to the Earl, Lady Edgerton had proved to have an unmistakably human side to her. Now, Vanessa found, there was a sense of humor too, somewhat submerged, but there nevertheless.

"Just yesterday, Aunt," Vanessa chuckled, "you accused me of being a whirlwind."

"True, child, but I am sitting out of the way now so you cannot have the servants set the room about my ears. Besides," she said practically, "you made sure it was put to rights yesterday. I don't think you will be doing it again so soon while you have the ballroom to supervise and your own costume to occupy you."

"I think I shall come as Charles the Second, mustache and all."

"Be serious for a moment. Our guests will be arriving in less than a week, their own costumes superbly thought out and executed. Should the Countess of Melcourt do less? I have it on good authority that your stepmother has ordered a flamboyant red dress. Ever since the Spanish ambassador told her she had the glamour of his countrywomen, Miranda has appeared as a Spanish dancer at every masquerade. I imagine it suits her purpose to let herself be known to her many admirers."

Vanessa looked startled and Lady Edgerton hastened to explain. "Did you think Melcourt the only one, child? Nonsense! And I shall not apologize for mentioning something you know. I give you credit for not being a weak-kneed creature." She took her niece's hand and patted it in an unexpectedly kind gesture. "There, child, where is that resolute Charldon pride? It cannot be so bad as you think. She is just another wench to Melcourt, while you, well, you are his wife, after all."

"Yes," she said, her lovely mouth twisted as though with pain. "I am, after all."

Lady Edgerton gave Vanessa's hand a final squeeze and deposited in it a large black key that she had withdrawn from the capacious pocket of her morning dress. "Jukes has given me the key to the attics in the west wing. Take one of the maids with you, or Jukes herself, if you prefer, and find something to wear that will out-Miranda Miranda. Oh, pshaw, Vanessa, you know what I mean."

To placate her domineering aunt, who asserted that she could not bear to be thwarted and was ready to escort her to the storage rooms herself, Vanessa accepted the housekeeper's services.

"Her ladyship was very firm, my lady," the woman explained as they mounted the stairs in the west wing. "She said we must find something to please you if we look all day." The housekeeper panted when they reached the upper floor of the mansion. "You'll have to forgive me, my lady. I don't often make this climb, and I'm not as young as I was," she said, excusing her shortness of breath.

"You would never know it, Mrs. Jukes," Vanessa told her. "Everything is in perfect order."

Jukes acknowledged the compliment to her housekeeping with warm appreciation as she opened a large trunk for Vanessa's inspection.

"I shall try not to keep you too long," Vanessa said as she impatiently discarded wig, gown, and tights that some aspiring Cleopatra had worn to a previous masquerade. "You must be frightfully busy with preparations for the ball."

"Not at all, my lady, thanks to you. We are all old hands at our jobs and go on the way we do every year. The only thing I must do is hire some temporary staff. One of our young footmen has come into a small inheritance and has decided to emigrate. He's taking one of the upstairs maids with him—a pretty little thing—so we'll be short-handed. It's a problem to come up with suitable help on such short notice, my lady," she continued worriedly. "You can't know the half of it. I beg pardon, my lady, you've been ever so helpful with sorting out our domestic problems, I can't help telling you."

"Not at all, Mrs. Jukes," Vanessa told her as the woman opened still another trunk. "Running a household has its many vexations, I see."

"Heavens, yes, my lady," she responded eagerly. "Why, just the other day her ladyship said to me, 'Jukes, we have to do something about cleaning out some of those old draperies in the attics. We'll never use them and I hate clutter.' I as good as told her it was a pity to throw them away as some parts of them are still good," Mrs. Jukes rambled on, "but you know her ladyship: once she gets an idea into her head . . . It's a pity, though. Just look! Such fine velvet."

Resignedly Vanessa looked at the discarded draperies, and then let her fingers caress the silken nap. Eagerly she went back to the first trunk. Even as she opened it, she was asking, "Are you sure Lady Edgerton meant the blue draperies, Mrs. Jukes?"

"Oh, yes, my lady, and she was very firm about it too. Said we had too much clutter in the attics to keep anything so faded. But as you can see, you can hardly tell where the original color faded."

"Well, if you are sure, and we can find enough that kept its color, I should like nothing better for my costume."

Puzzled at the Countess's strange selection, but pleased to have been of service to such a gracious and sympathetic lady, Mrs. Jukes promised to have the articles delivered to the sewing room.

"My abigail's a skillful needlewoman, child, and I know you can't sew a seam without a minor bloodletting," Lady Edgerton had told Vanessa. "Just tell her what you want."

Reluctant at first to donate her draperies, Lady Edgerton became more enthusiastic as time went on and had to admit, finally, that her niece had faultless taste. On the night of the masquerade Vanessa's long legs showed to advantage beneath the short blue tunic. Her charming page-boy costume proved more attractive than any painted dancing girl or Gypsy dress, and more modest than the multitude of Cleopatras and Aphrodites whose fly-away gauzes revealed what would have been better left concealed.

Vanessa, watching the guests arrive and looking for one in particular, paid no heed to a man in a black domino who stood near her, his back to the wall.

"Put not your trust in princes—nor in their favorites," panted a fulsome voice too close to her ear.

"Lord Gresham! You startled me!" Seeing him, she was suddenly relieved that her blue velvet tunic was braided and frogged up to a very high collar, and she wondered if he felt frustrated that he could not breathe down her neck.

"How flattering that you recognized me, dear lady; how sad that I must be the bearer of disappointing news. Do not look for your husband quite so soon. HRH has other plans . . . and Melcourt is with him," he said insinuatingly, his eyes seeming do devour her.

Vanessa searched out the guests, many of whom were known to her, disguise or no, and finally let her gaze fasten on a tall, masked Spanish dancer complete with high comb, mantilla, and quantities of black lace embellishing a daringly cut *Gros de Naples* gown. The Charldon rubies, so magnificently displayed upon Miranda's expanse of white bosom, were preserved to the family, as was the Manor, because of the entailment. Vanessa, aware that Melcourt did not dance attendance upon her stepmother, was generous enough to admit that Miranda provided the perfect setting for the gems. Her eyes scoured the room, looking for one man. Then, realizing how betraying her long examination of the ballroom was to Lord Gresham, she clenched her fists in self-disgust and sought to engage him in identifying the masked guests.

One tall, bewigged Cavalier stood out, although his identity eluded her. Apparently he did not have the same problem, for he addressed her by name in a faintly accented voice.

"Miss Charldon? Perhaps you remember me? André Vallier? We left Paris at the same time."

My God! Raoul! she thought, her insides churning. Outwardly she remained calm; only her sudden pallor and the unsteadiness of her voice betrayed her agitation.

"I was not sure, m'sieu, until you spoke just now," replied Vanessa and turned to Lord Gresham with a shaky laugh as she performed the introductions. "You could almost say that Monsieur Vallier and I were traveling companions, our paths crossed so frequently."

She turned back to the Cavalier. "However, m'sieu, I am Miss Charldon no longer; I have since become the Countess of Melcourt, although I cannot believe that our relationship will suffer because of that."

Raoul looked at her narrowly. If he knew her at

all—and he prided himself that after eight years none knew her better—she was unhappy and undoubtedly at loose ends. If a tight rein was not kept on her, she would be off on one of her mad escapades, which she always called "looking for something to do."

Neither of them noticed that Lord Gresham was strangely silent and looked at one and then the other of them at first in puzzled bewilderment, and later in dawning and perturbed recognition. The Chat d'Or in Vitry! He had been with Fouché. The two men who had slept in the room at the head of the stairs! Yes, the older had been tall and slender; the other . . . his eyes assessed Vanessa in her page-boy costume . . . the other had been no man. They had shared a room! Perhaps he could use this to his advantage.

"So this is Monsieur Vallier?" he said. "Why have we not heard you speak of him, Vanessa dear?" Miranda, who had appeared as if out of nowhere during the preceding introduction, raised sultry eyes to the Frenchman, all the while plying a large lace fan. "I am Lady Charldon. I feel sure my stepdaughter would like us to be acquainted with each other. Apparently she has lost her voice from the shock of seeing you. She had no idea that she would be meeting you after your trip. Surely if I had spent so much time with a gentleman, especially one so handsome, I would have informed my family, or at least my husband . . . or would I?"

"That is so, Vanessa, is it not? You had not planned to keep Monsieur Vallier's presence a secret, had you?" Miranda's voice was sweetly suggestive.

"Why, Stepmama, I would not dream of keeping anything from you. Whatever would you do with your nights if you had no . . . tales . . . to amuse you?"

Miranda made a quick recovery and addressed herself to Raoul, an inviting smile upon her carmined lips. "Surely, m'sieu, you will have pity on my ancient state and take tea with me tomorrow. I should so love to hear about your adventures in France."

Raoul bent low over the hand she extended. "My lady, I should be most delighted, were I to remain in Brighton. Unhappily, I have been called away for a time."

"Unhappily, indeed. I am sure we would have had a lot to tell each other. You must call upon me when you return," Miranda almost purred.

Lord Gresham was happy to find his presence ignored during the exchange between Lady Charldon and the Countess. His mind searched busily for the solution to his problem. He thought he had found it, thanks to his sharp eyes and Miranda Charldon's malicious insinuations. A few words dropped in Melcourt's ear . . . a little trouble between the Earl and the lovely Vanessa, and she would disappear, apparently with some lover. No one would be the wiser when Lyman Gresham returned to England. Now if he could cultivate Miranda Charldon. . . . She'd been playing deep lately—had sold her diamond tiara to Rundell and Bridge and had replaced it with some bit of trumpery. Bridge was a damned good businessman. Miranda must have been mad as hellfire! And then there were her diamond earrings. Surely she would like to have them back.

Gresham recovered himself in time to partner Lady Charldon in the next dance. A few words together proved them to be in total accord, and when Gresham finally escorted her from the dance floor, he stood once again with his back to the wall, watching Vanessa and Raoul.

In a pensive mood after the magnificent buffet supper so lavishly provided by the hostess, Miranda's gaze flitted among the assembled company and came to rest on Lyman Gresham. It was obvious he could not take his eyes from Vanessa. He almost drooled when he looked at her. She did not wonder at all that he would like to get his hands on her stepdaughter. True, the girl could be pushed into an *affaire*, she was sure, but it would be a pity to waste that exciting Frenchman on her. Surely, with Gresham's connivance, she could arrange something to ruin the chit— and get back her diamond eardrops as well!

CHAPTER TWENTY-TWO

"Three weeks of waiting! And the house party about to break up! Have you no news for me?" Lord Gresham was annoyed.

"Patience, my lord. I am just as eager for my diamonds as you are for your—shall we say—diversion. I would not have our chances queered."

"Answer me one thing," Gresham snarled. "How will you know when the time is ripe?"

"Our hostess required a new footman—need I say more?" answered his fellow conspirator.

The vice-riddled face broke into a smile, and Lady Charldon could barely repress a shudder. She was thankful it was her stepdaughter's body that would be exchanged for the eardrops lost at the gaming tables; she herself could never tolerate Gresham, even if he showered her with diamonds. Luckily his taste ran more to young virgins, and she was sure Vanessa still possessed that commodity so desired by him.

"I will rely upon you, Lady Charldon. Do not let either of us be disappointed," he said pointedly.

Assuring Lord Gresham that his confidence was not misplaced, and thanking him for the support of his arm on their short tour of the formal and geometric topiary garden, Lady Charldon returned to the card tables. It was after one o'clock when she finally made her way up the stairs, disgruntled at the loss of the quarter's allowance but determined to recoup her losses the next night. Everything, she felt, had gone wrong since the advent of her so charming stepdaughter. She could scarcely wait until Gresham took her.

Once Lady Charldon entered her room, it appeared she would have to wait no longer. A whispered disclosure on the part of the abigail, and a young footman was hurriedly admitted, only to leave almost as quickly as he had entered. She smiled as she disrobed, feeling as satisfied as a well-fed cat. Her spy had done his work! All that remained was for Gresham to be told.

Examining her well-endowed body in the full-length mirror, Miranda Charldon almost purred in anticipation of consoling Melcourt when he discovered his wife's infidelity.

Just before breakfast, and immediately after a tête-à-tête with Lady Charldon, Lord Gresham informed his hostess that he would be taking his leave.

"I cannot be sorry," Lady Edgerton told Vanessa, "for while my husband holds him in great esteem, one day of his company is sufficient to last me the season. I imagine, too, that you have found it a little uncomfortable with him about this last week."

"He has not bothered me while he has been here, yet I too cannot feel at ease with him, Aunt. And I do hope he will not beg a seat in my carriage, for I will surely refuse him."

"He has no business at Melcourt, my dear, none at all."

"Yes, of course; I am being foolish," said Vanessa, adjusting a fashionable sleeveless pelisse, whose lining matched the green ribbons on her bonnet. "Good-bye, Aunt. Please tell Meg that I like her young man."

"I will, if you tell your husband for me that I think he is a fool," said the outspoken Lady Edgerton as she escorted her niece to the waiting vehicle. "He will know what I mean."

"Perhaps. If I see him, which I am beginning to doubt." Vanessa kissed her aunt and entered the carriage in which her abigail was seated. She wished she could have confided in her aunt, for she had come to like and respect that formidable matron. If they kept to their schedule, they would reach Melcourt Castle late the next day, and she was looking forward to being alone for a little while before Raoul needed her. How lucky that she had found his note. Lately she did not remember where she put things, and it was very annoying, although not of any great import.

As the elegant traveling carriage traversed the long avenue of beeches, Vanessa sighed, untied the leaf-green ribbons of her dashing, straw-colored bonnet, and put it on the seat. Her maid promptly rescued it and placed it in a far corner, exclaiming, "The way this carriage fair rolls, my lady, one of us might crush your bonnet before we're able to sit up straight."

This was unlikely, since the Earl's coaches were exceptionally well sprung, but Vanessa did not comment. Realizing her employer was in no mood to talk, Iris, like the good servant she was, said nothing further. Resting her head against the comfortable squabs, and unaware that her maid had said anything, Vanessa decided it was nonsensical to do anything but sit back and relax. She stared sightlessly at the countryside, seeing neither green of forest nor green of water. There would be time enough to plan when she reached Melcourt, she mused. She would not think of Sylvester enjoying himself with Miranda—blast her!— Miranda, who had taken great delight in confessing that she and the Earl were still lovers.

Lapwings and linnets by the side of the road raised their voices in noisy protest as the wheels rumbled on, but Vanessa was so busy telling herself what not to think that she heard nothing of their piercing cries.

Brisk morning breezes carried the almost fishy smell of salt water, finally distracting Vanessa from her thoughts. She fell into a deep sleep, which lasted most of the morning, waking only when they stopped for refreshment. She would have liked to push on through the night, for the trip was of no great duration, but she could not bring herself to expend the energy to inform the coachman of her change of plans. Pacing and resting the horses had been her decision, but with a sleepless night at a Southampton inn behind her and once more confined in a vehicle that seemed to have become an instrument of torture, she felt she had again made the wrong decision. Thus the morning found her no less fatalistic than she had been the previous day.

Once she had crossed the Channel with Raoul, if that was what he needed her for, things would be different. If she returned, she promised herself, she would turn the tables on her stepmother. It would be so easy, if only that heavy feeling around her heart would go away. Vanessa almost hated herself then for being so melancholic and unwilling to fight for her rightful place at her husband's side.

As the chalk, flint, and thatch of isolated farms turned into the endless gray-gold stretch of shingle known as Chesil Beach, she knew she was home. But at Melcourt things were no better. The Earl had sent word that he would be arriving within a day or two, and although no one said anything, Vanessa knew that he would be traveling with Miranda. In spite of all she had tried to tell herself, it was a shock, and when the butler brought her a letter early one morning, it was as if someone else's brain registered the fact that Raoul's plans had changed.

She could be ready in an hour, as he had asked. No one needed her. The servants ran everything with only token assistance from her. Her presence was unnecessary to the smooth operation of the household, she told herself as she climbed into the carriage that had been sent to get her. Vanessa closed her eyes as if in pain and allowed a single tear to fall. At least Raoul needed her, she thought as the coach rolled on to its destination. Whatever it was he wanted, she would do it, even if it meant returning to France.

A semblance of a smile lighted Vanessa's face for an instant as she noticed the basket. Tucked into the folds of a snowy white napkin, Vanessa found Raoul's apology for his untimely haste: a fresh loaf of bread and a bottle of white wine that was pleasurably cool to the touch. No wonder she had felt so maudlin, eating hardly any breakfast and going off before luncheon. Miranda was nothing but a stupid cow and a liar to boot. When Sylvester arrived, she would have it out with him once and for all.

Vanessa broke off a corner of the loaf and poured a glass of wine. She decided that the least she could do was to show Raoul that she accepted his peace offering—and besides, she was very thirsty.

Sleepless nights at Melcourt Castle had taken their toll, and Vanessa curled up in the corner and closed her eyes. She was tired; she could hardly keep her head up. She felt peculiar—dizzy. Perhaps it was the wine—she had not eaten after all. How sick she was! Maybe she should get the coachman to stop. Vanessa willed herself to raise her hand, but it did not obey her. Her eyes closed, and her head lolled back against the cushions in a drugged sleep.

How long she had been unconscious, Vanessa was not sure. She knew only that it must have been for some time. When she had left Melcourt, it had been late morning. Now, judging from the lengthening purple shadows, it was late, almost evening, and she had no idea where she was or why she had been brought here—wherever "here" was. There was no doubt in her mind that some powerful drug had been added to the wine. She had had little or nothing to eat, as she recalled, which made the drug react even more strongly upon her body. Vanessa still felt the effects of it as she tried to raise her head. Her mouth felt furry and her head ached, sending sympathetic pains down to her neck and shoulders. In spite of her discomfort and because of the large dose of laudanum that she had been given, Vanessa slept again, but it was a shallow, fitful sleep.

When she woke, a man stood before her, a candle in his hand. At first she did not recognize him, and then she realized that it was Lord Gresham, a rather terrifying Lord Gresham with a gloating smile upon his face. As though conferring a signal honor upon her, he told her why he had abducted her and explained some of the doubtful pleasures in store for her at his knowing hands.

The metallic taste of fear was in her mouth as she listened to him. She was barely able to squeeze out one word from a throat gone suddenly parched. It began as a scream in her mind, but it came out a croak.

"Melcourt? Your husband's mistress will engage his interest, my dear Countess—Vanessa. So you need not worry that he will look for you. You and I will beat them at their own game, my dear."

Moisture gathered at the corners of his thick lips as he described in great detail how he planned to instruct her in what he called the pleasures of love. "I told you, dear child, before you foolishly refused my suit, that these young lordlings know nothing of initiating a maid in the delights of the body. They're too anxious for their own gratification and demand partners as experienced as they. They are also impatient with the virgin fears which a more seasoned lover would relish as proof of a girl's purity and freshness."

As he spoke, his eyes became bright and glassy, and a thin film of perspiration appeared on his florid face. He seemed to be whipping himself into a frenzy, Vanessa thought, as she tried once again to stand. This time, she blacked out completely, only to recover almost instantly to the sound of Gresham's voice berating someone for putting an overdose of laudanum in the wine. Vanessa forced herself to remain still and keep her eyes closed as a woman's voice answered him in an indistinguishable whine.

Vanessa heard Gresham snarl orders to the servant and then stamp out of the room, slamming the door behind him. She allowed herself to open her eyes to the gap-toothed smile on the face of an old harpy.

"Well, dearie, playing games with his lordship? If ye don't make him angry, it won't be too bad. Likes a bit o' a fight, he does, so's he has an excuse to be rough—makes him feel strong and manly, it does. Think o' somethin' pleasant when he's at ye, an' it'll be over and done with so fast, ye'll think nothin' o' it, and ye won't be hurtin' either. Now come and eat some o' the nice dinner I cooked. Ye'll need all yer strength." She howled with laughter and slapped her knees, acting as if it was the greatest of all jokes.

Vanessa gave her a baleful look. The thought of food was repugnant, but she would certainly have more strength if she ate something. All of her strength would be needed before this horrible night was over.

Vanessa allowed the woman to help her tidy her hair and straighten her creased and crumpled white muslin dress, more to bolster her own sagging courage than out of any desire to mollify her abductor. Vanessa wondered at herself in wry amusement. Once again, as she had in France, she was facing a distinctly dangerous situation without the flicker of an eyelid, when for months she had been shivering and trembling at every stray thought. No wonder both this lout and Miranda—not to say her own husband—thought her a weak, spineless creature who would allow all manner of indignities to be inflicted upon her. How often Raoul had said she was her own worst enemy! Yes, she decided, her imagination was her enemy—always borrowing trouble. Reality gave her courage where it often caused others to quake in their shoes.

As the old harpy ushered her into the shabby dining room, Vanessa was silently repeating, "Reality gives me courage," somewhat in the manner of one using a talisman against evil. She faced Lord Gresham with bravado, insisting upon her release.

"Sit down, my dear, and let us enjoy each other's company," he said, blandly ignoring her demand. "It isn't often that I can enjoy the company of a woman as beautiful as you without having many rivals for her attention."

Vanessa allowed him to seat her but continued to remonstrate with him. A look of annoyance passed over his brutish features. "My dear Countess, I will be

212

forced to think you don't look forward to my company, and that will get us nowhere."

"If you do not know by now that I am not happy to have your attentions forced upon me," said Vanessa, "I am surprised that you are capable of thinking anything at all. Somehow, Lord Gresham, I never thought of you as a stupid man, but if you think you shall get anywhere with me, perhaps I was wrong."

Gresham looked pained. He filled two glasses with wine and put one in front of Vanessa. "Let us enjoy our dinner before we have any arguments. I am quite hungry, and I know you have not eaten since you have been here. My cook is very good," he assured her as he placed a slice of roast duck upon her plate. "Of course," he said with sudden bitterness, "she is not up to the French chef you have at Melcourt. Quite apart from the delight I expect from your own beautiful self, it will be a pleasure to scratch some of the polish off your fine husband. He's always had everything the way he wanted—money, horses, women. He's always been lucky—until now."

"Do you think he will let you get away with this?" Vanessa asked calmly, giving the food on her plate her complete attention, as though it interested her more than his answer.

"By the time you return to the castle, he shall be convinced that you have been seeing your lover." Once again Gresham emptied and quickly replenished his glass. "I have it on good advice that he will not believe you."

Vanessa was stricken. Miranda! How her stepmother must hate her to do this terrible thing to her.

As for Melcourt—the less she thought about him, the better.

Vanessa forced herself to eat some of the food placed before her, then Gresham said something that caught her attention, and she risked a glance at him from under lowered lashes. He was busily engaged in dissecting a slab of blood-red sirloin that had been left on a sizable platter by, she supposed, that same crone who seemed to be cook, apothecary, and lady's maid.

"In spite of the fact that you and the Comte de St. Varres shared a room at Le Chat d'Or, you still have the look of an innocent. With all your fine husband's experience, I am astounded that he cannot see that. Is he so blinded by his lust for another woman that he cannot see the purity that is in your face? Pearls cast before swine, my dear, the way of the world."

The woman winked at her as she placed a ham before her employer, and Vanessa clenched her fists, but did not answer him. She must try not to become angry at anything he said. She would have to remain as calm as possible, listening, waiting. As the evening wore on and he imbibed more and more freely, surely his tongue would loosen.

CHAPTER TWENTY-THREE

Dinner, Lord Gresham's avowals to the contrary, was agony to Vanessa. The innumerable side dishes might well have been burned and the turbot soufflé seaweed, for all she tasted. By the time Gresham had broached his third bottle, Vanessa knew little more of his activities than she had known before.

"You are right about your cook; she is very good, but even Melcourt's chef cannot rise to the elegant dinners we had in France," Vanessa told her host with a slight thickening of her speech, as he escorted her into the salon.

"Naturally, my dear, the French really know how to savor the good things of life," he responded benevolently as he offered her a glass of brandy. She was almost tempted to drink herself insensible, but her head was still mizzy after being drugged, and she did not want to make it any worse. It seemed to her that even for oblivion one must pay a price.

The cool, damp breeze from the windows facing the garden made her shiver and wish she had something more to wear than a thin muslin dress. But the fresh air helped to dispel some of the remaining aftereffects of the laudanum.

"Well, my dear?"

Vanessa was startled. She had meant to listen to him and lead him into making some indiscreet remark. "Forgive me, my lord. I am still somewhat befuddled from the drugged wine."

"Since you are not going to come to me, I shall have to come to you." He laughed softly as he took her arm. She shuddered as his fingers dug into the soft flesh above her elbow. He moved one hand against her breast, and she attempted to free herself from his grabbing hands, but he was persistent.

"Come to France with me. You know as well as I that there is nothing here for you. I can give you anything you want—clothes, jewels, furs, your own house in Paris."

"How is this possible?" she demanded, suddenly standing very still.

"Never mind about that," he mumbled thickly into her neck. "Just say you will come with me tomorrow night."

"I do not know," Vanessa murmured, trying to fend him off.

He pulled her away from the open window, almost threw her onto the sofa, and fell upon her, covering her face with slobbering kisses. "After tonight you'll know who your master is." His weight was pushing her down into the soft cushions, and she felt smothered. She could feel his hand sliding under the smooth fabric of her dress, and she struggled like a panic-stricken wildcat, her nails raking his face. For a moment he loosened his grasp, but as quickly as she twisted from under him, he was on his feet. Moving swiftly for such a corpulent man, he caught her and pulled her within his arms once more.

His hand hooked at the neckline of her dress and ripped it to her waist. Eyes bulging at the sight of pink-tipped breasts cupped in the torn garments, Gresham subjected her to as many abuses and indignities as he could while trying to control her with one arm.

"Fight me, you little beauty, fight me. There'll not be an inch of your body I won't cover with bruises and kisses," he panted as he lowered his head.

She raised her knee with an abrupt movement, and he collapsed, moaning, at her feet.

"So you learned something from me, after all."

Startled, Vanessa turned and saw at the open window the tall, elegant figure of the Comte de St. Varres.

"Oh, Raoul," she sobbed as she ran to the shelter of his arms. "Thank God!" For a few moments she allowed herself the luxury of unrestrained tears, and then, in response to his urgent questioning, she calmed herself, the tale pouring out between sobs and hiccups.

"*Quelle femme!* What a woman you are, Vanessa, *chèrie*. Anyone else would be in a state of collapse after an experience like that—but you—you are magnificent!"

Vanessa stopped crying and looked up at him. "Which means, *n'est-ce pas,* that you think I have done enough crying," she said with a tremulous smile. "I am sorry to be such a watering pot."

"Not at all, *petite*," he sympathized, producing a large white handkerchief for her use. "It is only in quiet and peaceful times that you are fearful—and perhaps *un peu* tiresome when reasoning becomes fanciful."

"Just do not think that my reasoning has become fanciful when I tell you that Gresham is a spy!" she said with all the dignity she could command, as she wiped away her remaining tears and returned the borrowed handkerchief.

"Tell me!"

"He is a spy, Raoul! He saw us at Le Chat d'Or in Vitry."

"The man in the corner with Fouché! Quickly, Vanessa, what did he say?" Raoul commanded tersely, his hands clutching her shoulders in a painful grip.

Words tumbling one over the other, Vanessa told him all she knew. "It is not much. I am sorry. The rest is like a bad play with the part of the villain being overacted by an amateur. If I had not been so frightened, I would have laughed."

Greatly relieved by what Vanessa had told him, Raoul smiled and soothed her, then became momentarily expansive. "Never mind, *mignonne*; if he is the one who is to make the trip to France, as you say he plans, any papers or information he carries will be with him and not with an accomplice. We suspected as much, but we were not sure. The authorities will question him now."

Gresham was still moaning as Raoul ripped the neckcloth from his prostrate body and trussed him the way he might have a small bullock. He then removed his own coat and helped Vanessa into it. "This gown is even more revealing than the latest Paris fashions, so we will button the coat. But then, Jeanne will be able to tell you all about the fripperies our ladies are almost wearing," he continued.

Vanessa blushed and clutched the lapels of the coat tightly to her. "Jeanne? Then she is already here? Oh, wonderful. But then you did not need me after all."

"Exactly," he grunted, bending down to check his prisoner's bonds. "My thanks to your husband for her safe arrival. I too was surprised, and Abel was coming to you with a letter changing our plans when he saw you enter the carriage. He recognized Gresham's coachman and followed just to make sure they were taking you to this house."

As Vanessa looked at him in astonishment, he rose to his feet and led her through the garden window to where two horses were held by a boy she vaguely recognized as coming from the Rose and Garter.

"You might as well know that we have been watching Gresham for some time—thanks once again to the very astute gentleman you married. He distrusted Gresham from the first. Had your William Pitt paid more heed to Melcourt, the invasion might not have been the fiasco it was. No," he amended honestly, "in all truth, I will have to say that Pitt was sorely troubled when he found he could not discourage the Royalist commanders. They were prepared to accuse him of all manner of things if he did not present them with supplies and transportation at the very least."

Raoul's hands clenched into admirable fists, and his face was clouded with anger. "Pitt admitted to me that it was only your husband's doubts that kept him from sending English troops to be needlessly slaughtered by the very men the Royalists had armed. Fools!"

"Then Pitt is likely to grant Melcourt any favor . . ."
Such as arranging for a Parliamentary dissolution of
our marriage, Vanessa almost concluded. "I cannot explain now," she said, glancing at the boy who stoically
waited with the horses. "In any case, you should get
back to Gresham before his servant sets him free."

Raoul exchanged a few words with the boy and
then helped her to mount. "You will be all right with
the lad, Vanessa. I have told him to go slowly. When
you tell Melcourt what has happened, give him my
thanks. It may be some time before I can get back.
It all depends on what we learn from Gresham."

He patted the cold hands that rested so slackly on
the reins, and then waited until she and the young
groom moved off into the darkness before he went
back to his prisoner.

Numb in the aftermath of the harrowing experience, all that kept Vanessa going was the knowledge
that Sylvester had not been with Miranda! She wondered how many times he had been in France when
she had thought him philandering.

Although they kept country hours, the household
could not have been long abed, an exhausted Vanessa
decided as she bade her young guide a grateful farewell and entered the darkened castle. Relieved to have
escaped the curious eyes of all but the lone footman
on duty at the massive South Portal, she hunched
deeply into the borrowed coat and hurried up the
stairs and into her sitting room, where she remained a
scant few minutes before entering the dimly lighted
bedroom.

She had disrobed in the other room, and as she approached the bed, a solitary candle cast alternate day and night on her long, slender limbs. Somehow she sensed the Earl's presence and stood poised to flee—so pale she seemed not flesh and blood but marble.

"How long have you been here?" She fought an impulse to cross her arms over her breasts.

"Long enough," he said, deriving satisfaction from the way she flinched at his sarcastic tone. His eyes swept her, making her feel exposed to her very soul. He made no attempt to rise from the depths of the chair, preferring to observe the play of light and shadow on her bravely lifted face and exquisite body.

"You are not afraid of anything, are you?"

"Not of anything I can see," she murmured as she reached for the filmy robe which lay waiting for her at the foot of the bed.

"Perhaps a good healthy fear would add variety to your experiences." His voice was soft and caressing and so at odds with his words that Vanessa turned to face him, wondering.

There was something about the way he was looking at her that made her wish the robe was not so revealing. She wanted to turn from him, but fear—a sickening fear—had left her paralyzed. Not until Melcourt rose from the chair did she wrench herself into sudden movement, but it was too late for escape. Slowly and inexorably he drew her to him until the whole length of her quivering young body was against him.

"Have you been with your lover?"

She wanted to confide in him, be comforted by him, but now, at his words, she remembered Gresham's warning: "I have it on good advice that he will

221

not believe you." Vanessa clenched her teeth and struggled against arms that tightened about her in a cruel embrace.

"What?" he said softly. "No story springs readily to your treacherous lips to explain your absence these many hours? Perhaps you would care to try my kiss, madam wife, to compare?"

"Never . . . You will never lower me to that level," she hissed, angered beyond all reason.

It was the wrong thing to say, but she was past caring. He bent his head to her upturned face and pressed his lips to hers fiercely and angrily, until she shrank from the savagery of his embrace. He let her go suddenly, and she swayed blindly, her hands outstretched. With a hollow laugh that had no humor, he scooped her up in his arms and placed her on the bed. His hands lingered possessively even as he withdrew them from her bruised and shuddering body. His voice matched the bleak expression on his face.

"You make a man want you—but you are not worth it. And that's the hell of it, my dear. You are not worth it. . . . At least Miranda . . ."

He turned abruptly and started for the door. Vanessa leaped from the bed and snatched up the first thing at hand, sending it flying across the room to smash against the door.

"You pompous, arrogant beast. If I were a man I would run you through."

The Earl turned casually. "Since you are not, you shall have to rely upon some other fool to defend your honor." His voice told her he thought there was precious little to defend. "Perhaps Monsieur André Vallier would be your *cavaliere servente*," he told her with repressed savagery. With two swift strides he was at her side, grasping her arms roughly. "In the future you should tell him to be more gentle with you. You bruise easily."

Vanessa stared at him, startled, and he misinterpreted her expression.

"No need to look so surprised. I have seen marks like these on a woman's breasts before. I only wonder, with such a beginning, that you did not stay the night with him."

In a dreary voice she said, "Miranda did her work well."

"Do not scoff, my dear. Her information was not inaccurate, I judge, for you did not trouble to deny your acquaintance with the gentleman," he said curtly.

Vanessa faced him defiantly. "I deny nothing!"

The Earl let her feel the full weight of his hands as they slid from her arms to her neck.

"All that Miranda told me . . . is it the truth?"

"The truth? What is the truth?" she answered him tauntingly, heedless of the pressure his cruel fingers were beginning to exert. "The truth that I spent many days and nights with André Vallier? The truth that André Vallier and I were closer than two people could possibly be? That my bed was indeed that of André Vallier? Yes, and yes, and again, yes."

She had goaded him past all endurance, but she did not care. She almost wished he would put an end to her agony—permanently. He held her in a merciless grip. A mist obscured her vision and a rushing, a roaring filled her ears as the blood pounded agonizingly in her head. Her eyes sought his, accusing, imploring, reproaching. Then her vision dimmed, and she knew no more.

The dark of night had given way to an eerie predawn haze when Vanessa stirred, then shuddered convulsively. She did not know how long she had been lying there, half-conscious; she knew only that it was late, perhaps too late for everything. If only her head did not ache so, she might be able to think. She tried to pull herself up, using the edge of the bed for support, and as the blue damask walls seemed to come tumbling down on her, she closed her eyes. Her throat ached abominably, and the backs of her eyes felt gritty with unshed tears. She forced herself to make a final effort and eventually stood, clinging to the carved wooden post of the great bed. Hysterical laughter bubbled at her lips. How she had longed for her husband's sympathy, for his protection, perhaps for tender, encircling arms, a gentle kiss. And now this! It would be impossible to confide in him or ask him for comfort now. There was no way she could have explained the bruises on her body when he had made up his mind to condemn her.

Vanessa stood still, fighting the dreadful nausea that threatened to overwhelm her each time she tried to take a step. After a while the appalling weakness eased, leaving her devoid of all feeling. Her palms were cold and clammy as she dragged on the first thing that came to hand.

There was one more thing to do before she left here forever. Only one thing would she take from his house, aside from the clothes in which she stood—the locket with the Cosway miniatures. For the present he could keep everything else belonging to her. Once she was settled, she could send for her things. Meanwhile she would return to Charldon Manor. With what she knew about Miranda, her stepmother would not dare refuse her. After a time she would go away. She did not know where, but she would need money to set up her own *ménage*. As she recalled, Melcourt had made her some allowance, but she did not want to touch it now. Maybe later, when she had time to lick her wounds and the hurt disappeared, then she would think about it—not now.

As she let herself out by a little-used side door, Vanessa heard the library clock strike the hour. Only five o'clock, she thought. How strange. The start of a new day for some and, for her, the end of the world.

CHAPTER TWENTY-FOUR

"Mr. Charldon, my lord."

His lordship, roused from a brown study by his butler's grave tones, uncrossed his legs and laid aside the book whose pages he had quite neglected to turn for upwards of an hour. He approached his unexpected although very welcome guest with a smile and an outstretched hand.

"Andrew! It is good to see you."

"And you, Sylvester. You've been a stranger, not that I blame you entirely, you understand . . ."

My Lord Melcourt, with ease born of considerable practice, interrupted his guest's train of thought by the simple expedient of guiding him to a deeply cushioned armchair.

"Another glass for Mr. Charldon, Parker." Casting an eye at the bottle that had been at his elbow, he continued, "And another bottle of brandy."

"Can't stay much more above fifteen minutes," Andrew said. "Left my man walking the horses."

The servant departed with nothing more than a "Very good, my lord," but his whole demeanor was so very expressive of his disapproval that both gentlemen were hard pressed to control their mirth until the door closed.

"A regular mother hen, ain't he?" sniggered Mr. Charldon.

"Far worse. You would never believe the way he has been clucking over my excesses."

"Didn't think you had any. Used not to, you know."

"That was—before . . ."

Andrew waited for Melcourt to continue, but if he had any intention of pursuing this trend, Parker's return forestalled it.

"Will there be anything else, my lord?" he inquired as soon as he had placed a newly filled decanter upon the tray.

"No, that will be all, Parker. I will see Mr. Charldon out myself."

"Very good, my lord. Good night, my lord, Mr. Andrew."

As he withdrew, he gave Mr. Charldon a very eloquent look, as Andrew explained to his host, "I have the feeling that he was trying to tell me something, Sylvester. Haven't been dipping too deep lately, have you?"

"Not you too, Andrew! My butler, my valet—even my head groom—and now my best friend. This is entirely too much and most unfair."

"Don't know about your people, Sylvester, though I must say it's rather cheeky of them to involve themselves."

"My people, as you so quaintly style them," his lordship interjected smoothly, handing Mr. Charldon his glass, "my people know better than to express themselves verbally. One can find excuses for them because they have been with the family for many years, but others have no reason to concern themselves."

"Tryin' to slap m'fingers, eh? You'll not embarrass me, if that's your intent, milord."

His lordship raised his brows in polite inquiry. "No?"

"Don't turn up stiff with me, Sylvester. Thing is, know m'sister; you don't."

The Earl tensed almost imperceptibly and a drop of brandy slopped over the rim of his glass. He raised it to his lips, downed its contents, and immediately poured another drink, his hand steady this time.

"That's what I mean! She'd drive a saint to drink, and as you, m'friend, are far from that state of heavenly grace, I wonder only that you've put up with her starts this long."

With yet another drink to fortify him the Earl felt

equal to maintaining his imperturbable exterior. "Thank you for your interest, Andrew, but I must impress upon you that my family affairs are of no concern to anyone but my wife and me."

"That's where you have it all wrong, Sylvester. There's no living with her these days. She's been cutting up our peace until m'father, for the sake of self-preservation, was forced to give up his invalid's couch and escort m'stepmother back to town. Everyone else is almost ready to follow their example, no matter how thin of company London is now."

"And how do you think I may be of assistance to you, my friend?" The Earl looked at his discomfited visitor with unfeigned amusement. "Surely you must have some idea of how I might help you, or you would not have mentioned this."

"Damme, Sylvester, you make it deucedly hard for a man to talk to you, but I refuse to be quieted until I explain things to you."

"That will not be necessary, Andrew." His voice was suddenly cold and implacable.

"But damn it, man, she's your wife!"

"Exactly. And as my wife she will find a welcome whenever she decides to return. If there are any explanations due me, I prefer hearing them from her rather than from her emissary."

"If you think m'sister sent me to you, you don't know her very well, which is what I've been tryin' to tell you."

"My error. You will forgive me my mistake, won't you, Andrew? You see, it was a quite logical assumption on my part."

"Nothing to it, Sylvester," answered Andrew, meeting the Earl's winning smile with one of his own. "Only thing—isn't logical. Nothing about this—this farrago—has been logical. . . . Stands to reason. M'sister's involved. She won't come to see you. Says she won't see you if you call."

"Then there is no sense in my calling." The Earl's voice was strangely gentle.

"Thing is—might regret it. You know women—always changing their minds. But that's not what I came here to say."

"I think, Andrew, for the sake of our friendship, you have said enough."

Mr. Charldon, recognizing the steel beneath the quiet voice, extricated himself from the depths of the chair with an air of resignation. "Knew I wasn't the man for the job, but I had hoped . . ." He shrugged, obviously accepting the neutral position in which the Earl had placed him. "Good night, Sylvester. You put me through a few uncomfortable minutes back there," he confessed as Melcourt walked with him to the door.

The Earl, contrite, clapped him on the shoulder and owned himself to be in the wrong. "If she returns of her own free will, I shall ask no questions, but I shall not don sackcloth and ashes to parade beneath her window and cry *peccavi*—nor do I expect it of her."

Melcourt returned to the library after speeding his departing guest on his way. It was readily discernible from the frown on his face that he too had found the evening's conversation most disquieting.

The newly broached bottle tendered silent invitation, and he went so far as to fill the glass and raise it to his lips, but with sudden decision he swept the contents into the fire and watched the flash of blue in the heart of the blaze in the manner of one making an offering to some pagan god.

An uncertain summer sun was doing its best to overcome a lowering sky as the Earl came to terms with a late breakfast.

"A gentleman to see you, my lord."

Parker had entered in his usual silent manner and was at his lordship's elbow before the Earl was aware of his presence. "He neglected to give his name, my lord, but as Mr. Andrew directed me to request you see him, I thought you would wish to know. I showed him into the library, my lord."

"What? Is Charldon here? Why didn't you show him in?"

"Not Mr. Andrew, my lord; he left directly he gave me the message for you."

Parker's facial muscles were indicative of his feelings at this breach of good taste, and he almost sniffed, but the Earl, less high in the instep and much more approachable than his butler, unfolded his tall, loose-limbed body from the dining chair and left the room.

"You wished to see me?"

The man at the window turned, and for just an instant the Earl's face showed his rage. Then a cold mask slid over his features.

"Monsieur Vallier, I believe?"

CHAPTER TWENTY-FIVE

"Only since I have been in England—since July, in fact," Raoul confessed.

The Earl's hands unclenched and he relaxed visibly.

"You are very perspicacious, milord," the visitor remarked with a smile.

"If you do not mind telling me," the Earl drawled, "what is your relationship with my wife?"

"Ah! First let me tell you of the relationship between Vanessa and the one you call André Vallier."

"Yes?" Melcourt's voice was curt.

"In a word, there is none."

"Yet Vanessa herself confessed to knowing all about this mysterious person."

"I think, myself, she confessed to a lot more than that," the gentleman replied with a twinkle in his eyes.

"Exactly!"

"Well, then, does not Sylvester Vinton share the bed of the Earl of Melcourt without causing comment?"

"So that is how it is." Suddenly the Earl's eyes lighted up in a smile that made him seem very young and carefree. "The little vixen! She was punishing me!"

"It's the English side of the family, you understand. We French are more placid in our dispositions," he quipped.

"The Comte de St. Varres, of course!" the Earl exclaimed, realizing who his visitor was. "Then it is you we have to thank for unmasking Gresham as a French spy."

"And you to thank for seeing to the safety of my wife and small son."

Melcourt looked embarrassed and raised his hand as if to stifle further gratitude, and the Comte, understanding, continued. "As for the unmasking of Gresham, it was only confirming your suspicions, my lord; Mr. Pitt was not deaf to them, after all. But it was not I who was responsible for the actual trapping of the spy. It was Vanessa," the Comte said. Accepting the armchair an interested Melcourt belatedly offered, he recounted the tale of Vanessa's abduction.

"So you see, my lord, you were very effectively taken out of the way."

The Earl, who had seated himself in his favorite armchair, stood up and paced forward and back like a caged panther. "My God! What she must have suffered at the hands of that swine! I saw her that night—after she returned. I lost my temper in a fit of jealousy. . . . You are sure she is—unharmed?" His voice was hoarse, the words torn from his throat.

"Your wife, my lord, is a remarkably apt pupil with pistol, sword, and, in this case," he smiled, "a knee to the groin."

The Earl regained his composure, his voice cool, almost casual, once again, but moisture glistened on his brow. "Apparently I may consider myself extremely fortunate that I have not given my wife cause to try more of her tricks on me," he said as he returned to his chair, still shaken but outwardly composed.

Raoul nodded to himself, as though satisfied with something he had just discovered. "Surely you have had experience in dealing with pistols, swords, and—er—knees?"

"Enough to know that they are not always an effective defense. . . . You are . . . sure?"

"My word on it, my lord. In this case—and we are speaking of knees, are we not—it was my privilege to witness the *débâcle*, thanks to Abel."

Raoul's speech was suitably grave, although his eyes sparkled with wicked amusement as he watched the Earl's hands clench the arms of the chair until his fingers lost their color.

"Why didn't Abel come for me? He has been working with me all this time."

"It was as simple as this: I was there, you were not. It was planned that way, intentionally and deliberately."

"You are quite explicit."

"There is no doubt that Lady Charldon and Gresham had their heads together. I realized it myself at Lady Edgerton's masquerade ball," responded Raoul. "When it appeared that Vanessa had no one to protect her, they struck. You, my lord, appeared very unconcerned as to the fate of your wife—or so Lady Charldon believed."

"I see. Another thing for which I must blame myself."

"There has been no harm done."

"Not because none was intended. I have been

aware of Miranda's scheming, but it was my intention to turn it to my own advantage."

"Now it is I who must say 'I see,'" interrupted Raoul. "Lady Charldon, had she been of a more retiring disposition, would have made an excellent cover for your secret trips. Unfortunately, Vanessa is of the opinion that you have no need of her. Even as I am talking to you, her clothes are being packed and she is trying to talk Addy into going to Italy with her. I must tell you, my lord, that what she plans, she invariably executes without delay."

The Earl was patently startled, and Raoul pressed home his advantage. "Once she is out of England, it will be only with the greatest difficulty that you get her back."

"And your suggestion?"

"Vanessa rides to Shelburne Park every afternoon. She leaves Charldon Manor at two o'clock or thereabouts."

"And no one will worry if she does not return from her ride?"

Raoul smiled. "I think not. Not now."

"Good! I think we understand each other completely," said the Earl as he accompanied his guest to the door.

Melcourt, ever the man to prefer action to the spoken word, quickly made his preparations and chafed at the enforced delay. Well before time, he was booted, spurred, mounted, and riding toward Shelburne Park. Stationing himself in a small copse that overlooked the road, the Earl maintained a steady vigil. Despite thickly leafed branches, the small patch of trees afforded little shelter, but Vanessa would not be expecting anyone to be there, and the element of surprise would be his.

The waiting seemed interminable, and he cursed himself for leaving too early; as more time passed, he began to wonder if she had changed her mind and was even now preparing to set out on her journey. ·

The silence in the house was deadly. Vanessa flitted from one deserted room to another, looking for something to do, something to look at aside from the furniture in holland covers. Only a handful of servants remained to attend to her wants, and they were busy about their jobs in some other part of the Manor. Addy's unflagging attention to the packing was suspicious, but she was doing what Vanessa wanted, after all.

What with Andrew and Gwenyth tearing off to town after Sir Lucius and Miranda, she had no opponent with whom to cross swords, or at least none worthy of her steel. When she was with Sylvester, whatever else she was, she was never bored.

Shortly after one o'clock, feeling as if the very walls were about to close in on her, Vanessa slipped through the door to the kitchen gardens and hurried along the path, entering the stables from the rear. She saddled her mare and mounted from the block, avoiding Nelson, the head groom, and his lads, who were working in the paddock. Nelson sometimes attended her when she rode out, but today she wished for no company as she made a final pilgrimage to Shelburne.

A soft, silvery mist had come up before dawn. Now it blanketed the gardens, blurring the edges of the elm-bordered drive and muffling the thud of hoof-beats as she turned into a leaf-bestrewn track. In another month, the floor of the forest would be carpeted with red and gold leaves, but she would not be here to enjoy the change of season. All her senses were heightened, knowing that this ride was her farewell to a place she loved.

Traveling south for several miles through the rapidly thinning forests, Vanessa detected the tang of seaweed long before turning west into the Old Coast Road. Well past the sleepy little fishing village on Melcourt Bay, she dismounted and, breathing deeply of the bracing air, made her way up a slight rise until the very edge of the cliff seemed to fall away. Here, along the ridge, the white veil of mist lifted, dissolved, and trailed away, leaving a clear view of the far side of the bay, and beyond it the Channel, gray beneath the lowering sky. Directly ahead the massive rectangle of granite and Purbeck marble that was Melcourt Castle broke the skyline above the cliff like some warlike giant, its old stone turrets massive clubs upon the creature's shoulders.

A fierce gust of wind tugged at the skirt of her lightweight habit, and she shivered, wishing she had listened to Addy; not that the willow-green color was unbecoming or the riding-dress unfashionable, but it had been an unfortunate and unseasonable choice. The weather was changing, Addy had told her when she had brought the morning chocolate. And then she had added, "It's these old bones, my lady. They ache with the damp and the cold."

Vanessa, who had lain in the pleasant world between sleep and waking, had sat up suddenly. "There, you see! It will do you good to come to Italy with me," she had said, as if trying to clinch an argument.

"That's as may be, my lady, but a body gets tired of traveling at my age."

"You just do not think I should go," Vanessa accused, but no answer was forthcoming from the grim-lipped servant, who busied herself around the room. "Did you pack my things?" she queried almost sullenly.

"Aye, what there is of them. 'Tis a sin not to send to the Castle for your clothes." She began to put out Vanessa's underclothing and a pale blue muslin round gown. "Waitin' for the local dressmaker to stitch you up something. Tsk! And worthless too, I can tell you."

"I shall shop in Italy," Vanessa replied mutinously, setting her jaw as if tired of hearing criticism. "It's not at the end of the world, you know."

She had made a momentous decision. The fitful, restless hours of the night had come and gone and, with them, her hesitation. No longer could she bear to remain here, trying to hide her misery.

Her husband was much too busy with his own affairs to take the trouble to come after her. How unlucky she had been to fall in love with a rake. She had to admit now that she would never love another man. She felt cheated. She would never know all that marriage could mean between a man and a woman who loved each other. She would never go back on the off chance that he would deign to notice her, or indeed wish a child of her body—an heir.

He would accept her return, he had told Andrew, with no questions asked—like the return of a bitch that had accidentally strayed from the kennel, she thought bitterly. Looking once more at the Castle, which was both heaven and hell to her, she made her way, almost blindly, back to where she had left her horse. If she missed her footing and plunged to her death on the rocks below, who was to care? The greedy, sucking waters would carry her away from the shore; no one would ever know what had happened to her.

The sudden shrieking of a gull tore at her nerves and suddenly it all seemed too much. "Oh, God! How can I bear it," she whispered convulsively as she rested her head against the warm, satin-smooth flank of the mare. "I must go, or I shall truly die. One more night, only one more."

Dashing the tears from her eyes, she mounted from a large stone, nearly falling in her haste, and galloped off as though pursued by fiends.

Wild-eyed, dodging low-hanging branches that lashed out like hands trying to snatch her from the saddle, she saw a dark figure in every shadow. She was beset by visions of Lyman Gresham hiding behind every bush and tree. For a terrifying moment she could almost imagine a horse and rider concealed within a narrow belt of trees. She was conscious of the hard beating of her heart and shook her head as though to banish her morbid fancies.

Just when she thought she could stand it no longer the mare broke into a clearing. Vanessa didn't notice the other rider until he was neck and neck with her. She tried to evade him, but not even her superb horsemanship could keep her safe from him. She risked a glance from the corner of her eye, heard him give a short laugh as he suddenly shot ahead, and then she was torn from her horse and imprisoned within the circle of his arms. She silently endured the ride to the Castle, refusing to give him the satisfaction of asking his intentions.

Vanessa was surprised that she felt no anger—only a strange and not altogether unpleasant apprehension. Held across the saddle as she was, she could look up at the stern mold of his features. She was torn by two conflicting desires: to rake her nails across the dark visage so close to her, and the other—senseless, she was sure—to smooth away the frown from between his brows.

CHAPTER TWENTY-SIX

The smooth gait of the horse never faltered. Vanessa tried to stay as quiet as possible, but she must have stirred in his arms, drawing his eyes to her. Fearing her disturbing thoughts were written upon her countenance for him to see, she hid her face against his chest with an inarticulate murmur. Sylvester's arm tightened around her, and for a moment she imagined he had pressed his cheek to her hair, but she dismissed that thought as being unworthy of her.

He had never called on her—or written—not that she would have received him or read his note, of course.

The haze of anger with which she faced her own tumultuous feelings would not permit any reflection. She told herself that she had been an expedient, so how could she hope for anything—any feeling—from him. She was sure he had come upon her quite by accident. Surely if she had not ridden in this direction, she would not have had the misfortune to encounter him. He had obviously made a decision on the spur of the moment, and like many such, it would prove his undoing.

The Earl pulled up before the sycamores that hid the approach to the Castle.

"And what are you going to say to the servants when you carry me inside?" she demanded of him. "For I shall not set one foot inside any residence of yours of my own volition," she cried out triumphantly.

He looked at her coldly. "You should know by now that I need explain nothing to my servants."

Vanessa fell into a mutinous silence, and Melcourt laughed in a way that sent shivers down her spine. She tried to draw herself away from any contact with him, but it was impossible to escape from the arm that encircled her like a coiled spring as they proceeded at a walking pace. Sooner than she could have wished, Melcourt Castle was in view and she knew that no matter what she did, what she said, she was at her husband's mercy.

The Earl did not relinquish his precious burden as he slipped from the saddle. "Have Titan seen to, Parker," he told the unruffled butler as he stalked through the doorway. His hands tightened on her painfully as he felt her tense in his arms, and, as he ascended the stairs with her still within his embrace, Vanessa became truly alarmed.

"Your rooms have been kept in readiness," he mentioned casually as he entered her bedchamber, but the beating of his heart was anything but that, she knew. He placed her on her feet and withdrew his hands suddenly, causing her to stumble and to lean against his unresponsive chest for a fleeting second before she drew back.

"Since I have returned, willy-nilly, would you send word to the housekeeper that I desire to see the menu?"

Melcourt had to admire how quickly she regained her composure, and he was not able to keep this from his voice when he replied that he would personally see to their dinner.

"We will be two to dinner, then, Melcourt?" She raised her brows in mock surprise. "One would have thought you would have had something better to do than break bread with your wife."

He smiled, and a stray thought passed through Vanessa's mind that he looked almost wolfish, but putting this thought aside with a shiver, she reached out to him impulsively.

"Could we not talk this—everything—over after dinner, Sylvester?"

For a moment, looking at the shadows beneath her eyes, he was tempted to tell her that he knew the truth; that revelation would earn her friendship, but he wanted more than that. He tried to harden himself by thinking of the anguish he had suffered by thinking her unfaithful. His guilt at her torment was forgotten as he took the slim hand that rested on his sleeve and kissed the smooth skin on the inside of her wrist. "Talk? One does not steal a woman for talk."

Vanessa jerked her hand away and turned her back as though signaling his dismissal.

"May I do anything for you before I leave?"

"You may ask my maid to attend me."

To her ears his voice sounded suspiciously contrite as he said, "Did I not tell you? I sent her to London to await our return."

"Who, then, is to help me dress?"

"Tomorrow we will see about hiring some village girl."

"Tomorrow?"

"Surely you would not deprive me of the pleasure of assisting you?"

"You are insufferable! Get out!"

My Lord Melcourt bowed to his fuming lady and sallied forth to review his arrangements for dinner. On his return he found her bedroom in shadow and quickly lighted the branch of candles on the dressing table.

"I have not run away, if that is what you are thinking."

He followed her voice to the massive four-poster in the center of the room and drew a quilt up to her chin. "Stay there until the room is warmer," he said as he bent over her. He moved to light the fire. "Once again, I must apologize for not being prepared for your homecoming."

So she had been right, after all! Theirs had been an accidental encounter; he had brought her here because of some momentary fancy. How very sad. How totally and completely soul-destroying, she thought, as tears welled up and overflowed, dripping, unnot-iced, down her cheeks.

The fire well begun, the Earl strolled back to the bed and proceeded to tuck the covers about her once again. "What is this?" He sat on the edge of the bed and leaned over, detaching her fingers from the quilt she had drawn up to hide her face. "You are not crying?"

She turned, no longer avoiding his searching eyes, and answered him baldly, "Yes."

"Whatever for?"

"If you do not know, I am certainly not going to tell you," she snapped with a return of her old antagonism as she sat up and pulled the quilt about her knees.

He took her chin in his hand, not letting her draw back, turning her face this way and that. Then he bent swiftly to place a kiss on her lips and left her before she could so much as sputter.

Her eyes followed him as he crossed the room. She heard water trickle into the basin and quickly closed her eyes. He resumed his place beside her, and Va-nessa narrowly opened her eyes.

"Close your eyes," he told her peremptorily as he placed a wet cloth over her face.

"You are getting water in my eyes." She reached up to remove the cloth.

"I told you to close them," he remarked in an off-hand manner as he captured her hands.

"Now it is running down my neck! Sylvester! You idiot! Do something or I shall be soaked to the skin!"

He realized with a start that under the wet cloth she was laughing. The tension within him was re-leased as though a spring had been touched, and his own laughter rang out free and clear. He removed the offending cloth and patted her wet face with a towel. And then, without warning, he began to unbutton her riding-dress.

Laughter that had its origin in pure relief now stuck in her throat. "What do you think you are doing? Stop it this instant!"

"I am unbuttoning your habit, can you not tell, my dear?" mocked the Earl. "It will not do to have you soaked to your skin, and such pretty skin too." He placed a soft, lingering kiss in the lovely hollow at the base of her throat.

Vanessa shivered, not from the cold, but tried not to betray her weakness.

"Off with this wet dress before you say another word."

There was something compelling about his voice— something that made her obey, although part of her stood back and accused her of playing the fool.

She was suddenly shy. "I can manage now, thank you."

"Do you have a warm robe?"

"Behind the dressing-room door—if it is still there."

For some reason—it was not from the cold—she was racked with shudders she could not control. Seeing this when he returned with the robe, the Earl rang, and in a very short time a steaming bath had been prepared.

Melcourt poured something into a glass and held it out to her. Vanessa eyed it suspiciously. "Brandy?" she asked between shudders, wrinkling her nose at the sight of this amber liquid. "You know how I dislike it."

"Yes, it is brandy and you are to drink it—now."

She opened her mouth to argue and finally accepted it with a hand that shook beyond her control. She needed his help to get it to her lips. It felt like liquid fire as it burned its way down her throat, but she was glad of the spreading warmth it generated inside her body.

"Now take off the rest of your clothes."

Vanessa looked at him as though he was demented. He did not ask her again, but began the job himself, heedless of her protests. His hands and his eyes registered the silky softness of her white body, and his mind stored the information for the future. Paramount in the Earl's mind was preventing further suffering from the violent chill that had suddenly taken possession of her body.

Vanessa was no longer protesting as Melcourt helped her into the tub. She was merely grateful for the all-enveloping warmth that stopped the convulsive movement of her body.

With as much ease and apparent unconcern as if he had done it for years, he began to soap her back, only to have her utter the first excuse that came to mind. "Sylvester, your coat! You will ruin it." It was quite weak as excuses go, but if she felt any disappointment when he put down the soap, she did not show it. She was, however, surprised to see him remove coat and waistcoat and roll up his sleeves. Once more he took up the scented bar and permitted his fingers to run down her back. He was only amusing himself, Vanessa knew, but she could not help responding. She allowed herself the luxury of a small, contented sigh and relaxed under his ministrations.

245

"You smell of lilacs," he murmured, breathing deeply.

"As shall you, my lord, if you continue using my soap in this fashion."

"Do you think I shall qualify as a lady's maid?" he inquired with assumed concern.

"As a back scrubber you are superb," she told him with mock severity, "but a lady's maid—especially to a Countess—must have other skills as well."

"Shall I show you how well I can do the front?" He stepped around to face her, and she hastily crossed her hands over her breasts. "Oh, no!" he said with a laugh. "We are playing my game now." She could sense his underlying anger, though what right he had to be angry, she could not imagine. She was the aggrieved party.

"Are you making the rules of this—game?" she parried.

"As it is my turn now, yes, I am making the rules, and the first one is that you do just as I tell you. It will be so much easier if you obey me at once, for I shall win in either case, Vanessa. If I am crossed, I may well wreak my vengeance upon your lovely white body, as I have been tempted to do so often in the past."

A thought occurred to her that he meant every word.

"You are my wife, even if you have not given much thought to it. Is it not time to consummate our bargain?"

Vanessa flinched at his choice of words, but realized her only hope was to sway him from his anger. He held out a huge towel for her. Apparently she was expected to get out of the tub in front of him. She shut her mouth on angry words. After all, he was her husband, and he had just seen her enter the tub, and she not wearing a stitch.

Making up her mind, she said, "I shall obey you—play your game, as you call it, Sylvester, if you will carry it a step further."

"Well?" His voice was as uncompromising as his expression.

"Will you pretend with me? Pretend you have just married an innocent young girl who trusts and loves you? Would you not then teach her of love and would you not find more satisfaction in this, rather than in forcing her to your will?"

He wrapped her in the towel as she stepped from the bath. "Does this add spice to the game you play with your lovers?" he asked casually, but she could see the corded muscles of his powerful arms suddenly tense.

For a few seconds she did not know what to say, then she decided that only the truth would answer. "I know you will not believe me, but I have never known a lover."

There was a strange expression on his face.

"I said you would not believe me, my lord." There was no bitterness, only sadness in her voice.

He bowed. "So you did, my lady."

She winced at the coldness of his voice, not realizing the enormous strain he was under to control himself—to keep himself from possessing her at that very minute. She looked up at her husband, her eyes wistful.

"Once it would have been 'my love.'"

Melcourt turned on her so wrathfully that Vanessa blanched and took an involuntary step backward. His eyes blazed with savage ferocity.

"It would be so easy . . . so easy to use your beautiful white body . . ."

She sat down on the bed, suddenly weak from the shock of his words. "Why do you torment me so?" she cried.

"I? Torment *you*? My God, when I think of the sleepless nights, imagining you in someone else's arms! It does not bear thinking of!"

"And what of your doxy?"

"Miranda and I have not been lovers for some time. She is too soiled even for me, my sweet."

"But the notes from her . . . You always went to her when she sent for you!"

"The notes? Ah, yes! They were on Miranda's letter paper, were they not? A good ruse, Mr. Pitt thought at the time—especially if I seemed to take up pursuit of Miranda once again. The letters went from Pitt to me, on her paper—and it was on my crested paper that they went the other way 'round. Even Miranda's unexpected visit to Shelburne served only to confirm the suspicions of the local gossips that I was a rake with nothing more pressing on my mind than my neighbor's wife.

"I was certain that Gresham had traveled between France and England on more than one occasion. But all I could do was put Abel to watching him whenever Gresham was in the neighborhood. Pitt couldn't take action without proof, because of Gresham's friends in Parliament.

"Something was going on—something dangerous to the crown, but what it was we did not know precisely until Gresham fell into our hands. His final coup for France was to have been the abduction of His Majesty while he was sea-bathing in Weymouth—a masterstroke if it had succeeded. If Gresham had not involved himself with you at the last, our Farmer George would be in France now."

That was important, to be sure, and at a later time, no doubt, Vanessa would consider her part in it. Right now all she could think was that Sylvester and Miranda were not lovers. She must have said this out loud, for he answered her.

"I have taken no woman since I met you—and I think it past time to remedy that."

Hugging the towel to her body with one hand, she appraised him, but his face gave her no clue to his feelings. Vanessa's breathing was harsh, as if it pained her, and her words seemed torn from her throat. "Have it as you will. I shall not resist you, but if you can find it in your heart to be gentle with me, I will give you kiss for kiss, caress for caress; I will do anything you wish."

He was about to speak, but she silenced him with a wave of her hand. "No, wait! I realize it is asking a lot of you to—pretend—but I see no other way if there is to be any life for us—afterward."

"Would it not be equally hard for you to pretend?" His voice was thick, almost unrecognizable.

It took her a full minute to master her breathing. "Perhaps. I . . . do not . . . know." She turned to him, her eyes blazing with a deep amethyst fire.

The Earl was shaken in spite of himself, but he forced his cutting voice to continue. "You are a fine actress, my dear. I am sure you will give an excellent performance as an eager, love-starved virgin. I am also sure that I will enjoy every minute of it."

"How can you be so cruel?" Vanessa asked, the words almost wrung from her.

"Cruel? Have I not given up my plans for rape and revenge?" he said, still intent on his purpose.

"Someday you will know the truth, and you will never forgive yourself if you have hurt me."

"The truth? Who, aside from you, my sweet wife, knows the truth?"

"Andrew will tell you."

"Andrew is in London. No doubt you expect me to deliver you there so that you can escape me again. Well, not this time, my girl! You have made me a very generous offer, one I would be mad indeed to refuse. I intend to take you up on it. In fact, the more I think on it, the more appealing it becomes. Perhaps by this time next week I myself shall believe that you are my young, innocent bride."

"Next week? But . . ."

"Enough!" His anger scorched her. "I will keep you a week, a month, a year . . . However long I choose. As you say, we may find we can rub along together—afterwards."

"I was wrong," she cried, suddenly distraught. "There can be no future for us—not together."

Melcourt ignored her frantic words. "And now I shall leave you to dress for dinner. If you wish for my help, knock on the door."

Once again he was cold, and she was totally confused. Vanessa could not decide which she preferred: his icy restraint, or his passionate but loveless embraces. He bowed formally and left the room, without touching her in any way. To Vanessa this signified his utter contempt—perhaps even disinterest—and suddenly she was furiously angry—angry because just looking at him made her knees weak. His touch was capable of turning her insides to water, while he seemed to be unaffected by any emotion save anger.

Her own fury turned to determination, and she turned to her wardrobe and reached for the most daring and seductive ensemble she had ever worn: an overdress of heavy reembroidered lace buttoned high under her breasts to frame a diaphanous silk nightdress, which revealed every contour of her body; the skirt, slit high up the sides, showed tantalizing glimpses of hip and thigh through a thin layer of white silk gauze. It was a deliberately provocative bit of drapery and she knew how successful it was when she entered the sitting room and found the Earl awaiting her.

"If your intent was to entice me, you have achieved your aim." He walked around her, holding his quizzing glass to his eye. "Is this being worn for the first time, or have you tested its efficacy on your other lovers?"

"Sylvester! You promised!"

"Promised? I did not promise, I merely agreed that your proposal might be worthy of a trial. But I will promise now. I promise that before the night is over, you will know that love is not a game for children; you will know what it means to be loved by a man." His promise was all the more chilling because it was uttered in a completely dispassionate tone.

"And now, madam . . ."

He led her to the table and seated her with exquisite courtesy, leaving a kiss upon her nape, where the curls were still damp from the bath, and causing her to shiver delightedly.

Vanessa admired the beautifully set table as the Earl poured champagne into sparkling crystal glasses. The delightful aroma of fine foods and delectable sauces arose from the serving platters as he uncovered them to serve her.

"Ummm . . . Lobster has not tasted like this since the last time I dined with you here at Melcourt," she said.

"Do we compliment the chef, or do I take that as a personal compliment, my lady?"

She blushed, and sipped at the champagne to cover her confusion. The Earl leaned over to refill her glass, whispering, "No hands but mine will serve you, no eyes but mine will see you this night."

Vanessa, speedily recovering her aplomb, responded pertly, "A very pretty speech, my lord. As well planned as your menu. Kisses with the lobster, caresses with the partridges . . . and what may I expect with the jam tart?"

"You have a devilish quick tongue, my girl. Has no one ever told you it could be to your disadvantage?"

"Yes," she retorted readily, "my nurse. She told me I should never get a husband unless I learned to hold my tongue!"

He grinned wickedly, one eyebrow climbing to meet the lock of hair that fell casually across his forehead, making her long to brush it back. He saw the change in her expression and stiffened. "You are not eating," he pronounced abruptly. "Let me help you to a tart. As I recall, you displayed a fondness for them.

Perhaps we can find out what comes after the kisses and caresses, aside from more of the same."

With succeeding courses, she knew not what she ate, but only that she herself was being devoured at his leisure. It set her teeth on edge, and she began to ache with an emptiness he alone could fill . . . but not this way. This way led only to despair.

Vanessa got up from the table with a swiftness that took him by surprise. "Do you mean it? All the words, the kisses? If not, it is no good." She walked to the window and stared out, seeing nothing, not even the reflection of the room in the glass. "Is this how one begins an *affaire*, meaning one thing, having one purpose in view, fooling each other with pretty speeches, kisses. . . . You see, I would not know. I have never taken a lover." Vanessa took a deep, ragged breath. "I am in love with you, and you are making a mockery of everything I believe in. Let me go, Sylvester. Please!"

She did not hear him get up—he moved silently for so big a man—but she saw his reflection in the glass as he came up behind her. He took her in his arms and buried his face in her hair.

"Too late, Vanessa. I cannot let you go now. I can never let you go. Your sweetness, your courage, everything about you . . ."

Her voice trembled. "But you cannot love me; you only pretended for a little while." The next words came in a whisper. "As you are pretending now!"

"Is there any need for me to pretend, now that you have admitted your love for me?" He turned her until they were face to face and halted her answer with kisses—teasing, demanding kisses that left her breathless and trembling with fear and desire. She obeyed an overwhelming urge to put her arms around his neck as the strange feeling deep inside her pulsed and spread, until her very fear of him seemed pleasurable and with every atom of her strength, she responded to his fierce embrace.

Even as he scooped her up in his arms, Vanessa was torn with doubt. "You will keep me then? You will not send me away?"

"Send you away?" he laughed joyously. "I told you I shall never let you go."

"But I do not understand . . ."

"Little fool," he told her lovingly, "I thought I should never get you to admit your love—and I was so afraid you would not believe anything I said that I did not dare tell you how I felt."

"As I was afraid to admit it, in case you should use it against me," she confessed.

"Two foolish people, Vanessa. I have loved you since the night you came to me at Melcourt Castle."

His lordship's bride whispered something in his ear which must have been extremely satisfactory.

"So long ago as that?" he murmured against her ear as his arms tightened possessively about her. "If I had known, you would be my wife in more than name."

His Countess looked up at him with sparkling eyes. A dimple appeared in her cheek as she said, "Then it is quite your fault, my lord, and entirely up to you to do something to remedy it."

The Earl, never one to shirk responsibility, accepted all blame and carried her to her room, prepared to correct his error to his lady's satisfaction.

INTRODUCING...

The Romance Magazine For The 1980's

Each exciting issue contains a full-length romance novel — the kind of first-love story we all dream about...

PLUS

other wonderful features such as a travelogue to the world's most romantic spots, advice about your romantic problems, a quiz to find the ideal mate for you and much, much more.

ROMANTIQUE: A complete novel of romance, plus a whole world of romantic features.

ROMANTIQUE: Wherever magazines are sold. Or write Romantique Magazine, Dept. C-1, 41 East 42nd Street, New York, N.Y. 10017

INTERNATIONALLY DISTRIBUTED BY DELL DISTRIBUTING, INC.